Tara Heavey

Making It Up
As I Go Along

TiVOLi

Tivoli

An imprint of Gill & Macmillan Ltd
Hume Avenue, Park West, Dublin 12
with associated companies throughout the world
www.gillmacmillan.ie

© Tara Heavey 2006
ISBN-13: 978 07171 3908 8
ISBN-10: 0 7171 3908 5
Print origination by TypeIT, Dublin
Printed by Nørhaven Paperback A/S, Denmark

*The paper used in this book is made from the wood pulp
of managed forests. For every tree felled, at least one tree is planted,
thereby renewing natural resources.*

A catalogue record is available for this book
from the British Library.

1 3 5 4 2

For Marianne

Acknowledgments

Acknowledgments are funny things to write, because half the people you're thanking have yet to do what you're thanking them for.

Take the following members of staff at Tivoli: Dearbhaile Curran, Nicky Howard, Chris Carroll and Paul Neilan – sincere thanks in anticipation. Tana French and Aoileann O'Donnell: for your sterling work so far and in the future, I thank you kindly.

To my editor, Alison Walsh. I thank you, as usual, for your hard work and your understanding of the trials and tribulations – real and imagined – of being a writer and mother. Thank you especially for talking to me for an hour and a half on Good Friday when I'm sure you had many more pressing and fun matters to attend to (Stations of the Cross? Gutting fish?). But most of all, I'd like to thank you for not resembling remotely the editor in this book.

As always, heartfelt thanks to my agent, Faith O'Grady, and to my family and friends for their unwavering support. This time, I'd particularly like to mention my appreciation for my Uncle David and Aunt Lorraine. To Alison Norrington for those enjoyable chats and cups of coffee. And I acknowledge you acknowledging me in your book. To Sarah Webb, for providing such great quotes for my last two books and for endeavouring to assist me with the title to this one. To Fran and Frank, without whose babysitting services this book would never have been written. To Margaret Kennedy for that inspirational trip in her black Beetle. Rory specifically asked me not to mention him this time, so I won't, except to thank him for not getting angry when I threw the map out of the window.

I'd like to acknowledge *The Spanish Armada 1588: The Journey of Francisco de Cúellar – Sligo to the Causeway Coast*, by Jim Stapleton and Francisco de Cúellar, a book that assisted me greatly in the telling of this story.

A final thanks to everyone who has ever read or bought any of my books. I hope you like this one.

Prologue

My father left us when I was very small – tiny, in fact. All dreams of a tearful reunion were dashed when, a few months later, he was knocked down by a bus. So it does happen in real life. Let's hope he was wearing clean underwear at the time. I was well aware that this was the type of grisly end a father might come to in a novel, especially if he happened to be superfluous to the plot. I knew this as an avid reader of books – and an occasional writer of them. At this the time of our meeting, I am about to embark on my third novel. That's if I ever work out what the hell to write about.

Back to my father. I knew precious little about him, although I had concocted many a wild theory over the years. When I was aged from four to six, he was a lion-tamer in a travelling circus; from seven to nine, a cowboy and rodeo star; from ten to twelve, a bullfighter; from thirteen to twenty-three, a complete bastard. And from then on he was a shadow, an enigma, a dark shade that coloured all my relationships with men, rendering them disastrous at best. I never once stopped to consider that I might bear some responsibility for the failure of these unions. It was so damned handy to blame dear old Dad. It wasn't as if he could answer back.

His enigmatic status was enhanced by my mother's steadfast refusal to discuss him. Now a large, square, strawberry-blonde woman in her late forties, she remained unrelentingly bitter towards my father – despite the fact that she had managed a successful marriage in the meantime and presented me with two half-brothers to lessen the blow. I knew she was proud of her unyielding hatred and viewed her spectacular capacity to bear a grudge with great pride.

Her attitude resulted in me being certain of only one thing: my father had black hair, olive skin and brown eyes. I knew it every time I looked at myself in the mirror, or at my mother across the kitchen table. I would marvel, once again, that I had ever been a scrunched-up morsel of flesh inside her belly. No doubt she marvelled at it too, at this changeling daughter who sold daydreams for a living. When I tested her patience – as I frequently did – she would lose her legendary temper and tell me that I was just like my father.

1

It was a jewel-coloured day, the first day of spring. Not St Bridget's Day – the first of February, when it's brass monkeys and half the population is still reeling from the flu; I'm talking about the *real*, unofficial first day of spring. It's a bit like the Queen having two birthdays. It might occur around St Patrick's Day, when January's clean slate has been well and truly sullied; more often than not, it happens at the end of March, about the time when the clocks go forward. The feeling is unmistakeable. It's the same feeling that the plants in the ground must get when they know it's time to grow again. That of sap rising.

This particular year, I got the feeling as I was walking past Trinity College one Friday evening, coming from the bookshop where I worked – the bookshop I had vacated, as if shot from a catapult, a few minutes previously. A car cruised by with the windows rolled down, 'Love Is in the Air' playing on the radio. It was still bright, and some inspired person had mown the lawn at the front of the college, for what could have been the very first time that year. There were ice-cream colours in the windows of the boutiques, and creme eggs were being bought and sold in newsagents' all over Dublin (I liked to buy them by the half-dozen and store them in the egg compartment of my refrigerator). And on all the flower stalls and outside all the florists, sturdy, Dutch-looking tulips had appeared, in reds, yellows, pinks and whites.

I merged with the throngs of people crossing the road and heading into Grafton Street, getting caught up in their collective

1

Friday-evening excitement. The street was abuzz. For the first time that year, there was a real gentleness in the sun. There were young girls with rolls of puppy fat spilling out over hipster jeans, pierced bellies protruding like sweet, milky puddings from beneath their cropped T-shirts. A large crowd, consisting mainly of young men, had gathered to listen to a busker in his forties pick impossible notes out of his electric guitar. Some of them were clearly students; others, just a few years older, were newly be-suited and short-back-and-sided, still dreaming about jacking in the day jobs and becoming rock stars. But for me, for now, the delights of Grafton Street would have to wait – because I had a date.

So there I was, in the restaurant, waiting for George. How can I accurately describe my feelings at that time? I can still see myself sitting there in my vintage black dress. My hair was pinned up, and a silver and turquoise pendant adorned my neck. I might even have looked a little sophisticated. I certainly didn't feel sophisticated. I felt nervous – final-exam nervous, first-night-performance nervous. I looked down at my hands and played with my silver and turquoise rings. I also felt euphoric – a dangerous emotion for me; the flip side of depression. But this wasn't misplaced euphoria, bordering on hysteria. This high had a raison d'être.

My gut clenched as George walked into the restaurant. He was wearing his brown crombie. His hands were deep in his pockets as he walked swiftly to the table.

George was in his mid- to late forties. His hair had once been a very dark brown, verging on blackness; in fairness, he was still hanging on to it pretty well. He had a goatee beard for which, arguably, he was a little too long in the tooth, but I felt he had enough aplomb to carry it off – and, judging by his air of blatant confidence, he felt the same way. His eyes were the darkest brown. They crinkled up at the corners whenever he smiled at me. Not for the first time, I reflected on how much more interesting older men's faces were, how much more character they possessed. In comparison, a younger man's face was as disappointing as a blank page.

But George wasn't smiling now. Why wasn't he smiling? Panic rose in my throat, and I reached up to catch it with my hand. I stopped myself and fiddled with my necklace instead.

Stay calm. I forced myself to smile at him as he sat down heavily. He removed his crombie, and a waiter discreetly spirited it away.

'Well? Did you tell her?' I searched his spaniel eyes.

'Let me have a drink first.' Before I could object, he had called the waiter back and ordered himself a scotch on the rocks and me another gin.

To take a break from staring at my own rings, I stared at his: a gold signet ring on the pinky of his right hand – pure Mafia boss – and, on his wedding finger, a gold band.

The drinks arrived, and he took a giant swig – damn near emptied the glass. I followed suit. Still he said nothing.

'George, please. I'm about to explode here. Did you tell her or not?'

'Oh, I told her all right.'

'That you were leaving.'

'Yes.'

'Oh, thank God.'

I slumped back in my chair, the tension draining from my shoulders as if someone had released a valve. Scanning his features for clues, I leaned forward again and clasped his hands in my own. 'Well done. It must have been so difficult for you. How did she take it?'

3

'She wasn't too happy.'

'Well, no. She wouldn't have been. But it can't exactly have come as a surprise.'

He said nothing, just drained his glass and gestured for another.

I exhaled deeply and cupped my face in my hands, my elbows leaning on the table. My mind was positively whirring. At long last, I'd be able to leave my kip of a flat. I'd already given my landlord notice; I knew it had been a bit previous of me, but I'd been so excited, when George told me he was leaving his wife and moving in with me, that I hadn't been able to wait. Where would we go? I fancied Rathmines or Ranelagh – not too far from work, but not so close that you couldn't put it out of your mind on your days off. We'd rent at first, buy later. We wouldn't need much space – not in the beginning, anyhow – although we'd need a spare bedroom for when his kids came to visit. Hopefully they wouldn't resent me too much. They were teenagers – old enough, surely, to realise that their parents' marriage had been over a long time before I came on the scene. I'd be their stepmother!

It was finally happening, after a year of excuses. He'd tell her as soon as they came back from their summer holiday – it had been booked for ages, she'd booked it without asking him first. Then he'd tell her as soon as the frenzy surrounding their twentieth wedding anniversary had died down. And then it had been when their daughter Judith finished her Leaving Cert. The complex and convoluted reasons had been legion. But now he'd actually gone and done it.

I looked at him fondly. His hair was almost completely pewter, but streaks of black still permeated his beard, lending him a slightly odd, badger-like appearance. He was still fiddling with his glass.

'Liz. There's something else I have to tell you.'

'What?' I was immediately on high alert.

He took a deep breath. 'Judith's pregnant.'

'Oh. Oh, dear. I'm so sorry, George. That's terrible. I mean, she's so young.' I reached over and took his hand encouragingly. 'But it needn't be the end of the world. Lots of young girls have babies and go on to lead successful lives nowadays. And at least she's got her Leaving Cert out of the way. She'll probably just need to take a year off college. Do you know who the father is?'

He was looking at me now with pure horror in his eyes. 'No,' he said softly. 'You don't understand. Not Judith, my daughter. Judith, my wife.'

My brain started to whirr again, more slowly this time, not quite as efficiently. Judith – his wife – was pregnant. For a second I was about to commiserate with him again: his unfaithful wife had been having it away with another man. But no – no…it couldn't be…

'You mean,' I said slowly, 'Judith, your wife, the one you haven't slept with for over three years?'

His Adam's apple bobbed up and down. Why wasn't he denying it?

'Well?' I snapped.

'It only happened the once. I swear. She got me drunk one night. It was a moment of madness. But you understand that I can't possibly leave her now, not when she's so vulnerable…'

His lips continued to move, but I was no longer listening to him. I was too busy concentrating on the fact that my whole world was crashing down loudly about my ears. I knew there'd be hurt. I knew there'd be tears. But not yet. First came the rage. It built up like a steam train inside my head.

'You bastard,' I said quietly. George was still speaking, but I ignored him. 'You despicable, low-life, miserable, lying, cheating, fucking bastard.' With each word, my voice became louder. By the last 'bastard', our waiter and the neighbouring diners were starting to look distinctly alarmed – as well they might. An explosion went off in my head as I literally launched myself across the table at George.

'You fucking scumbag!' I yelled. At this point, I had one foot on the floor and the other knee on the table. I started to pummel at his head with all my might.

'How dare you?' I screamed. 'How could you do this to me?' I threw his drink, followed by my own, into his face.

'Madam, please!' The waiter was beside me, hopping up and down frantically. I ignored him.

'I hate you! I hate your guts. You bollox, you shit…' With each statement I whacked George around the head as hard as I could. He attempted, in vain, to shield himself with his hands.

All of a sudden I felt myself lifted into the air from either side. I kicked my legs fruitlessly as I was carried towards the exit and plonked unceremoniously before the door.

'May I remind you, Madam, that this is a respectable establishment?' the maitre d' said furiously. 'I believe this is your coat.' He shoved it at me and held the door open.

'Prick,' I said. It was the only insult that I hadn't already used up. I didn't shout this time, but it was certainly loud enough for all the nearby diners to hear. Then I found myself standing alone in the rain on Baggot Street. Couples sharing umbrellas strolled happily by, completely oblivious.

Now it was time to cry.

2

'I'm looking for a novel. It was on *The Late Late Show*.'

'Last night?'

'No. About a year ago.'

'Right. Do you remember what it was called?'

'No.'

'OK, do you know who wrote it?'

'No. It was a long time ago, you know.'

'Yes. You said.'

'Oh!' The woman looked excited.

'Yes?' Oh, sweet anticipation.

'It had a white cover.'

I sighed. 'Did it, now? Well, you know what you should do?'

'What?'

'Do you see that man standing over by the Sports section? Yes – the one with the beard. Ask him. He's bound to know.'

'Oh, right. Thanks for your help.'

'My pleasure.'

I idly watched the exchange for a couple of minutes – the woman gesticulating theatrically, and the mounting frustration on Tom's face. He shot me a putrid look. I would have sent one back, but I didn't have the energy. Instead, I turned back to my book for comfort. It was my custom to keep whatever book I happened to be reading hidden beneath the cash desk, but today I couldn't be bothered, even though I knew that the owner of the shop was due in at any moment. I was reading *One Hundred Years of Solitude*, by Gabriel Garcia Marquez. I could have done with a bit of solitude myself – a break from pesky customers. I'd nearly phoned in sick that morning, but the thought of spending a whole day dwelling upon the decayed ruins of my former love life had stopped me.

A man approached me shiftily and placed a book, face down, on the counter.

'I'll take this, please,' he murmured, glancing surreptitiously from side to side. I guessed that it was either a sex manual or a book on incontinence, impotence or explosive diarrhoea. Yes – there you go: *The Joy of Sex*. As if I gave a toss about what he read, thought, bought or did in his spare time. I watched him as he shoved the bagged book inside his coat and left the premises in the manner of a shoplifter. Usually, I would have felt a little compassion for someone in his position; but today he just made me wonder why men were such a bunch of stupid assholes.

'Thanks for that, Elizabeth.' It was Tom.

'What?'

'You know what. Lumbering me with that mad old bat.'

'Oh, shut up. It's your job, isn't it? Did you work out what book she was talking about?'

'God, no. But she mentioned that she wanted it to read on her holidays, so I convinced her to buy a book about Lanzarote instead.'

'Clever boy.'

'I know.' He did, too.

When first I was introduced to Tom, I thought he was gay. Then I was introduced to his wife, Mindy (her real name is Ursula. Well – wouldn't you?), who I assumed was a dyke. Then I met their two-year-old daughter, Clarissa, and revised my opinion.

Tom has dark hair, a beard and a paunch. He wears outrageous sideburns and a wicked grin. When we first met, almost three years

8

ago, he harboured acting ambitions far above his station. Later he transferred his ambitions to publishing and found an outlet for his thespian proclivities in amateur dramatics and the local musical society, where he spent many a happy hour torturing middle-aged women who, in his opinion, took the whole thing far too seriously. He was arrogant and pompous and said 'indeed' far too much, but better company could seldom be found on either side of the Liffey. When I first found out he was straight, I considered him as a potential romantic partner for several seconds, as one does with all new males. True, he was married. That was one point in his favour. But he was far too young for me, a mere year and a half older than I was, and he cared far too much about his cuticles for me to take him seriously. There had also been the odd cravat-wearing incident.

He peered at me closely. 'You all right?'

'Yes. Why?'

'You look a bit funny. Puffy-eyed. Have you been crying?'

'No.'

'Yes, you have.'

'No, I haven't.'

'Have.'

'Leave me alone, Tom.'

I saw Tom's eyes widen in alarm as my own welled up. Again.

'Jesus, there is something wrong.'

Pulling a bedraggled piece of tissue from the sleeve of my cardigan, I dabbed at my eyes frantically.

'Are you on one o'clock lunch today?'

I nodded.

'Me too. I'll book a table at Gotham.'

I nodded again. It was all I could do, apart from feel pathetically grateful. I checked the clock: almost midday. I just had to hold it together for one more hour. I could do that. I blew my nose, as noiselessly as possible, and glanced around the shop. Not a bad place to be when your life was falling apart, I reflected.

Grainger's Bookshop was almost a century old. One hundred years of commerce. It had been founded by the current owner's great-uncle, who had died without issue. There had been a few lean years in recent times – competition from the smarter-looking bookshops that sprang up around the city from time to time. But the punters always returned, drawn once more by the unique, brown mustiness of Grainger's. It never changed; when the current owner's father had died a few years back, the old-fashioned tills had been replaced by up-to-date versions, but that was about it. The original shop-front remained. A bell on the door still pinged to alert us to the presence of a new customer. Rare titles had to be accessed by means of a ladder that slid along the wall. And it was still undoubtedly one of the best-stocked bookshops in Dublin, with the best staff – apart from me.

I was probably the worst employee in the history of Grainger's. The only reason I hadn't been sacked long since was that my best friend, Helen, was the shop manager. It wasn't that I didn't know my stuff; it was just that imparting the information to customers made substantial inroads into my valuable reading time. And I could never get my till to balance correctly, either. It was always way off, and I could never work out why. Luckily Helen knew that I was no thief – just completely incompetent. She was always covering up for me, bless her.

Helen and I had met in Trinity College, where we had both studied pure English. If I put my mind to it, I could still recall the paralysing sense of intimidation I had felt in those early college days. It seemed ludicrous to me now. When I walked by the gates of the college these days and watched the students loitering on either side of the iron railings, they seemed so very young, with their Trinity scarves draped self-consciously around their pink necks. But when you're little more than a child yourself, and when you come from the unfashionable end of Phibsboro, and most of your classmates come from the fashionable end of Foxrock; and when you've been dragged up sideways in the local community school, with Tracy whose ultimate ambition is to work behind the checkout at the local supermarket and Doyler who now reigns supreme in C wing of Mountjoy Prison, while your new classmates have spent the last six years in the most expensive private schools in the country, with Humphrey Plonkington-Smythe and Hilary Plinkington-Plonk…

Helen had come from one of those private schools. Destiny had sat us together in the first week, at a less than illuminating lecture on Dante's *Inferno*. She had shyly invited me for a cup of coffee in the Buttery, and I had shyly accepted. So had begun an alliance that had withstood the strain of countless disastrous romantic and not-so-romantic dalliances, not to mention the vicissitudes of my writing career.

Old Mr Grainger had taken great interest in my then-embryonic writing career. I recalled him vividly, although I'd only met him a handful of times when I first started in the job. He had been a very old man, crumbling with decrepitude, but his heart had still beaten with a passion when it came to books and his beloved shop. As for the current owner…

The door pinged. It was George. *Oh, God…* I held my breath, but he didn't even look my way. He walked straight past me.

'Afternoon, Mr Grainger,' chorused the staff on the floor.

'Afternoon, everyone.'

Young Mr Grainger. It was like an episode of *Are You Being Served*, I thought bitterly. He continued through the shop and disappeared behind the door that led into Helen's office.

Did I mention that George – George Grainger, my former lover,

11

the man with whom I had been having an affair, the man whom I had verbally and physically assaulted and publicly humiliated just the night before – was my boss?

He was in there for an age. I stared anxiously at the clock. What could they possibly be talking about? It took one poor woman at least five minutes to get me to take for *How to Heal the Gaping Hole in Your Head*, from our Mind, Body, Spirit section. And she was the only one in the queue at the time.

At long last, the office door opened. It was Helen; I was soon to discover that George had pulled a fast one and escaped out the back door. She met my gaze anxiously.

'Come on,' she said, 'let's go and get some lunch. Are you coming, Tom?' she called over her shoulder.

'But it's only ten to one.'

'We'll make an exception.'

I shrugged. Who was I to complain about an extra-long lunch break?

'I wonder if I need my coat,' I mused. 'No, I don't think I'll bother; it's quite warm out.'

'Liz. I think you should bring your coat with you.' I noticed then that her eyes were red-rimmed.

I made my way to the storage room out the back. On the way, I was treated to the rare sight of a customer with one of my books in her hand. It was the second one. Grainger's was probably one of the few bookshops in Dublin – in the entire universe – that still stocked it.

I couldn't resist approaching her. 'That's very good,' I said. 'I'd highly recommend it.'

'Really?'

'Yes. And I happen to know the author personally. If you like, I can even get it signed for you.'

'Ah, I don't think I'll bother. I read her first one, and I found it disappointing.'

Having fought back the urge to bludgeon her to death with the few remaining copies of my book, I entered the storage room. Eric, the lanky blond person whose job was to take deliveries and unload boxes, dropped the book he was reading.

'Just a tad obvious, Eric.'

He smiled, picked up his book again and sat back down on the box he'd been using as a chair.

'Have you seen my coat?'

'Is that it over there?'

It was on the floor, underneath twenty-odd copies of *Bridget Jones: The Edge of Reason*. I knew how she felt. I picked it up and dusted it off.

'Are you all right?' Eric looked at me a bit strangely – probably because I looked a bit strange.

'Never been better.'

3

It would have been hard to find three more mismatched figures walking down Grafton Street that lunchtime.

To my left, we have Helen: long, curly, honey-brown hair; long, straight, honey-brown legs; tall, confident, competent. To my right, Tom – loud in both manner and dress, and leading with his paunch. And then there was me, the little piggy in the middle. And, make no mistake, I felt exactly like a pig that day – both inside and out. My shoulder-length black hair was a haze that mercifully covered up most of my sullen face and hid my swollen eyes. My floor-length black coat, which I had brought along on Helen's advice, covered up my soon-to-be-discarded shop uniform.

With each step I took, my sense of dread grew. I'd never thought I wouldn't want to arrive at the Gotham Café. But there we were. No going back. No putting it off. No way out.

We took our favourite table by the window, and Helen determinedly perused the menu she knew off by heart – classic delaying tactics. Feeling even sorrier for her than for myself, I decided to put her out of her misery.

'He fired me, didn't he?'

She drew a deep breath. 'Yes.'

'That's why you were crying.'

'Yes.'

'And that's why you told me to bring my coat with me?'

'Yes, it is. George said you needn't come back to work if you don't want to. He'll pay you two weeks' wages in lieu of notice.'

'Well, isn't that very fucking noble of him? The low-down, sneaky, good-for-nothing…'

'He sacked you? Why?' asked Tom.

Helen and I looked at each other.

'Be my guest,' I said.

'Liz has been having an affair with the boss.'

'Not Gorgeous George?'

'The very man.'

'No! You mean that married man you've been banging on about for the last year – it was Grainger all along?'

'Yep.'

Tom clapped his hands together and widened his eyes and mouth as far as all three orifices could go. 'I don't believe you.'

'It's true.'

'That's the best bit of gossip I've heard all year. You've surpassed yourself this time.'

'Gee, thanks, Tom. Your praise means a lot.'

'I mean, your married boss – how wonderfully clichéd! I love it!'

'Again, Tom, thanks.'

'But, Jesus – your job… That's rough. He can't do that, surely. Can he, Helen? Sack her for – how will I put it – for being a tart?'

'Excuse me!'

'Well, you know what I mean. Can't she do what Eric the Viking did and take him to one of those industrial-strength tribunals – countersue for sexual harassment or something?'

'It's *industrial* tribunal, you moron. I don't know if she can, really. It was different for Eric.'

Eric the Viking was Tom's name for Eric. He hadn't had to stretch his imagination too far to come up with that one: Eric was tall and bony, with white-blond hair and Nordic cheekbones. George had fired him because he wore his headphones all the time

15

while he worked in the stockroom. The Viking had succeeded in proving that his incessant music-listening didn't affect the quality of his work, and had won the right to be reinstated. I remembered how furious George had been at the time.

'But why is it different?' Tom persisted.

'It just is.' Helen seemed embarrassed.

'What is it?' I said.

'Well, he says he has other grounds.'

'Let me guess. Incompetence.'

'Well…yes. I'm so sorry, Liz. I really did try and talk him round, but he wasn't having any of it. I take it things are over between you?'

And I was off – crying in public, again; making a show of myself, again. Helen took my hand and stroked it. Tom rubbed my upper back, right between the shoulder blades. It was very soothing, actually. Then he beckoned to the waiter, who'd been hovering impatiently. He ordered us all our usuals.

'And you'd better bring her a beer, too,' he added. 'On second thoughts, make that three beers – and one each for me and Helen.'

When his beer arrived, he held it as if it were a prop, laughing silently to himself between sips. I could tell he was having a great time. I pictured him telling Mindy the latest. I could see her throwing back her head and letting out one of her enormous, raucous, man's laughs, and then going down to the local, where she would down six pints of Scrumpy and tell all her butch friends what a sad cow I was.

The waiter returned and placed three opened bottles of Heineken before me.

'*Gracias*,' I said, dabbing my eyes and guessing his country of origin. Immediately, his face lit up and he launched into a stream of incomprehensible babble. I blinked and looked at him blankly.

'He thinks you're Spanish,' Helen explained.

16

'Oh – no, no.' I shook my head and managed a weak smile. The waiter shrugged and walked off, looking disappointed.

'So what happened? You were meeting up with George last night, weren't you?' said Helen.

'Yes. He told his wife about us.'

'Really? God! I never thought he'd do that. What did she say?'

'That she was pregnant.'

'Really?' said Tom. 'Judith? She's hardly a spring chicken.'

'She's only forty,' I snapped, ludicrously defending my ex-lover's wife. I was mindful that I myself would be forty one day, not all that far in the dim and distant future. And it seemed a damn sight closer now that I was single again.

'So,' I said, 'the bastard was sleeping with her all along.'

'The cheek of him, having sex with his own wife,' said Helen.

'Well, that's just great, Helen. I could really use your sarcasm just about now.'

'Look, I feel bad for you, Liz; I really do. But, honest to God, forgive me if I have just a little sympathy for his family. The man has two kids, after all.'

'Two and a half,' chipped in Tom. He really was having the time of his life.

'They're practically grown up,' I said.

'They're only teenagers,' said Helen. 'They still need their dad. You, of all people, should understand that.'

Sensing I was losing the battle, I decided to bring out the big guns. 'I can't help it,' I said, almost smugly. 'I'm psychologically programmed to be attracted to older men.'

'Oh, come on, Liz. You've been using that "I'm searching for a father figure" line for far too long now,' Helen said, sounding quite cross.

I stared at my so-called friend in disgust. I had known all along

17

that she didn't approve of my relationship with George, but I'd failed to understand the full extent of her disapproval. It was all right for her, with her perfect Stepford family.

I turned to Tom for affirmation. 'I suppose you think I'm a cold-hearted little home-wrecker who's getting her just deserts, too?'

'No. I just think it goes to show that you should never poo on your own doorstep. Speaking of desserts, I think I'll have the Key lime pie. Are you guys going to have something?'

We both shook our heads – Helen because she had the discipline of a Buddhist monk, and me because I always went off my food when I broke up with a man. This was partly because it was, temporarily, the only thing over which I felt I had any control, and partly because I was all too aware that I had been shunted back onto the singles market and therefore did not have the luxury of letting myself go. As it was, I had barely fiddled with my favourite Flatiron pizza.

We were silent for a little while, all digesting what we had to digest, be that edible or non-edible. Every once in a while I allowed myself a comforting little sob into my sodden serviette, and Tom resumed rubbing my back. I was ever so grateful.

'Seriously, Liz,' Helen said, 'what will you do for money? Will you be able to afford your rent?'

'I can always get another job.'

They looked at me, then looked at each other, then looked away.

'Well, thanks for the vote of confidence. I'm not completely useless, you know.'

This time they didn't look at me at all.

I sighed. 'I suppose I could always move back home.'

'Oh, God. Seriously?' Helen sounded genuinely sympathetic. She had met my family.

'I don't have a lot of choice. I can barely afford the flat as it is.

18

No, I'll go back home. I'll concentrate on my writing – that's what I'll do. I'll have lots of free time on my hands. This next book will be the best one yet. You know, I honestly think this might be the best thing that's ever happened to me.'

'Yes,' Helen said weakly. I could feel her trying to be supportive. 'It might be a blessing in disguise.'

I caught the look on Tom's face.

Bloody good disguise.

4

I can't have been the only person in Dublin who had noticed that
the heart was being ripped out of the city. In any case, I identified.
These days it was downright depressing walking down Charlemont
Street – a street once brimming with character. Now, all the elegant
old red-bricks had been demolished to make way for progress, in
the shape of hotel chains and faceless apartment blocks. Not that I
was in a position to complain, living as I did in one of these
apartment blocks – though not for long.

I let myself into my flat, and the sound of the front door
slamming reverberated into the silence. I was home – not that it felt
like home any more; not that it *was* my home any more. Not after
today. The four weeks' notice I'd given my landlord were almost up,
and I wouldn't have been able to afford next month's rent anyhow
– not now that I'd been sacked.

The sooner I got this over with, the better. I stood decisively on
my bed and dragged my battered brown case from the top of the
wardrobe. I looked around, considering where to start. In spite of
everything, I was more than a little sad to leave. We'd shared some
good times, this room and I. This was the end of what had been –
for the most part – a very good era. And now I was going back
home, backwards... *Don't think about it. Just pack.*

I started with my most treasured possessions. I took my Fern
Fennelly original off the wall and wrapped it protectively in a
cashmere pashmina, purchased on a trip to New York. I removed
the strings of coloured beads and chiffon scarves draped across the

mother-of-pearl frames containing various snapshots of cherished childhood pets, and stacked the frames in my case.

Then I tackled the jumble beside my bed. I'd always thought you could tell a lot about a person by what she had on her bedside table, or failing that, on the floor beside her bed – as in this case. There was my bedside lamp, of course – the bulb was red, to lend a certain ambiance – and my itty-bitty book light, for nights when I had company and didn't want to disturb with my nocturnal reading. Most importantly, there were books: *The Lives and Loves of a She-Devil*, which I'd just finished, and *The Girl's Guide to Hunting and Fishing*, which I was just about to read. I could do with some guidance; it was clear that I had veered way off course a long time ago and had yet to find my way back. Then I had an antique *Cosmopolitan*; a notebook, in case inspiration struck in the dead of night or in case I had a flummoxing dream that I wanted to record and analyse in the cold light of day; half a glass of water, full of bubbles and containing one long black hair; two Solpadeine tablets; one box of tissues; one purple scrunchie; three pens, one working; one dead spider; one tube of walnut and rosemary hand cream; a watch that had yet to be wound one hour forward; a travel alarm clock that worked when it felt like it; a passport-sized photo of George (which I ripped up and threw in the bin); a pair of Totes rolled into a ball; and a bottle of red nail polish. I think that was it. All in one square foot. It was a veritable microcosm of my life: chaos.

It was time to move on.

I finished packing and indulged myself with one last nostalgic look around the room. Now devoid of personalising details, it revealed itself to be nothing but a tiny, rectangular boxroom with barely the space for a single bed. *Adios.*

I closed the door and phoned for a cab.

When the taxi pulled up outside a row of terraced houses in Phibsboro, it was teatime, and the road was empty – except for a scutty little terrier that cocked his leg against the rear wheel of the taxi before trotting off home for his own tea. I heaved my case laboriously to the front door and let it down with a thud, cringing at the thought of my precious breakables. I couldn't find my key, so I rang the doorbell.

'Somebody get that,' I heard my mother yell, above the theme tune of *The Simpsons*. After a pause, I heard footsteps on the lino in the hallway, getting closer, accompanied by a string of curses, getting louder.

My mother opened the door and stared at me for several seconds in surprise. She had a tea towel draped over her left shoulder and her cheeks were flushed. The aroma of burgers and peas wafted out of the kitchen into the hallway. My mother looked me up and down.

'You're not *still* wearing that coat?'

Familial reactions to my homecoming were mixed. I'll own up to being parsimonious with the truth. I neglected to tell my mother that I had been sacked following an affair with my married boss. I just said I had given up my job voluntarily in order to pursue my writing career with renewed vigour, the only slight drawback being that I could no longer afford my rent. My mother was none too impressed with this course of action. I comforted myself with the knowledge that the truth would have been even less palatable.

When I'd first told the mammy that I was to have a book published, her initial reaction had been amazement that her wayward sprog might yet amount to something. Then came the pride – at last, something to boast to the neighbours about – and then the pleasure. I had been thrilled to elicit such a response. But that had been over three years ago. Since then, my two books had scarcely managed to cause a ripple of interest on the Irish literary scene. I was horribly aware that it was make-or-break time, and that the success of book three was crucial. My mother had realised a while back that her visions of being flown to the Oscars on a private jet were just that – visions. And she looked at me again with old eyes.

As for the rest of my family...

My stepdad – Graham – was rendered predictably uneasy by my mother's displeasure, but he didn't seem too put out personally. My brother Jim, on the other hand, was less than pleased at my return. 'You needn't think you're getting your bleedin' room back.'

'You needn't worry. I don't want it. I'd only have to fumigate it and bring in industrial cleaners.'

'Fuck off.'

That was Jim – Jamser to his mates. And what a collection of mates they were. They all looked and acted – and were – exactly the same. They all had the same stupid hairstyle, which they achieved with the application of too much hair gel; their clothes were identical. I was willing to bet that they all read *Nuts* magazine and had posters of Jordan on their bedroom walls. And I suspected that they had all secretly auditioned for boy bands. They frequently went to rock festivals and slept six blokes to a four-man tent, asphyxiating on one another's farts and B.O.

Then there was Tim. (Yes, Jim and Tim. Legend had it that my mother had wanted to call me Kim, but my father had saved me from this fate by naming me before his departure.) Tim was fourteen. Each time I came home, I expected him to have mutated

23

into a horrible teenage creature – his brother had become a teenager at age eleven and, at twenty, was still struggling to become an adult – but no: Tim was as sweet as ever. He was currently going through a *Lord of the Rings* phase – at least, I hoped it was a phase. He had read all the books three times and had all the films on DVD, even though my mother and Graham had yet to purchase a DVD player – but Tim lived in hope. When I became the only family member to agree to a challenge match in his role-playing *Lord of the Rings* board game, his happiness was complete. So I think I can safely say that Tim was pleased to have me home.

It was eleven o'clock of a Sunday morning and I was already nursing my second cup of coffee. I sat dreamily at the battered kitchen table, scarred as it was by a thousand such coffee cups. I was royally attired in bed-socks and a fluffy, plum-coloured dressing-gown.

Somehow, being back at home made me think about Dad more than usual. I didn't know why this should be, although I had to admit that George's abandonment had probably gone some way towards stirring up all the old feelings again. It wasn't as if I'd ever lived with Dad in this house. I had no happy memories of playing swingball with him in the back garden, or of snuggling up together in front of *Blake's Seven* in the sitting room – no memories at all; just a sense of longing. Sometimes it was vague, but at other times it was overwhelming – times like now, when I felt like an alien in my own family. I couldn't help but think about how differently things might have turned out if Dad had lived. My parents might have got back together. They might have had more children. I might have had a sister. Or two.

Something else that George's abandonment had stirred up was

a desire to look for my father's family. It was a thought that surfaced from time to time, but I was usually quick to quash it. What if they weren't interested? It wasn't as if they'd ever tried to look *me* up...

Jim entered the room, clad in a pair of striped pyjama bottoms and a black T-shirt with red writing on it. 'Shit happens,' said his T-shirt. It certainly does.

Without even looking at me, Jim opened the fridge and stared into its depths for about fifteen seconds. Then, scratching his arse with one hand, he took out a carton of orange juice with the other and began to drink directly from it.

'Don't do that, Jim. It's disgusting.'

'Fuck off,' he replied, wiping his mouth with the back of his hand and replacing the carton.

'Is that the full extent of your vocabulary?'

'No. Fuck off, *bitch*.'

'You know, you've grown up to be such a lovely young man.'

'And you've grown up into such a lovely old woman.'

I took a large gulp of coffee and decided to start again. 'So what are you doing with yourself these days?'

'What do you mean?'

'Well – are you working?'

'I'm an apprentice welder.'

'Really?' I started to giggle. 'Like the girl in *Flashdance*?'

'Fuck off.'

I started singing 'Maniac'. I knew it wasn't exactly mature, but I couldn't help myself. My family always brought out the worst in me.

He flounced out of the room, muttering obscenities.

'What's wrong with you?' I heard my mother's voice in the hallway. She bustled into the kitchen, pulling a navy cardigan over her uniform as she went. 'Don't you be starting with him, Madam. He's hard enough to deal with as it is.'

'I didn't say a word.'

'Hmph!' She clearly wasn't fooled.

'Do you want a cup of coffee?'

'No, thank you. Some of us have to go to work.'

Ouch.

My mother was a nurse. She'd always been a working mother, thanks to my father's untimely departure. Her nursing background made her the type of person who could discuss periods and bowel movements with an alarming lack of self-consciousness. I'd never quite mastered this myself, which meant that we managed to embarrass each other in equal measure.

'Look, Libby.' She stopped what she was doing and stood with her hands on her hips, looking down at me. 'Did you really give up your job, or did you get the sack again?'

'No!' I was indignant. 'I told you. I left so I could concentrate on my writing.'

'But it was only a part-time job. Could you not work and write at the same time?'

'No,' I said. 'My writing *is* my career, you know.'

'No, dear. A career pays you money. Your writing is a hobby – a very nice hobby, mind you, but a hobby just the same. It's about time you realised that.'

I was furious. I said nothing, just gripped the handle of my mug until my knuckles went white.

'You can't just waltz back in here and expect me to support you again. I've enough mouths to feed as it is.'

'I don't expect you to support me.'

'Well, what were you planning on doing?'

'I'll sign on.'

'Oh, will you now? Isn't that very ambitious of you? Wake up, Libby, and join the rest of us in the real world. Jesus Christ, you're just like…'

The unfinished sentence hung in the air between us.

'I've had enough of this. I'm off,' she said abruptly, grabbing her keys off the table and exiting swiftly into the hall.

My family really knew how to make a person welcome, that was for sure. I mean, I hadn't expected the red-carpet treatment, but this took the biscuit. But I'd show her! Book three was going to be a masterpiece. It would be that rare hybrid of a book – critically acclaimed and a runaway bestseller at the same time. She'd be sorry! Stuck at home, cooking burgers and peas, while I was living it large at the *Vanity Fair* after-show Oscar party – because they'd be bound to make this one into a film. I fantasised about what I'd do with all the money …

I wouldn't waste another second. I'd start immediately. First thing tomorrow morning. Now where had she hidden the biscuits?

5

It was now tomorrow morning – already – and I was about to start writing. I'd just put the kettle on and have another cup of tea first.

It was Monday morning. The house was completely quiet; everybody else was at work or at school. Perfect writing conditions. I'd clearly done the right thing by coming home.

I wandered around the sitting room, cup of tea in hand, looking out of the window for inspiration. All I saw was that scutty little terrier, pissing on anything that didn't move and couldn't object. I turned my attention back into the room. Best make up my bed.

I was sleeping on the sofa-bed – hardly ideal, but beggars and all that. I tidied it away and considered my surroundings. Bloody awful. Rummaging around in my case, I took out the two mother-of-pearl picture-frames. I put one on the coffee table and the other on the television, beside a pink plastic pot containing a cactus. There were cacti growing all over the house. Apparently you hardly ever had to water them, just dust them.

Speaking of the TV… I flicked on breakfast television. I'd just watch it while I was having my tea. A young female author was giving an interview about her latest book. It was only chick-lit, but I decided I'd better watch it just in case, for research purposes. I finally switched off the telly when they switched to a feature extolling the virtues of Tupperware. Even I didn't have the capacity to sit through that.

I switched on my laptop, and the blank screen stared back up at me. I changed the font from Times New Roman to Tahoma and back again. Then I wrote 'Chapter One' in bold italics. Then I underlined it. There.

God, I really missed George. This time four days ago, I had been planning a whole future with him. Now here I was, back home again, sleeping on a lousy settee and living with the Addams Family. Did that make me Wednesday Addams?

It was no use. I needed to stretch my legs first. I pressed Save and sauntered into the kitchen, searching for random tasks to complete. I unloaded the dishwasher. Three brownie points. I calculated that I'd have to earn another one thousand, four hundred and ninety-seven to get back into my mother's good books. *May as well make a cup of tea while I'm in here...*

I brought it back into the sitting room and switched the television back on for my tea break. *Cagney and Lacey* was just starting. Excellent! Hard-hitting, groundbreaking, superb dialogue and great story lines... I might be able to pick up a few tips. I fancied writing for TV someday.

When the programme was over, I went upstairs to the loo (all that tea). I rambled in and out of the bedrooms. It had been a while since I had seen any of them. I wasn't snooping or anything. There'd be no opening of drawers or exploration under the beds.

Tim's room was exactly the same as I remembered it, save for six massive *Lord of the Rings* posters on the walls. He appeared to have a marked preference for Aragorn. Come to think of it, he had insisted on playing him in the game last night. I swiftly made the bed and left the room.

Next came what used to be my room, now occupied by Jim the Usurper. I opened the door and recoiled. Everything was black and red. The curtains were still drawn; they were red and they lent the room an eerie, crimson glow. The Laura Ashley wallpaper was long gone – well, that was no bad thing. The walls were plastered from

29

floor to ceiling with posters of Metallica, the Red Hot Chili Peppers, Nirvana and their ilk. The bed was unmade, and it could stay that way. The pungent aroma of Lynx body spray seemed to be masking a much darker, murkier scent…what was it? Ah, yes: teenager. Smells like teen spirit. I closed the door without even going in.

And how about the mammy and stepdaddy's room? I was starting to feel like Goldilocks. I'd be tasting everyone's porridge next. The bed was unmade here also, but I'd soon remedy that. Two more brownie points (one thousand, four hundred and ninety-five to go). I sat down on the made bed, alongside my mother's bedside cabinet. What was she reading? Jesus. Did the woman have no taste?

The door of the bedside cabinet was slightly ajar, and I couldn't resist taking just one tiny peek… Videos. I hesitated. Did I really want to know if Graham and my mother watched porn together? But by then it was too late: I'd already seen the title of one of them.

Oh, good Jesus! I couldn't bear it. *Julio Iglesias – Live in Concert*. And there were about six of them, too – all Julio. I chuckled to myself and considered blackmail. Who'd have guessed it? The most practical, sensible woman in the world, hankering after some mushy romantic crooner. If her employers found out about this, she could lose her job.

This I had to see. Filled with glee, I ran back down the stairs and popped one of the videos into the VCR. And there he was – tangerine skin glowing, black hair shining, white teeth gleaming. He was standing on a stage in front of a horde of women, singing a ballad. The women were collectively transfixed, as if witnessing a vision or a moving statue. Midway through the song, he crouched down onto his hunkers at the edge of the stage and began to sing directly to one of the women in the front row, as if she were the only

30

woman in the room. He clasped her hand against his chest and stared intently into her eyes. She cried, silent, blissful tears… I hit the fast-forward button. I was allergic to cheese.

The next song was slightly more acceptable. Julio was strolling along a beach, hands in pockets, canvas trousers rolled up, waves lapping gently against his toes. Next was that song with Willie Nelson. I quite liked him.

Before I knew it, I was halfway through the tape. Credit where credit was due: Julio really was a very good-looking man. A bit on the orange side, but still, I think I preferred him to his son. And, while the style of singing wasn't exactly to my taste, he did have a fine pair of lungs on him.

I all but leapt out of the chair when the front door slammed. Panicking, I fumbled around for the remote control, barely managing to hit the stop button before Jim stuck his head around the door.

'What are you doing here?'

'Nothing. What are *you* doing here?'

'I came home for my lunch. What are you up to? Your face is all red.' I could feel my cheeks burning. Shit!

'Were you watching porn?'

'No, I was not!' It was far more shameful than that. I threw a cushion in the general direction of Jim's head. It hit the wall, narrowly missing him. His head disappeared, but I could hear his evil laugh travelling down the hallway and into the kitchen.

Urgently and furtively, I rewound the tape and pressed the eject button. What had I been thinking? Watching a Julio Iglesias video in broad daylight – and enjoying it! And fancying him! How sad was that? I found the case and picked it up. As I did so, a photo fell out from inside the back cover and fluttered to the ground. I picked it up off the floor.

A young girl with strawberry-blonde hair and blue eyes was beaming into the camera. She was wearing a simple white dress and holding a bouquet of freesias over a mound of belly in a hopeless attempt to hide it. She was arm in arm with a slightly taller man. He had thick black hair, dark-brown eyes, a swarthy complexion and a moustache like a ferret. Someone had inserted the head of a yellow freesia into his lapel. The suit screamed seventies.

I felt kind of sick – and not just because of the revelation that my father had worn a moustache. It was the first time I had ever seen his face.

6

From the moment she got home that evening, I stalked her silently and relentlessly, waiting for the opportunity to get her on her own. Waiting to pounce.

The closest I got was after dinner. Jim and Tim had left the table. Graham was still there, drinking his tea and reading his gun magazine. My mother was opening and closing presses, humming to herself, looking for the packet of biscuits that she had hidden (and which, unbeknownst to her, Jim had scoffed two days previously). She was in the best mood I'd seen her in since my homecoming.

'Can I talk to you about something, Mam?'

'Hold on a second, I'm just looking for something. Graham, have you seen the chocolate biscuits?'

'I never touched them.'

'I never said you did. Have you seen them, Libby?'

'No. Mam, will you please sit down so I can talk to you?'

'All right, all right. Hold your horses.' She stopped looking and sat down opposite me. She even smiled. I started to doubt myself. Maybe I shouldn't confront her until she was already in a bad mood. That way, I wouldn't have as much to lose.

'Did you get much writing done today?'

'Yes. Loads.'

'Really? Well, that's something, I suppose.'

'Look, Mam, I found something when I was tidying your room today.'

Graham's head shot up out of his magazine. He was starting to say something when Tim burst in.

'Libby, will you play *Lord of the Rings* with me?'

'Not now, Tim.'

'Please. You can be Galadriel.'

'No, Tim. Later.'

'But—'

'No!' I shouted.

Looking surprised and hurt, Tim shut up and went back out. I'd make it up to him later.

'What's this about, Libby?' My mother was starting to look worried.

You may have noticed that my family call me Libby. I changed my name to Liz when I started secondary school; I thought it had more of an edge to it. Now I was thinking of changing it back, as part of a general desire to return to my roots.

I drew the photo out of my pocket and placed it on the table in front of Mam. She looked down at it for a long time without saying anything – without seeing anything, or so it seemed.

'What were you doing rooting around in my room?' Her voice was controlled, contained.

'I wasn't rooting around. I was making your bed. The cabinet door was open; I saw a video and decided to play it, and the photo just fell out.'

'You had no right.'

'And you had no right to keep this from me. A photograph of my father! You told me you'd burnt them all.'

She didn't respond – not in words, anyway. Her body language spoke decibels. She sat with her arms crossed tightly and her lips pursed shut. A splotch of red had appeared on each of her cheeks and she stared straight ahead, as if concentrating on making the cabinet doors fly open by the power of thought alone.

'You knew how curious I was about him – all the questions I asked growing up… This photo would have meant so much to me.' I could feel my voice cracking.

Still she didn't say anything. Her silence fuelled my outrage.

'How could you be so cruel?'

'That photo is private.' She accentuated each word with frightening precision.

Graham's head shot up as she spoke. He looked at me fearfully, as if to say, *You've done it now*. I didn't care.

'I don't give a shite about your privacy,' I said. 'I've gone through my entire life not even knowing what my own father looked like. Do you have any idea what that can do to a person? What else have you been keeping from me?'

'I've kept nothing from you. I've told you everything you need to know about that man.'

'You've told me virtually nothing about *that man*, as you so charmingly call him.'

'Your so-called father abandoned us both when you were a baby, for his bloody music.' Her tone was getting angrier.

So was mine. In truth, 'anger' was no longer the appropriate word. It was rage, rising up like bile into my gullet, making me feel that my head was about to explode, turning my voice into a cross between a bellow and a screech. I loathed this side of myself, but I appeared to have no control over the beast that had been unleashed. It had been contained for too long.

'That was over thirty years ago. Get over it! The man is dead, for Christ's sake!'

'Don't you shout at me, Miss. After everything I've done for you.'

'Oh, here we go. All the sacrifices you've made for me, getting pregnant with me ruined your life, blah-de-blah-de-blah.' We were both on our feet, squaring up to each other across the kitchen table like a couple of prizefighters.

'Now, come on, girls. That's enough,' said the normally ultra-passive Graham, sounding like he meant business. 'You can both sit down and discuss this like adults. And don't swear at your mother, Libby.'

He surprised us both into sitting down again. I took a deep breath and made a massive effort to control my temper.

'Look,' I said finally, 'I've given this a lot of thought, and I want to try and contact his family.'

To my horror, my mother started to cry. My mother never cried.

'Why are you trying to hurt me?'

Oh, God. This was awful. 'I'm not trying to hurt you. But I have a right to find out about my own family.'

'You already have a family. Are we not enough for you?'

More than enough. 'Of course you are. But that's not the point. It's nothing personal; it's just…'

'Why can't you leave well enough alone?'

'I've done that for the last thirty-one years, Mam. I'm not prepared to do it any longer. Where did his family live?'

'I told you before. They were from the inner city.'

'I need an address.'

'I don't have one.' And with that, she left the room, sobbing.

I sat motionless, covering my face with my hands. My breathing felt harsh and ragged, and I had a horrible, nauseated feeling in the pit of my stomach. I picked up the photo and stared into the face of the man for whom I had searched in the faces of countless men.

'The Coombe,' said Graham.

'What?'

'The Coombe. That's where your father's family is from.'

36

7

I felt like the walls of the house were closing in on me, and I mean that in an Indiana Jones kind of a way – as if the walls were covered with spikes that would pierce your flesh before the walls themselves crushed your spirit as well as your body. I had to get out of that house.

So I rang Helen, to arrange to meet for a drink. I rang Tom, too, but he had to babysit; Mindy was in the semi-finals of the darts tournament down at their local pub. On second thought, I was glad it was going to be just Helen and me. I decided just to call around to her house; her parents had a well-stocked drinks cabinet.

On the bus into town I sat upstairs, at the front, where the views were positively panoramic. The sense of space was liberating, and it felt good to be on the move; it made me feel as if I was taking some action. The bus stopped outside the Ann Summers shop on O'Connell Street and I people-watched the people getting on and off. I needed some refreshment to go with this entertainment. I rummaged deep inside my coat pocket and found a fluffy mint. Making sure that nobody on the half-empty bus was looking at me, I popped the mint into my mouth. Not bad, although every so often the fluff tickled my throat and made me cough.

Somebody tapped me on the shoulder. 'I thought it was you.'

'Hi, Eric.' Oh, no. The last thing I needed was to make small talk.

Eric the Viking folded his long body into the seat behind me and removed the headphones from his ears. With an inward sigh, I put on my sociable mask. I twisted my body towards him and put my feet up onto my own seat. I knew it was a fineable offence, but I wasn't in a law-abiding mood. There ensued a pause, in which I was embarrassed by the fact that I was eating a sweet while he wasn't.

'Would you like a mint? They're a bit fluffy, but they taste all right.'

'No, thanks. Is it true you got the sack?' Oh, God. They must all be talking about me back at the shop.

'You don't beat about the bush, do you?'

'Is it true?'

'Yes.'

'Why?'

'Didn't Helen say?'

'She said you left for personal reasons.'

'There you are, then. Personal reasons.' I was surprised at his line of questioning. Eric was famous for keeping himself to himself – virtually to the point of rudeness – and minding nobody's business but his own. If *he* was this curious, I could only begin to imagine the wild speculations of the rest of the staff.

'Are you all right?' he asked.

'Fine, thanks.'

'Because you look a bit – shaken up, or something.'

'I'm absolutely fine.' I concentrated hard on the view, but I could feel him regarding me closely, as if trying to evaluate something.

'Tyrone Power,' he said eventually.

'Pardon?'

'Tyrone Power. He's my solicitor. When George sacked me that time, he got me my job back – and some compensation. I was able to buy a new set of amps. I can give you his number if you like.'

I turned to look at him again. Not for the first time, he reminded me of a young Stewart Copeland in the early days of the Police. Although – Jesus – he might not even have been born when the

Police had their day. He probably thought of Sting as that sad old codger who'd sung a duet with Craig Davis.

'You're all right. I don't really want to go down that road.' I could just imagine the tribunal having a good old discussion about my incompetence. 'Are you a musician, then?' I was eager to change the subject.

'Yes. I'm in a band.'

'Really? What's its name?'

'Eric and the Vikings.'

'Really?' I started to laugh. 'Does Tom know?'

'Tom who?' He looked slightly put out by my laughter.

'Tom in the shop.'

'Don't think so. Why do you ask?'

'No reason. Oh, Jesus – this is my stop.' I ran down the stairs, swaying precariously, and alighted on the pavement for all the world as if I hadn't almost landed on my snot.

One more short bus ride and I was outside Helen's. I liked to fantasise I lived there, on occasion – like every time I walked up the path to the front door, flanked as it was on either side by verdant banks of lavender plants. Sweet, lowly clumps of crocus were scattered beneath blossom and magnolia trees and in random patches on the otherwise bowling-green-like lawn. It was never made fully clear who was responsible for this sylvan beauty. Certainly not Helen's French-manicured mama; and daddy was always in the office. My money was on the Filipino gentleman – determinedly unmentioned – whom I'd seen going quietly about his business a few times. My own mother had set eyes on Helen's parents' garden just the once and hadn't stopped drooling for a week.

'Come in.' Helen's smiling, beckoning form materialised at the front door. I followed her into the light-filled kitchen – all granite worktops and solid oak carcasses – and perched, with some difficulty, atop one of the leggy kitchen stools. My lower limbs dangled like a child's.

Helen chatted amiably whilst popping two pyramid-shaped tea-bags into cream-coloured Denby mugs – linen, I think she called them. I confess I wasn't really listening. Just watching.

Helen was perfect. When she was born, her parents must have known how beautiful she was going to become and named her after Helen of Troy accordingly. She was Helen of Templeogue. Her hair looked and felt as soft as if she washed it every day in rainwater. My own hair was coarse in comparison, and it had a split personality: depending on the humidity and the conditioner I was using, it resembled either a silken sheen or a badly constructed crow's nest. Tonight, it veered towards the latter. I put that down to stress. Stress is very bad for the hair – makes it fall out and everything. It was astonishing that I had any left.

Helen wore real diamond studs in her ears at all times; I wore earrings that were too big, inappropriate or mismatched, or none at all. Helen bought her clothes in Next, Pia Bang and Principles; I bought mine in second-hand stores in Temple Bar and in the Oxfam shop, even when I wasn't broke. One woman's crap is another woman's vintage. I really brought down the side rather badly. And there always seemed to be some small thing letting me down – a scuffed heel, or lipstick on one of my front teeth. And, no matter how carefully thought out my outfit, I always got something wrong. The hair and the dress might be good, but the shoes disastrous; or the shoes and the jacket might be right, but as for the scarf... And the coat never failed to let the side down. I'd been wearing my long black coat for three years now, and not once had anyone ever said anything along the lines of 'I like your coat'. This told me all I needed to know. Girls are always quick to heap lavish praise on any item of clothing that they find vaguely attractive, but not one compliment had my coat merited. Somehow that just made me love it even more, as if it were the ugly dog in the pound, with no house-training, that nobody wanted to take home. Helen had mounted a one-woman campaign to get rid of the coat. I was proud to say that so far she'd failed monumentally.

'So what's the big emergency, then?' She settled down on the stool opposite me, her long, bare, slender foot casually grazing the limestone tiles.

'This.' I laid the photo on the table in front of her and told her everything.

'He's good-looking.' Helen held the photo aloft and inclined her head. 'Shame about the moustache.'

'It was the seventies. Lots of men had dodgy facial hair in those days. Remind me to show you a picture of my dad when he was in college. Wicked sideburns. He looks like a member of Slade.'

'Really? Your dad?' I had never seen Helen's father minus his briefcase and Louis Copeland three-piece.

'I'm not kidding. And wait till you get a load of his platforms.'

I took my photo back from her and peered at it thoughtfully. 'He looks nice, though, doesn't he? Kind.'

'Yes, he does.' Helen smiled at me and offered me a chocolate Kimberley. 'You seem to be taking this very well. Very calmly.'

'Well…I was furious at first. But I'm so worn out from being angry all the time lately that now I just feel – I don't know. Shattered.'

She nodded. 'Hardly surprising, after everything that's happened. So you're going to try and contact your family, then?'

'Yes.'

Your family. My family. That sounded weird.

'Are you sure about that?'

No, I wasn't sure. The family I already had was hard enough to contend with. Was I mad, seeking out yet more relatives? 'No, I'm not sure. But I'm going to do it anyway. Will you help me?'

'Of course.'

'Thanks, Helen. The trouble is, I don't know where to start.'

'I do.' Helen hopped off her stool and marched out to the hall. She returned moments later with a phone directory and a very smug expression.

I frowned. 'Are we looking up private investigators?'

'No, my dear. We *are* the private investigators. And we're going to look up all the Clancys living in the Coombe area.' She started flicking towards the C's.

I discovered that I didn't want her to. I needed more time to adjust to the idea. 'I don't know, Helen...'

'Look, do you want to find your father's family or not?'

'Well...yes.'

'Right, then.' She travelled down the column of Clancys with her finger, pausing every so often at one that interested her. Suddenly she stopped and looked up at me, her expression triumphant.

'There,' she said, tapping the page and handing me the directory. There was a Clancy in the Coombe, all right. An Elizabeth Clancy.

'Let's ring her now,' Helen said.

'What! We can't do that.'

'Why not?'

'I don't want to. It's too soon.'

'For what?'

'Just too soon. I need time to think.'

'I know you, Liz. You'll drive yourself mad thinking about it.

42

Better to get it over with. Do it right here, right now, with me here for moral support.'

She was right.

'OK.' I took out my mobile – quickly, before I could change my mind.

'Yes!' Helen almost punched the air.

I dialled the number.

'Hello.' The voice belonged to a middle-aged woman with a strong Dublin accent.

'Hello,' I replied, sounding more confident than I felt and resisting the urge to hang up. 'Can I speak to Elizabeth Clancy, please?'

'She's not available right now. Would you like to make an appointment?'

'Would I like to make an appointment?' I looked at Helen. Her eyes widened and she nodded her head like mad. 'Yes, please.'

'She has an opening at half past seven on Thursday evening.'

'That's fine.'

'Can I have your name, please?'

A name. Oh, God!

'Um…Tallulah Jones.'

Helen pulled her jumper over her head to muffle the laughter.

'We'll see you then, Tallulah.'

'Bye.'

'*Tallulah*?' Helen asked.

'Well, I don't know, do I? I was put on the spot.'

'Even so – Tallulah! What's wrong with Susan or Ann?'

'Never mind the name. I have an appointment in three days' time with a woman I don't even know, and I have no idea what it's for.'

'Maybe she's a chiropodist.'

'Or a chiropractor.'

43

'A tax consultant.'

'A dentist.'

'With evening appointments? And why doesn't it say beside her name in the phone book?' Just what did this mysterious woman do for a living?

'What's all the giggling about, girls?' Helen's mother came into the kitchen.

'Nothing,' said Helen, her tone brooking no further enquiry.

Helen's mother was looking ridiculously young, as usual. She was often mistaken for Helen's sister, which delighted her and annoyed Helen. Helen said she wasn't just mutton dressed as lamb, she was dinosaur dressed as foetus, and her youthful looks were the result of frequent visits to her friendly neighbourhood plastic surgeon.

'And how are things with you these days, Liz?'

'Great, thanks, Olivia.'

I was acutely aware of Helen rolling her eyes behind Olivia's back. I really thought Helen was a bit harsh on her mother. She seemed all right to me – always friendly and welcoming, despite my somewhat scruffy appearance. But maybe we're all programmed to be irritated by our own parents, no matter how inoffensive they might appear to the outside world.

Having said that, I couldn't deny that Olivia had developed a significantly greater interest in me since I'd been published. I was used to this, though. I'd meet a person at a party, for instance – male or female, it didn't matter. We might chit-chat briefly, and I'd quickly register the lack of interest in their eyes; then somebody would inform them that I'd had a couple of books published, and – hey presto – their eyes would ignite and I would suddenly become the most scintillating conversationalist in the room. Certain people who'd known me for years had developed a renewed interest in me overnight; they would study me closely, searching for something that they felt they must have missed before. And then there were my family and friends, who knew that I was still, at heart, an idiot, albeit a published one.

Olivia finally floated off to her cocktail party, I think it was, and we were alone again.

'Do you fancy something stronger?' suggested Helen.

'Do I what!'

'You know,' said Helen, slipping comfortably into her second glass, 'you're not the only one making major changes to your life.'

'Oh, really? How so?'

'Well, I've come to the conclusion that I take myself a little too seriously.'

'Surely not!'

'Are you taking the piss?'

'Yes.'

'Well, don't. I'm being serious.'

'I thought you were giving that up.'

'Liz!'

'Sorry. Carry on.'

'I just feel – I don't know. I suppose I'm fed up with trying to be perfect all the time. I just want to…'

'Hang loose, man.'

'Yes! That's it exactly. I want to hang loose. Will you help me?'

'Of course.' If there was one thing on which I was an expert, it was being imperfect. And if I hung any looser, I'd fall apart at the seams.

Helen rooted around on the counter and produced a spiral notebook and a Parker pen. I watched as she wrote 'How to Be Less

Perfect' at the top of the page and underlined it twice. Then she wrote '1)'.

'Now.' She looked up at me expectantly. 'Begin.'

'Number one,' I said. 'Stop writing lists.'

She began to write, then stopped; then looked up at me. 'Very funny.'

'I mean it, Helen. If you're serious about not being so perfect, you're going to have to stop living your life by lists.'

'But how will I get anything done?'

'You'll still get the important stuff done. But this way, you can go with the flow at the same time.'

She looked at me uncertainly and frowned. Then she went to put the notebook away. Then: 'No, I can't.'

'Jesus, Helen. That was the easiest thing on the list.'

'Oh, God. I don't think I can do this.'

'Yes, you can. And stop looking so serious. You're defeating the whole purpose.'

'You're right, you're right.' She visibly relaxed her shoulders, and the lines on her forehead disappeared. 'Maybe I can just write this one last list and then no more after that?'

'Go on, then.'

She beamed and picked up her pen again. 'What's number two?'

'Eat a dessert every single day.'

'I couldn't possibly—'

'Helen!' I had to be strict.

'All right, all right.' She wrote it down. 'Number three?'

'Get rat-arsed one night per week.'

She looked up at me, and I gave her my best schoolmarm look. She wrote it down.

'Number four: learn flamenco dancing.'

'What's that got to do with being less perfect?'

46

'Nothing, really, but I've been wanting to learn and I don't want to go on my own.'

'But I'm a crap dancer.'

'All the more reason to take lessons. Oh, please! I've always fancied it. And we might meet men.'

'No chance,' said Helen. 'Those sorts of classes are always teeming with desperate women.'

'No, they're not. Oh, come on, Helen. It'll be fun. And all that shaking your booty is bound to help you loosen up.'

'Oh, all right, then.'

'Great!'

'What's next?'

I leaned back on my stool. Now we were having fun. 'And the last item on the list…'

Helen looked up at me, pen poised expectantly.

'You have to shag a complete stranger.'

She threw her pen down in disgust. 'Oh, come on!'

'I'm afraid I can't help you, then. You'll just have to stay perfect.'

Helen's near-perfection had always been a source of both attraction and irritation to me. I was fascinated by her poise, her efficiency and her punctuality, her ability to navigate the most difficult situations and emerge with never a hair out of place, but sometimes I just wanted to whack her around the head.

She sighed. 'All right. I'll consider it.'

'*Really*?' *Holy shit!*

'I only said I'd consider it.'

'Good enough for me.'

She'd never do it. I knew that. I myself had grown out of meaningless one-night stands a while ago. Let's face it: who wants to wake up with a stranger farting like a brass band in the bed beside you? I hate the smell of napalm in the morning.

I began to backtrack in my head. 'I don't want to be blamed if you get a venereal disease.'

'You won't be – and I won't,' she said, the angelic expression on her face belying the topic of our conversation.

'Unless,' I said suddenly, 'you've already met someone.'

'Course I haven't.' Was she blushing, or were her cheeks merely flushed from the wine?

'You have so. That's what this is all about – you're trying to impress someone!'

Helen laughed through another mouthful of wine. 'I'm telling you, you're barking up the wrong tree. There's no one. Honest to God. I'm doing this for myself.'

I was almost convinced. 'Right, so. Here's to the new, dis-improved Helen Staunton.'

8

Elizabeth Clancy's front garden was a demonstration of extraordinary tackiness – unless she was trying to be kitsch, which I seriously doubted. This looked like an authentic case of tack to me.

The pillars on either side of the front gate were topped with white concrete poodles. Then there were the gnomes – literally dozens of them, in clusters on the sparse lawn and perched on the wall. One little fellow with a fishing rod was balanced at the edge of a plastic wishing well. In between the groups of gnomes (what do you call a group of gnomes? a shoal? a pride? a gaggle?) someone had positioned little black cauldrons full of pansies, to hide the more threadbare areas of grass. I had to admit it was colourful. And did I mention the lions? There was one on either side of the front door, giant head resting on massive paws. Possibly they had something to do with feng shui.

The ancestral home. No wonder Dad went a bit mental.

But by far the most extraordinary thing about Elizabeth Clancy's front garden was the queue of young women winding its way halfway down the footpath. It appeared to emanate from the depths of the hall, where several plastic chairs had apparently been provided. She was certainly very popular – I'd give her that. But why, exactly?

I eavesdropped on the two girls ahead of me in the line.

'Tell me again what she said to you last time.'

'That I should enter the Rose of Tralee.'

'Jaysus, I forgot that. Are you going to?'

'I sent in me application form last week.' The girl had long yellow hair, an orange face, bright-red lips and matching stiletto boots. She looked like a hooker, but she probably worked in an office. Her sidekick was a mousier version.

'That's bleedin' brilliant, Jade.'

'I know. I can't wait.'

'What else did she tell you?'

'That Macker wasn't the one for me.'

'I could have bleedin' told you that!'

'Only 'cause you know him, Jacinta. She could tell he wasn't right for me and she's never even met him. She's bleedin' brilliant, so she is.'

'Yeah. Brilliant. Are you going to break it off with him, then?'

'Already did.'

'Fuck off!'

'Excuse me for butting in,' I said, butting in, 'but can you tell me what you're waiting for?'

The scarlet-lipped one looked me up, down and back up again. She took in the coat, the barely-there make-up and the mussed-up hair and seemed satisfied that I'd be no obstacle on her road to the Rose of Tralee title.

'We're waiting for the fortune-teller, of course. Why? What are you doing here?'

'Oh. I'm here to see the fortune-teller too.'

They gave each other funny looks and me even funnier ones. 'Is this your first time?'

'Yes.'

At this admission, they immediately allowed me into their club. They took me under their wings with all the zeal of two middle-aged aunties discovering that their favourite niece has fallen pregnant for the first time.

'Jaysus, I wish it was my first time,' sighed Jade.

'Me too,' sighed Jacinta.

'Have you been many times before, then?'

'I've been fifteen times,' said Jacinta proudly. 'But that's nothing. Wait till you hear how many times Jade's been. Go on, tell her, Jade.'

'Twenty-two times.' Jade nodded her head solemnly for emphasis. 'I'm going to her two year now. I'd go every week if I could afford it.'

'Why – how much does she charge?'

'Thirty euro.'

'Thirty euro!' I was outraged.

'I know. It's brilliant, isn't it? And she gives you a tape and all.'

'Jade's been to loads of different fortune-tellers,' said Jacinta admiringly. 'Haven't you, Jade? Go on – tell her.'

Jade proceeded to reel off a list of fortune-tellers spanning the length and breadth of the country. She was able to tell me the price each one charged and the accuracy of their predictions, on a percentile basis. The girl had a photographic memory. She also had a serious addiction. I could picture her forty years from now, down at the bingo hall every night playing five cards at once.

And all the while, a thought kept popping into my head. Surely, if you got your fortune told once, that should be enough? You wouldn't need to keep going back again and again – not to the same person, anyway. Naturally, I didn't have the nerve to say this to Jacinta and Jade.

I had, in fact, been to a fortune-teller once before. About ten years previously, Helen and I had gone to see a woman in a caravan in Bray, one afternoon when we were skiving off college. The woman had told me that I'd have three children by the time I was thirty and that I'd work in science. I never found out what she said to Helen, because Helen refused to tell me. She emerged white-faced and shaken, and hardly said a word all the way home on the bus.

'Mrs Clancy's the best in the business,' Jade concluded.

So you're a fortune-teller, are you, Elizabeth? Predict this!

Approximately one hour – and two near-cases of bottling out – later, it was my turn.

'Tallulah Jones!'

They had to call out the name three times before it registered. In I went.

A massive statue of the Virgin Mary dominated the room. At a guess, I'd say it probably glowed in the dark. In the room's centre was a table. On either side of the table was a chair; on the table were a crystal ball and a pack of Tarot cards; and behind the table was Elizabeth Clancy.

The old woman's eyes remained glued to my own as she rose slowly from her seat and blessed herself repeatedly.

'God bless us and save us,' she said. 'God bless us and save us. Elizabeth. I always knew you'd come.'

Years later, I'd still cite that moment as one of the strangest of my whole life. I still recall the scalp-tightening, skin-crawling, hair-raising sensation as my grandmother, Elizabeth Clancy, and I, Elizabeth Clancy, recognised each other instantly.

We both stood rooted for what was probably only half a minute, but seemed a lot longer. Finally, my grandmother came around to my side of the room and gripped me by the arm, as if to check that I was real. She walked me over to the chair and sat me down.

'Did the cards tell you I was coming?' I asked, dazed.

She laughed, a forty-cigarettes-a-day-for-forty-years laugh. 'No, love. Sure, I'd know you anywhere. Aren't you the living image of your Auntie Aggie, may the Lord have mercy on her soul.' She blessed herself again. 'For a minute there I thought she'd come back to haunt me.'

I didn't have the presence of mind to come up with a response to that. So I just sat and stared at her.

She was quite elderly, of course. I'd give her eighty. I was considerably taller than she was – and that doesn't happen to me too often. She couldn't have been more than four foot ten. Her hair was dyed an aggressive, boot-polish black and her eyes were dark brown. I felt as if I'd looked into those eyes many times before.

'You gave a false name,' she said. 'You must have known who I was.'

'Well, I guessed you were a relation.'

'You were looking for me, so?'

'I was looking for my father's family.'

'What took you so long?'

I really didn't know. Had I been reluctant to hurt my mother? Loyal to Graham? Afraid of rejection? Terrified of the unknown? Maybe I'd just reached a stage in my life where I needed to know where I came from. But all I said was, 'I don't know.'

I badly wanted to ask her why she hadn't looked for me, but the words wouldn't come out.

'I wish Kit was here to see you. She'll never believe me when I tell her.'

'Kit?'

'Your Auntie Kit. Your daddy's sister.'

Of course – I had aunts. And uncles. And, very possibly, cousins. This was just too weird. My brain couldn't process all this mind-blowing information at once.

'Can I get you a nice cup of tea, love? Plenty of sugar. You look a bit pale.' I *never* look pale.

'No, thank you. You know…' What should I call her? I couldn't possibly call her 'Granny'. 'You know, Mrs Clancy, this has all come as a bit of a shock. Do you mind if I go now and come back and see you again soon?'

'Come for your dinner on Sunday.'

'OK, then. I'll do that.' I got up to leave.

'Two o'clock.'

'I'll see you then.'

My grandmother crossed the room and clasped my hands in her own. I looked down and saw that they were gnarled with arthritis. Would I get that?

'It's been good to see you, love. Very good indeed.'

I nodded and, disengaging myself from her grip, left the room as if in a trance.

'You mind yourself now, getting home. It'll be dark soon,' she called down the hall. I turned and nodded. Then I stepped out into the front garden and took two huge gulps of air. The remaining girls in the queue stared at me, wondering what on earth the fortune-teller could have told me – wondering if what she would tell them would provoke such a reaction. I doubted it.

9

Thomas Street had an urban beat to it that reminded me of Kilburn High Street. I liked it, but I could have done without the junkie shooting up in the corner. Unfortunately, he couldn't – do without it, that is.

My hands were shaking as I dialled Helen's number on my mobile – which, according to Jim, was a hopelessly outmoded and uncool model. They all looked the same to me. I only had this particular contraption because – bizarrely – it had come free with a set of pots. I didn't know how to use those properly either.

Helen answered instantly. 'Well?' she said. 'How did you get on?'

I was about to tell her when, suddenly and inexplicably, I started to cry.

'Liz, are you all right? What happened?'

'She's my grandmother,' I sobbed.

'Really? Well, that's good – isn't it? She didn't kick you out or anything?'

'No, no. Nothing like that. She was nice. I'm going back to see her on Sunday.'

'But that's great. It's what you wanted.'

'Yes.'

'Why are you crying, then?'

'I don't know.' I started to laugh. We both did.

'I wish I could have gone with you,' Helen said. 'Damn George and his late-night openings. So what was she like? Tell me everything.'

I was about to when somebody far bigger and stronger than

myself grabbed me from behind, twisted my left arm behind my back and rammed me against the wall. I felt the breath escape my body. A young, male, Dublin voice hissed into my ear: 'Gimme the phone or I'll break yer fuckin' arm.'

His breath reeked of stale cigarettes and something underlying and far worse. I could feel him trying to wrench the mobile out of my hand. I relaxed my grip and he was gone, taking the phone with him.

I immediately started to scream. In an instant, a large black man was at my side.

'Are you OK?'

'Yes. He's got my phone.' I pointed after the fleeing figure.

Without missing a beat, the man flew after my assailant. I watched as he caught up with him, in remarkably few strides, and brought him to the ground with a flying rugby tackle. I started to shout something incomprehensible and ran towards them. The commotion attracted the attention of three men walking along the other side of the street.

'What's wrong?' they called out to me.

I pointed to the two men wrestling. 'He mugged me!' I shrieked.

We all ran in the direction of the struggling men. Just as we reached them, my attacker managed to wriggle free and bolt off into the night.

'Get him!' I heard one of the three men yell. Then they all descended on my rescuer and started punching and kicking him.

'Not him – it wasn't him!' I screamed.

An hour later, I had given my statement to the police and called back a frantic Helen – on my state-of-the-artless mobile phone, which had been returned to me. I never found out my hero's name.

As soon as I managed to drag the three men off him, he had disappeared. They'd tried to shake his hand but he had walked away, looking back at them disdainfully. I ran after him, thanking him; in an awkward gesture that I would later be ashamed of, I thrust a twenty-euro note at him. He just waved it away.

'I'm glad you're OK,' was all he said, before disappearing down an alleyway.

The police dropped me home in a squad car. This caused great excitement amongst the neighbours. My mother ran out of the house to meet me.

'What happened?' It was the first time she'd spoken to me in three days.

'I got mugged.'

'Jesus! Are you all right? Look at your face!' I had a graze above my right eyebrow where I had been shoved against the wall.

'I'm fine, Mam.'

'Did he take anything?'

'He tried to take my phone, but I got it back.'

'Thank God you're OK. Where did this happen?'

'Thomas Street.'

I saw the realisation on her face and watched as her demeanour changed.

'You should have a bath,' she said, her tone considerably cooler. 'The water's on. I'll bring you up a cocoa afterwards.'

Except she didn't. Instead she sent Tim up with the cocoa and a tube of ointment for my face.

'There you go.' He handed the cocoa to me. 'I put the baby marshmallows in myself.'

'Thanks, Timmy.' It was hot and comforting and tasted like childhood.

For the next five minutes, I had to endure Tim's incessant

questioning. Did the mugger have a gun? A knife? A syringe? Did I lose control of my bodily functions? Did I get a detective or a uniform? What was the inside of the squad car like? Did they break all the red lights on the way home? Did they put the siren on?

'You're so jammy,' he said. 'I always wanted a go in a squad car.'

'Well, with a bit of luck, you'll get mugged soon.'

'Can I ask you something else, Libby?'

'Not if it has anything to do with being mugged.'

'It doesn't.'

'Go on, then.'

'You know the way you dye your hair?'

What? 'I do not dye my hair.'

'You do so. I've seen you.'

Shit. Who else knew? 'I don't dye my hair, Tim. I enhance the colour sometimes, to bring out the shine. Why do you want to know, anyway?'

'I want to dye my hair.'

'Why on earth would you want to do that? Your hair is a lovely colour.'

Oh, no. Was he getting teased in school? Both Jim and Tim had inherited Graham's red hair. Age had toned Graham's down to an acceptable level of auburn, but Jim and Tim were still wildly ginger.

'I want to look like Aragorn.'

'What! But that's mad, Tim.'

'No, it's not.'

'The kids in your class will tease the hell out of you if you turn up one morning with different-coloured hair.'

'I don't care about them. They're all gobshites anyway.'

'And Mam would kill you – and me, too, if she found out I helped you.'

58

'I'll tell her I did it myself. I'm going to do it anyway, whether you help me or not.'

I looked at his intense little face. 'Oh, all right, then.' At least I might be able to stop him from turning it blue by mistake. 'But on your own head be it.'

That Saturday, I introduced my little brother to the wonders of Roche's Stores' toiletry department. He was agog at the sheer range of gloop that women could buy to rub on themselves. He looked to me for a logical explanation, but I was at a loss.

My strategy was to pick out a colour that would change Tim's noggin as little as possible. I scanned the light browns: Chestnut Glow, Soft Amber, Barely Brown...

'Hello there.'

Eric the Viking took out his headphones.

I looked up at him. Then I looked down at the box of hair-colour in my hand. 'It's not for me,' I said, instantly regretting the words and blushing to the roots of my colour-enhanced follicles.

'Are you holding it for a friend?'

His humour was lost on me. 'For my brother, actually. Eric, this is my brother, Tim. Eric works in Grainger's.'

'I'm dyeing my hair to look like Aragorn.'

Oh, God. I'd have been better off pretending it was for me. This was bloody typical. Any time you try to do something confidential in this town, you meet somebody you know – like the time I bought a home pregnancy test in Boots, and our nosy next-door neighbour was behind me in the queue. The whole street watched my stomach like an army of circling hawks for the next nine months.

Eric, however, appeared unfazed by Tim's announcement. He never seemed to get fazed about anything. I half listened as they discussed the merits and demerits of the *Lord of the Rings* movies versus the books. When Tim began to show off his extensive knowledge of the Elvish language, I decided enough was enough.

'Come on, Tim. Hurry up and pick a colour. I'm sure Eric has better things to be doing.'

'Not really.' The Viking smiled a rare smile. He was a nice kid, really. Tim could have done with a big brother like him, instead of Jimmy Rotten back home.

'Did you ring that solicitor I told you about?' Eric asked me, as soon as Tim was out of earshot.

'Oh…no. I'm not really interested in doing that.'

'You can't let Grainger get away with it.'

'I…' I didn't know what to say. What was it to him?

'If I were you, I'd threaten to tell his wife if he doesn't give you your job back.'

'How did you know…?' But he already had his headphones back in and was walking away.

I felt a furious flush on my face. Then I just felt furious.

Then I realised that he was absolutely right.

Why hadn't I thought of that?

10

George would have to wait, though, because I had a dinner to attend. I told my mother that I was going to Helen's for Sunday lunch. If she suspected otherwise, she didn't show it.

What do you bring on your first visit to your long-lost grandmother? I played it safe with a jam sponge and a bunch of daffodils, hoping that she didn't suffer from diabetes or hay fever. It was frightening how little I knew about her.

This time, there was no queue of expectant young women in the front garden. It was just the gnomes and me. I stood on the front doorstep for a full minute before ringing the doorbell.

A bitter-looking woman in her fifties opened the door. Golden loops adorned her ears, and her hair was drawn back from her face into an unforgiving bun. She used the same hair dye as her mother and it was equally unconvincing on her. 'You must be Elizabeth,' she said.

'Kit?'

'That's right. Come in, and you're very welcome.'

It appeared that she was actually pleased to see me. The bitter expression was habitual.

'Me mother was right,' she said. 'You're the spit of Aunt Aggie.' They were going to have to show me a photo of this Aggie woman.

I stepped into the hall. And the tack continued. I had been too distracted to register the full horror on my last visit. The hallway was dark and narrow; in an attempt to brighten it up, they had put in rose-pink plush carpet scattered with large white flowers. This was offset by the type of wallpaper I'd only ever seen in hotel lobbies. The background was a creamy yellow and the pattern was an embossed, velvet-looking, dark-red leaf; it was more like material than paper. It was truly vile. Not content with this nightmare of visual overload, somebody – I had yet to identify the culprit – had festooned the walls with cutesy prints of little blonde girls cuddling kittens and little blond pantaloon-wearing boys cuddling puppies.

Kit led me into the minute kitchen. 'Don't mind me,' she said. 'I'm getting the dinner. Go out and say hello to the mother. She's out back, hanging out the washing.'

I laid my gifts on the kitchen table and went out back. The garden was surprisingly large. Of course, the house had been built in the days before they stuck as many houses as possible into as small a space as possible.

Sure enough, there was the grandmother, hanging out her smalls on the rotary line – not that there was anything small about her smalls. And why would there be, at her age? She was hardly likely to wriggle into a thong. She was standing on a small stepladder – this being the only way she could reach the line – and wearing a pair of tights on her head. The two legs hung down to her backside, like a couple of plaits.

'Oh, howya, love. I didn't see you there.' She swiftly removed the tights and climbed down onto terra firma. 'Come in with me out of the cold.' She looked up at me, smiling. 'Let me have a look at you again. You're a grand, tall girl, aren't you?'

Well, that was the first time anybody had ever said that to me.

Back in the kitchen, dinner preparations appeared to be reaching their final stages. I watched in fascination as the two women manoeuvred about each other in the tiny kitchen, with the ease of people who'd been following the same routine for years. It didn't stop them bickering, though.

'You didn't put enough cornflour in the white sauce, Kit.'

'Would you ever leave the sauce alone? It's grand. Take up the spuds – and don't be boiling the arse out of them again.'

'There's nothing wrong with the way I cook potatoes. I've been cooking them that way since before you were born. Look at that: gorgeous and floury.'

Dinner consisted of boiled bacon, the aforementioned floury spuds, cauliflower and white sauce and mushy peas. I watched in horror as, for no particular reason, my new granny managed to handle every morsel of food on my plate.

'There!' She handed it to me with a proud flourish. 'Take that with you into the room on your left.'

A table was laid. I suspected that the good tablecloth, placemats, silverware and glasses had been brought out in my honour. The result was hideous.

Kit and Granny followed me into the room, plates in hands, and we sat down to share our first meal together as a family.

And it did feel like family – right from the outset. I wasn't sure why. A sense of familiarity hung over the scene, as if it were a TV programme I'd watched as a child and long since forgotten. The lack of either an air or a grace on either woman's part also contributed to the sense of comfort. They quizzed me endlessly about my 'bukes'; Granny was excessively proud of my published status, and immediately asserted that my writing abilities had originated from her side of the family. Who was I to dispute it?

After dinner, we retired into the 'good' room for dessert. Kit carried in the jam sponge, which was served with viscous tea and soft custard creams. The 'good' room meant the room where the most magnificently tacky objects in the house had been gathered together. There was barely room to sit down, what with all the ornaments. If they could have got away with putting a few gnomes about the place, they would have done. Personally, I loved the room – because it was full of photographs. And there began my trip down a Memory Lane of which I had no memory.

My grandfather had been a tall, malnourished-looking man with very little hair. There was a picture of their wedding day, my grandmother not much higher than his waist. She was wearing a blue dress that she'd made herself; it was wartime, and nobody had reams of white satin to spare. The couple had six children, four surviving: baby Elizabeth had been stillborn, and then there was Dad. Apart from Kit, who had never married, my other two aunts and my uncle lived in Australia. I was shown new colour prints of them and their broods – my cousins.

Then there was the famous Auntie Aggie. She featured in one group photo. She was a small, serious-looking woman, her face partly obscured by a veil of thick black hair. I had to admit that the resemblance was striking.

But we all knew what I'd really come to see. For this, all the old albums were taken out and dusted off.

My father. Dad. Robert. My grandmother's youngest son, Kit's cherished brother. They brought me on his life-journey, cradle to grave.

Slowly, almost tenderly, my grandmother sat down beside me on the couch. She placed an old, black photo album across both of our knees and opened it up at the first page.

'He was six weeks old there. I was just after changing him. He was after doing a bloody big shite that went all the way up his back.'

So much for me and my romantic notions. I laughed in spite of it all.

My father, at six weeks, had possessed the maddest head of black curls I'd ever seen, and the goofiest expression. Something beyond the photographer's left shoulder had attracted his attention, and he was staring at whatever it was in goggle-eyed fascination. He was gorgeous. Was it strange to want to pick up your own father and cuddle him? Shouldn't I want him to do that to me?

'That's him on his First Communion day. He was a holy terror that day, so he was – stuffed himself with sweets and got sick in his uncle's car on the way home, all over his sister.' Dad was instantly recognisable and looking anything but holy. He sat on a short wooden bench in short trousers, all dimples and no front teeth.

Confirmation day: 'I had a devil of a time trying to get him into that suit. I made it meself, out of an old one of his daddy's. He nearly had to be bet into it, so he did.' Sure enough, there stood Dad, sporting his rosette, dark eyes resentful.

He posed with the guitar he'd been given for his thirteenth birthday – a glimpse of the man he was to become. He leaned against a motorbike, mouth wide open, laughing with two of his mates. He was sixteen years old and his future stretched into infinity. My grandmother had been strongly opposed to the motorbike; she'd told him it would be the death of him.

The box of Kleenex kept on the table in the fortune-telling room was brought in and all but emptied.

There were no snaps of my father on his wedding day. I showed Kit and my grandmother the picture that I now carried with me wherever I went.

'How's your mother keeping?' asked my grandmother.

'She's fine.'

'Did she ever marry again?'

'Yes. I have a stepdad, Graham, and two little brothers.'

'Did she become a doctor?'

A doctor? 'You mean a nurse? She's a nurse.'

'No, I mean a doctor. She was all set to go to college and study medicine. Full of plans, so she was.'

This was news to me. 'No. She's a nurse,' I said again.

Again, the question that had been battling to get out all afternoon came to the forefront of my mind: *Why didn't you ever try to contact me?* But in it stayed.

'So do you know where you get your dark looks from, then?' said Kit.

'From Granny?'

'Before that. Tell her, Mother.'

My grandmother grinned, showing lots of white teeth (all her own?). She settled herself more comfortably into her seat to tell the story.

'Back in 1588,' she said, with relish, 'three of the vessels belonging to the Spanish Armada were shipwrecked off the Sligo coast. Your ancestor was one of the survivors.'

I looked at her incredulously – but she actually had evidence to back this up. She got Kit to unlock a bureau in the corner and take out a detailed copy of the family tree – she'd employed the services of a genealogist – and a map of the area where the Spanish sailor had been washed up.

The story went something like this:

In September 1588, three Spanish vessels – *La Livia*, *La Juliana* and *Santa Maria de Vision* – had been blown off course by unseasonable storms. The badly damaged ships moored off Streedagh Strand, on the Sligo coast. Four days they remained there – until another vicious storm dashed them against the unforgiving rocks. Of the thousand-odd Spaniards on board, most were drowned. Of those who made it ashore, many were cut to pieces by British soldiers who lay in wait for them. As if this wasn't enough to contend with, hundreds of Irish 'savages' were on hand to relieve these bedraggled creatures of their valuables and clothes.

Miraculously, a few of these men managed to escape. Luckily for me, my ancestor was one of them. He struggled onto dry land, possibly injured, and was very probably stripped and robbed by the Irish. He must then have found a safe hiding-place for himself until the British threat subsided. From Streedagh, he somehow made it to the castle of McClancy, at Rossclogher on Lough Melvin. Here, he would have received a warm welcome from this well-known enemy of the English. He managed to impregnate a woman by the name of Mary McClancy before resuming his journey home, via Antrim, Scotland and the Spanish-held Dunkirk. No one knows for sure what happened to him after that, or if he ever made it back to his native Spain.

I was fascinated. I wasn't just a boring old one-hundred-per-cent-Irish fart, after all.

I went into town on the way home. In HMV, I purchased *The Best of the Gypsy Kings* and Gloria Estefan's *Greatest Hits*. I drew the line at Los Ketchup.

11

My first thought when I woke up the next morning was: *Thank God.* That had to be why I'd enjoyed Julio so much. It wasn't my fault; just some genetic throwback over which I had no control. I was reminded of the Woody Allen film where a character receives a blow to the head and becomes a Republican.

I'd had a restless night, plagued by weirdly vivid dreams. A dripping-wet Spaniard in a funny helmet had fired me from my job. Then I'd walked in on Eric the Viking in bed with George Grainger's wife. In the adjoining room, my grandmother was having her fortune told by Enrique Iglesias, while my teenage father polished his motorbike in the corner.

My waking thoughts were similarly mixed. I had so much stuff in my head that I didn't know where to begin. So I just lay in bed for far longer than I should have, mulling it all over.

But one thought wouldn't leave me alone. It pestered me until I had no choice but to act on it. I flung back the covers and vacated my bed as if propelled from an ejector seat. I padded over to the phone and, without allowing myself to think about it, stabbed in a number I knew by heart. It rang six times; then the machine answered. I felt both deflation and relief.

'Hello, this is George Grainger. Please leave your message after the tone.' Crisp and businesslike – like the man himself.

'Em, George. It's me...Liz. Elizabeth Clancy. I need to talk to you. Urgently. Call me back. You have my number, I think.' Clearly there wasn't a crisp or businesslike bone in my body.

I replaced the receiver and sighed. He probably wouldn't ring back, but at least I'd taken the first step. I'd done him the courtesy of ringing him at work – this time. If he didn't call back, I'd try him at home. That should put the skids under him.

It was almost midday. To distract myself from the guilt of another wasted morning, I decided to listen to my new CDs. Ms Estefan first. I'd never heard 'I Don't Want to Lose You' sung in Spanish before. It sounded so much more – meaningful, somehow.

I played it again. I didn't have a hairbrush handy, so I rolled the *RTÉ Guide* into a microphone and sang at my reflection in the TV screen. The song was wasted on Gloria. I lolled on the unmade sofa-bed in various provocative poses, mouthing earnestly into the magazine – words I didn't know in English, let alone Spanish – and imagining an entire alternative video, starring me as the tragic Spanish heroine. By the time I had listened to 'Rhythm's Going to Get You' twice and writhed around to 'One, Two, Three, Four (Come On, Baby, Say You Love Me)' one, two, three, four times, I was in a state of high excitement.

Giggling foolishly to myself, I ejected Gloria and inserted the Gypsy Kings. Feeling inspired, I dragged my half-unpacked case out from under the sofa-bed and threw items of clothing hither and thither until I found a long, red, tiered skirt I'd bought in Petticoat Lane market two years previously. I wriggled it up over the white T-shirt I'd been wearing as a nightdress – and I was ready.

Bamboleo!

I shimmied, I sparkled, I spun; I whooped, I whirled, I whooshed; I flamencoed, I flounced, I fandangoed. I lifted up my skirts and danced barefoot around the gypsy campfire, whipping back my hair and clicking my imaginary castanets in time to the music. I wanted to live in this song forever.

'Bleedin' hell, Jamser. What's your one at?'

Unfortunately, Jim had chosen this lunchtime to invite two of his workmates – Deego and Doyler – home for a sandwich.

'Don't mind her, she's fucking mad.'

'Get out!' I yelled, as soon as I managed to unfreeze myself.

'The state of her. Is that the one that writes the dirty books?'

Oh, to have a room of my own!

George didn't ring back the next day, or the one after that. So, the next evening, I rang his house. I decided in advance that I'd hang up if his wife answered, but I didn't have to: George picked up himself.

'Hello.'

'Hello, George.'

There followed an interminable silence, in which I could hear George's mind ticking away.

'What do you want?'

'Now, that's not very civil, is it?' I impressed myself greatly with the coolness of my tone.

'What do you mean by ringing me at this number?'

'You leave me very little—'

He hung up. The bastard hung up.

The next night I called to his house. Yes – in person. I didn't tell Helen what I was up to; she would have skinned me alive. It was awkward enough for her as it was, having to work with George when she was my best friend, not to mention the one who had got me the blasted job in the first place.

George Grainger's house was massive and posh. Not a gnome in sight. It was surrounded by a high stone wall to keep out the riff-raff – and you couldn't get much rougher riff-raff than me. There was also a security camera on the gate. I buzzed the buzzer.

After about ten seconds, a high-pitched, friendly, girlish voice said, 'Hello.' George's daughter. I hesitated, immediately feeling like scum.

'Hello?' The voice was still friendly, but more enquiring. I would have run off if it hadn't been for the camera.

'Hello. Can I speak to Mr Grainger, please?'

'Hang on a second.'

My breathing became increasingly shallow. I forced myself to inhale slowly, trying to recall tips from an ancient yoga class.

'Hello.' George's voice, deep and impatient.

'It's me.'

I heard him curse under his breath. 'Stay right there. I'm coming out.'

This suited me fine. I had no desire to enter his lair. I had been at his house before; he'd snuck me in while his wife was working. She was 'in PR'. As far as I could gather, this entailed looking glamorous and handing around canapés at functions. I imagined it was a hobby for her. It wasn't as if they had to struggle to pay the mortgage.

I heard the rapid approach of footsteps, and something caught in my throat. It was almost excitement. Potentially, it was a very romantic situation – standing here under cover of darkness, inhaling the scent of the evergreens hanging over the wall, watching the daffodils on the landscaped lawn bobbing pale yellow in the moonlight: the perfect setting for a secret lovers' tryst. But there was nothing romantic about this rendezvous.

'What the hell are you doing here?' George's eyes flashed angrily, and I couldn't help fancying him all over again. He was having a rare casual moment: his blue pinstriped shirt was open at the collar

71

and the sleeves were rolled up to the elbows, revealing dark hairy forearms. I remembered what they felt like. This was going to be even harder than I'd thought. *Focus, Liz. Just focus.*

I stuck out my chin out and glared at him. It took every ounce of effort I had to feel dignified, standing there on the road outside his home – to all intents and purposes, stalking him.

'I want my job back.'

'What? You've got a nerve. I'll never be able to show my face in that restaurant again. My wife keeps asking me why I won't bring her there.'

'Is that all you're worried about, you son of a bitch? My heart bleeds for you, it really does.' My great plan to be cool, calm and collected had, alas, already fallen by the wayside. 'I've lost my flat, my job, all my hopes for the future. You fed me such a pack of lies, George Grainger...' *Don't cry! Don't!*

'They weren't lies,' he said quietly.

Please don't look at me like that. 'You told me you hadn't slept with Judith for years.'

'I hadn't. I meant it when I said it was just a one-off.'

Don't fall for it!

'If it weren't for the baby...' George let the words hang in the air.

He took a step closer. I took a step back. I could feel him trying to reel me in.

'Look, just tell me I've got my job back, and I'll leave you alone.'

'OK.'

'What?'

'OK, you can have your job back.'

'Really?'

'Really.'

'Oh. Thanks.' *What are you thanking him for, you big eejit?*

'There's a pub down the road. Fancy a drink?' he said.

'You're unbelievable.'

George shrugged and gave me the sheepish grin that he knew I found irresistible. I'd told him so often enough.

'No. I think I'll just go now.'

Sounding more decisive than I felt, I clip-clopped off into the night, in the shoes I'd worn to impress George Grainger.

12

Helen rang me the next morning. I assumed that George had told her to offer me my job back, which he had – but that wasn't the only reason she was ringing.

'Guess what? There's a flamenco-dancing course starting tonight.'

'You're kidding.'

'No. Still want to go?'

'Course.'

This was typical of the way Helen and I operated. I might come up with the ideas, but she was invariably the one who put them into practice. If it hadn't been for her, virtually none of my schemes would have got off the ground.

I was going to be a flamenco dancer! No wonder I'd always wanted to do it. It was clearly in my blood.

Ay, caramba! I was practically a señorita already.

Helen got there before me, even though she'd been multitasking all day long and all I'd had to do was make sure I got to the class by half six. So I arrived in a sweat, worried she'd be annoyed with me. I needn't have been: she practically ran – no, *skipped* – out to meet me.

'Liz, Liz!'

'What is it?'

'You were right about meeting men.'

'I was?'

'Just wait till you see this guy in the class. He's the only man in it, mind you – but, my God, what a man. He's only gorgeous!' She rolled her eyes to emphasise his gorgeousness.

'Show me the way.' I must admit I was surprised. I really hadn't expected there to be any decent men here.

'You won't believe it. He's sooo good-looking – and perfect for you.'

'How?'

'Well, you said you were on the lookout for a gorgeous Spaniard. And they don't come more gorgeous than this one.'

'How do you know he's Spanish?'

'He has to be. He's so dark and exotic-looking – and he's taking a flamenco class, for pity's sake. Liz, he's like a young Ricky Martin.'

'Ricky Martin *is* young. What is he? Three?'

'Don't be silly. Come and have a look.'

So I went to have a look.

I stood stock-still in the doorway and gawped. 'I don't believe it.'

'I told you,' Helen whispered excitedly in my ear.

'It's not that. I know him.'

'What?'

She had to wait for the next instalment, as our dance instructress chose that moment to clap her hands together and usher us into the centre of the room. The Ricky Martin look-alike (my arse) watched us as we walked in. After giving Helen a good going-over, he turned his attention to me. I saw his brow furrow; then recognition crossed his features, and he smiled and nodded in my direction.

'You actually *know* this love-god?' Helen hissed to me, her eyes just about as wide as they could get, while the instructress fiddled around with the troublesome CD player.

'The love-god was in my class at school. He's no more Spanish

75

than I am. I mean, I'm more Spanish than he is. You know what I mean.'

'What's his name? What's he like?'

'Phil. And he's a fool. Phil the Fool.' I started to laugh.

'Phil.' She tried out the name for size. 'I've always liked that name. But just because he was a fool in school—'

'He's Phil the School Fool.' I laughed even harder.

'Stop it, Liz. Just because he was an idiot back then, it doesn't mean he's one now. It's…how long since you left school?'

'More years than I care to remember.'

'Exactly. He's probably changed completely. I bet you have.'

'You're not wrong there.'

'So give him a chance.'

'He's hardly an authentic Spaniard, is he?'

'Shh. He's coming over.'

Sure enough, Phil had taken the opportunity to head our way. I thought Helen was going to erupt. *Mount Saint Helen*, I thought, trying not to giggle again. I was really going to have to get out more.

'Lizzie Clancy. Is it really you?'

''Fraid so.' I blushed, remembering the creature I had been back in school – the pain of being dragged kicking and screaming through adolescence into adulthood.

'Wow. How long has it been?'

'Since we were both seventeen.'

'That long!' Phil's eyes kept flicking over to Helen. She was looking like a teenybopper about to meet her pop idol. I decided to put her out of her misery.

'Phil Gallagher – this is Helen Staunton.'

'Lovely to meet you, Helen.' He shook her hand, holding it for far too long and flashing her a smile of such blinding whiteness that

I was reminded of the cheesier moments of that Julio video. It was clear that Phil still fancied himself tremendously.

Back in school, Phil had been a heartthrob to all the little girls in the lower forms. Those in his own year knew what a wanker he was. He was the mainstay of the choir and appeared in every school play, often as the romantic lead. But his shining moment had come when the drama teacher decided to stage *Jesus Christ Superstar*. Phil had played Jesus Christ – and, by God, did he think he was a superstar. I remembered somebody telling me, years ago, that Phil had gone busking around Europe – something about escaping the irate father of a girl he'd knocked up – but that could easily have been bullshit. They were a bunch of vicious gossips around our way.

When Phil finally released Helen's hand and returned to his spot on the dance floor (how typical of Phil to be the only man in a dance class; I was sure it was an excellent way to pick up women), she directed her glazed gaze back to me. Eyes aglow, face aglow – even her goddamn hair was aglow. I knew what was coming.

'So...' she said.

'Yes?' I said.

'Are you interested?'

'Oh, for God's sake, Helen. Who are you kidding? Go for it.'

'Really?'

'Absolutely.'

'Are you sure you don't mind?'

'Quite sure. Be my guest.'

'Oh, thank you – thank you!' She all but clapped her hands in glee, jumping up and down like a woman with a horrendous case of cystitis.

Which – I don't mean to be cruel – is what her attempts at flamenco dancing looked like, too. She had no rhythm whatsoever. But, since I was the woman who had put the idea of the classes into her head in the first place, I merely smiled encouragingly at her wild jerks – even when she accidentally kicked me in the shins. I just hoped she hadn't noticed the dubious looks she was getting from our fiery-looking instructress. *No, Helen Staunton, the rhythm is most definitely not going to get you.*

Did it have me? I'd like to think I had my moments. There were times when I certainly felt that I was in the flow. But then, maybe Helen felt that way too.

As for that other wild jerk, Phil Gallagher…I hated to admit it, but the boy was good. He flowed across the floor like hot oil. The instructress – who I was willing to bet had acquired her own mini-crush – held him up as an example so many times that it began to get annoying.

But Helen can't have been annoyed. Because at the end of the class, when Phil sidled up to her and asked her out, she responded with a resounding yes.

13

The next night, Tom and Mindy had Helen and me over to dinner, in order to celebrate my return to Grainger's. I had been sworn to absolute secrecy about Helen's impending date with Phil.

Tom answered the door, sporting a hat he'd purchased in a drunken moment in Torremolinos. It was the only thing he'd brought home with him, apart from a bad case of the squirts. It was a red straw sombrero, with a brim that extended at least a foot around his head. He had to stand at a funny angle just to let us in. I'd always known that someday he'd have trouble fitting his head through a door.

'*Buenas noches, señoritas!*' he boomed.

Mindy handed us each a bottle of San Miguel on our way into the sitting room. The theme of the night was becoming clear. I had told Tom about my new Spanish connections. No wonder he had asked me to bring along my Gypsy Kings CD.

Their daughter Clarissa was still up with a vengeance. The child appeared to need approximately one hour's sleep per night. I hadn't seen her for a few months. She now looked like a miniature version of Tom, without the beard.

'She's the image of you,' I told Mindy.

Two hours later, we had managed to polish off four plates of paella, four bowls of ice-cream and six bottles of wine. I had been duly toasted ('To the prodigal daughter on her return to the Grainger fold'), and everyone had clinked glasses – except for Clarissa, who had held her plastic beaker aloft. This was, of course, the perfect moment to introduce the home karaoke machine. Mindy was the opening act, with 'Viva España' – we all contributed to the chorus. Then Tom serenaded his wife with 'Blue Spanish Eyes', which made her cry because she was pissed. This in turn made Clarissa cry, so, to make amends, we had to do all the actions while she sang 'La Macarena' four times in a row.

Following this, the adults collapsed into a heap while Clarissa stampeded around the room like the Duracell bunny on speed, to the accompaniment of the Gypsy Kings. Twice she attempted to take slugs of Spanish plonk when she thought her parents weren't looking. Definitely not adopted. Then Mindy served the coffee. In actual fact, she placed four mugs on the table and poured the contents of the coffee pot over the general area. I'm sure some of it landed in the cups.

'So,' said Tom, dragging on his ninety-ninth cigarette of the evening (at least he wouldn't have stained fingertips; he was using his new faux-ivory cigarette holder), 'you never told us. How exactly did you convince old Georgie Porgie Pudding and Pie to give you your job back? A bit of the old hanky-panky, rumpy-pumpy, how's your father, hide the salami – was that it?'

'Nothing like that. I just went round to his house.'

'You did what?' Helen spluttered on her mouthful of coffee and tried, unsuccessfully, to raise herself from the beanbag in which she was trapped.

'I went round to his house and I said, "Oi, you – you great big bastard! Give us me job back or I'll take your arse to the cleaners." I mean, "I'll sue your arse and take you to the cleaners."'

'Did you really?' said Tom admiringly.

'You betcha I did. And he was shit-scared, and he said to me,

"Elizabeth," he said, "you can have your job back immed—immed— straight away.'

'Good for you,' cheered Mindy.

'Well, I think it's disgraceful,' said Helen. 'Going around to his house like that. What if his wife had answered the door?'

'Fuck his wife,' I said, spilling red wine all over Tom and Mindy's new cream carpet.

'He already did,' said Tom, doubling over with laughter.

'Well, I think you're a disgrace,' repeated Helen. What was it to her? Silly, moralistic cow!

'A toast! To Liz the disgrace!' cried Tom, standing up and tripping over his own shoe.

With a bit of luck, Helen wouldn't remember any of this in the morning.

Whether she did or not, she was too sick to do anything about it. As for me, when I finally opened my eyes the next morning, I felt like the horse's head in the Godfather's bed – or, if you prefer, as if someone had poured a giant vat of glue all over my face. My head was apparently glued to the pillow; my eyes were glued shut, my nostrils glued over, and my lips felt as if someone had glued them together. I staggered into the shower and turned on the heavenly spray.

My thoughts turned to Grainger's. Was I mad, asking for my old job back? It was all very well letting George know that he couldn't push me around – but did I really *want* to work in that shop again? Seeing George's self-satisfied mug, day in, day out, was hardly going to help me get over him. And – even worse – Judith might make the odd appearance: glowing, blooming, blossoming Judith. Still… what was done was done. And I needed the cash.

Feeling slightly more human, I emerged from the shower and – slickly avoiding looking in the mirror – stumbled into my room. Then something truly terrible happened. The phone rang.

It was my editor. She caught me completely off guard – which was, I supposed, her intention.

'Liz. How are you?'

'Oh, hi, Marian.' I tried – unsuccessfully, I knew – to keep the horror out of my voice.

'I haven't heard from you in a while.'

'Yes. Sorry about that. I've been very busy.'

'Writing, I hope.'

'Oh, yes, writing – of course.'

'Well?'

There was a pause.

'Well what?' I said finally.

'What have you been writing about? Are you going to give me a clue, or do I have to guess?'

I laughed, a sickly laugh. Marian had never used this tone with me before. We had always had such a good working relationship. She was the one who had 'discovered' me, and she had been my champion all along, backing me up even when her bosses thought my ideas were mad. But I sensed I might have stretched her patience too far this time. I felt even less blasé than I sounded. The truth was that I was in a state of sheer and utter panic about my writing. Whatever ability I'd once possessed seemed to have vanished into the ether, and I wondered if it would ever come back. Hope did not spring eternal. In fact, my hope seemed to have sprung a leak some time back.

'Of course,' I said weakly. 'Well…remember that idea I had, about a fictional account of the life of Queen Maeve?'

'Yes,' Marian said slowly, cautiously.

'Well, I've been working on that.'

'Didn't we discuss that idea before and decide it was a non-runner?'

'Did we?' *Oh, fuck* – we had, hadn't we? Another sickly laugh. 'Well, I had a good think about it and decided it was worth another look. And I must say that it's going very, very well.'

'Really?'

'Oh, yes. I'm extremely pleased with it.'

'Any chance of seeing a few chapters?'

'Ah...well...that might be a bit tricky. You see, I've been writing it in longhand.'

'Well, perhaps now might be a good time to start typing it up.'

'But you see, if I do that, I might interfere with the creative process.'

'You might. Interfere. With the creative process.' *Oh, dear...* 'Liz. As you are well aware, you were meant to have sample chapters in to me three months ago.'

'I know, Marian. I'm really sorry—'

'You're not the only person under pressure, you know.'

'I know, Marian. I know you're under pressure—'

'Henry will have my guts for garters if this book isn't ready on time.'

'I know. I'm—'

'You're sorry. Yes, I know. Look, Liz, I'll give you a ring this time next week and you can let me know how your *creative process* is going. OK?'

'OK, Marian.'

'Goodbye.'

'Goodbye, Marian.'

I put down the phone. Now all I had to do was arrange to be dead by this time next week.

14

I often wondered what Helen must think of our house. Whatever her opinion, she kept it well hidden. It was the next day, and she was due around any second, to fill me in on her date with Phil – and on any filling in that might have gone on.

The bell rang. Sure enough, Helen was standing on the doorstep, a grin of Cheshire-cat proportions splitting her regular features in two.

'Well, well, well,' I said. 'Somebody had a good time last night.'

She waltzed right by me, straight down the hall and into the sitting room. By the time I followed her in there, she was stretched out on the couch, her smile even more feline.

'Come on, then. Details, please.'

'Oh, Liz, it was amazing.'

'Really?'

'I think he could be the one, Liz.'

Oh, Christ, no. Here we go again. If I'd heard that once... Helen thought every new man was 'the one' until he inevitably showed signs of imperfection, somewhere around the third or fourth date. And Helen's standards of perfection were frighteningly severe. The last unfortunate had been dumped because he'd bought her a bunch of chrysanthemums from a *service station*. Blaming the flowers for the man who'd brought them, Helen had fired them directly into the bin in disgust (as far as I knew, this was known as transference). OK, the purchasing of garage flowers isn't exactly a redeeming feature in any woman's book, but it was hardly a sackable offence in mine. All he needed, in my view, was a little floral education.

'Go on, then. Why do you think he's the one?'

'He's just so...'

Don't say it.

'Perfect.'

Oh, God.

'Helen, I really don't want to rain all over your parade, but this is déjà vu all over again. No man is perfect.' *Especially not that fool.*

'I know, I know. But I think he might be the perfect fit for me.'

'Physically?'

She giggled. 'In every way.'

Helen was quite coy when it came to sexual matters. This was about as much detail as I could hope for.

'Well, congratulations on how fast you're working through your list.'

She really was flying through her 'How to Be Less Perfect' list. She'd got herself drunk as a skunk in Tom and Mindy's – and on a school night, no less! I force-fed her a dessert of truly stupendous, American-style proportions every time we had lunch together. (Did I just want to make her fatter? Surely not.) Unless she was doing it on the sly, I hadn't seen her writing any lists lately. And she was well on her way to shagging someone who could fairly be described as a stranger – if she hadn't done it already.

'In fact, you're doing so well that I might even let you write another list as a reward.'

'I don't need a list,' she said softly. 'I have Phil.'

Oh, sod it. Let her have her romance. It might help loosen up those tight seams she was so worried about. 'When are you seeing him again?'

'Tomorrow night.'

85

'Helen! I thought I heard your voice. Libby, why didn't you tell me that Helen was coming round?' The top half of my mother's body had appeared around the sitting-room door.

'Must have slipped my mind,' I murmured.

But she didn't even hear me. She was already sitting on the couch beside Helen, who had rapidly adjusted herself into a seated position.

'You don't even have as much as a cup of tea in your hand. What have I reared? Libby, would you ever go and make Helen a cup of tea – and one for me, while you're at it. And there's a packet of chocolate Goldgrain in the cupboard under the sink, behind the basin.'

Dragging my feet like a sulky teenager, I headed for the kitchen to do her bidding. Helen was *my* friend, wasn't she? Why did my mother always have to muscle in like this? I'd forgotten why I hadn't invited Helen around to my place in an age.

With particularly bad grace, I carried the tea tray back into the sitting room and slapped it heavily down onto the coffee table.

'Helen was just telling me how well she's getting on in the shop. You never told me that George put her in charge of *all* the buying.'

'That must have slipped my mind too.' *Why don't you just tattoo 'My daughter is a failure' on your forehead and have done with it?*

Helen gave me a slightly guilty look. She knew how I was feeling, but I could tell she was lapping it up, all the same. Who wouldn't enjoy the attentions of such an ardent fan?

'Chocolate biscuit, Mam?' I offered her the whole plateful. It was the only way I could think of to shut her up.

The next night, I had just sat through a particularly disappointing episode of *Coronation Street* – I wouldn't mind, but I'd expected that to be the highlight of my evening – and was foraging about in the kitchen, wondering how Helen was getting on with Phil, when the phone rang.

'Hello.'

'Liz...'

'Helen? Why... What's wrong?'

'He stood me up.'

Helen had waited at the entrance to the Stephen's Green shopping centre for a full hour. As the minutes ticked by, her elation had turned to worry, which had turned to despair. Eventually, she had slunk away in shame, feeling that every passerby could see the 'reject' mark stamped clearly on her forehead.

I brought her out and got her exceedingly drunk that night. It was the least I could do. It took her mind off Phil, it took my mind off the impending phone call from Marian, and it gave me a well-earned break from not writing my book.

15

It had been almost a week since the phone call from Marian. Maybe she'd forgotten about me. Maybe she'd had to go to London or New York on urgent business. Or maybe, I thought hopefully, she'd got the sack. She'd been let down by one unreliable author too many, and her bosses had given her the old heave-ho.

I knew I'd better try and write something, just in case she was still gainfully employed; but, again, the words just would not come. Why had I ever thought I'd be able to do this? Why had I ever believed I had it in me to write a novel in the first place? I was a two-hit wonder, that was all I was – and they hadn't even been hits!

Sod this, I decided. *I'm going to Granny's.* She always made me feel better. Fortune-telling wasn't her only gift.

My grandmother was a little upset that day, because some scoundrel had made off with her favourite gnome – the lad with the fishing rod who had been perched on the side of the wishing well. She shook her head sadly. What was the world coming to?

It was just the two of us. Kit – a trader in Meath Street market – was working on her stall. I'd brought Granny an African violet, and she gave it pride of place on top of her new, plasma-screened television set. She was in casual mode today: she wore carpet slippers and tights that wrinkled about her slightly swollen ankles. I silently sympathised; it must be difficult to get tights to fit legs that short. Her skirt was floral, and so was her headscarf.

'You know,' she said suddenly, 'I never did tell your fortune that day. Will I do it now?'

'Ah, no. I don't really—'

'Come on into the fortune-telling room. Cards, palm or crystal ball?'

She wasn't taking no for an answer. I followed her in. 'Ball.' *Or should I say balls?*

Granny drew the curtains before sitting down at the table. In spite of myself, I felt a prickly sensation at the back of my neck as I sat down opposite her. Then I tried not to giggle as she passed her hands theatrically over the crystal ball, all the while peering intently into its depths. I prepared myself to be told about tall, dark, handsome strangers and overseas travel.

'You already know your soulmate,' she said abruptly. I already knew that. Pity he was already married. 'But you don't know he's your soulmate yet.'

Oh?

'You need to learn to see him with new eyes.'

I'd need a bloody eye transplant, judging by the men I knew.

'Don't worry, he's a lovely lad,' my grandmother said, smiling benignly at me. 'You're going to have a long and happy life together.'

How nice.

'I see a lot of money and a lot of success,' she said. 'Your books will sell across the globe.'

That sounded promising. All I had to do was write the bloody things.

'But you have a lot of blocked energy you have to shift first.'

Nothing, I'm sure, that a bowl of All-Bran couldn't sort out.

'Family issues.' Her voice was stern, and she looked up at me pointedly. 'You have to sort these out first, or you'll never get anywhere.'

And just how am I supposed to do that? I wondered, thinking of the unsolvable problem of my mother.

'I'm not just talking about your mammy. I'm talking about your daddy, too.'

I stared at her, shocked. 'How do I do that?' I said, aloud this time.

'I can't tell you that. You have to find your own way. All I can tell you is that you must trust in God and your gut.'

Good catchphrase.

When she had finished the reading, I couldn't work out if I felt better or worse. But at least I didn't have to pay thirty euro. There were some perks to being related to a fortune-teller. I watched Granny as she draped a dark-grey cloth reverently over the crystal ball.

'Did you ever think you might be psychic yourself?' she asked.

The question threw me. 'I don't think so. I mean…I never gave it much thought. Why?'

'We have a long history of psychics in this family. You've never had any dreams that came true? Or seen anything strange that nobody else could see?'

'No. Well – now that you mention it…'

'You have?'

'When I was little…' I couldn't believe I was telling her this. I hadn't even thought about it for years. 'I thought I saw a fairy sitting on a gate. It seems ridiculous now…'

'Was it betwixt the two lights?'

'What?'

'Did you see it at twilight?'

I thought for a few seconds. 'Yes. It was dusk. We were visiting my aunt down the country.'

'I used to see fairies all the time when I was a girl.'

'Really?'

90

'Oh, yes. You have the gift, all right. You just have to learn how to use it.'

My mother handed me the phone literally the moment I walked in the door.

'It's for you. It's Marian.'

Of all the lousy timing... There was no point in asking my mother to lie for me. My heart sinking, I took the receiver from her hand.

'Hello, Marian.'

'Liz! You're a hard woman to catch. I was trying you all afternoon.'

'I was out.'

'So I gathered. And your mobile was powered off.'

'I forgot to re-charge the battery.'

'That would explain it. So, Liz, how many chapters do you have for me?' There was a note of challenge in her tone.

'Well, you see...there's a bit of a problem.'

'Oh, yes?'

'My computer is giving me gyp, and I can't get stuff to print off. I've left it in to be—'

'Liz.' Marian's voice was big.

'Yes.' Mine was small.

'Would you like an extension on your deadline?'

'What?'

'I said, would you like an extension on your deadline? I was thinking six months.'

'Oh, Marian, that would be just brilliant! Oh, thank you so much – you're a life-saver.'

'Don't thank me too much, Liz. You're rapidly running out of chances here. You're just lucky another writer submitted her manuscript way ahead of time. You know Harriet Hayes? We've given her your slot instead.'

I felt a pang. I knew Harriet, all right. She was my arch-rival, no less. The bitch always seemed to be one book ahead of herself. Still, I was hardly in a position to complain.

'I really appreciate this, Marian. And I'm sorry for putting you to so much trouble.'

'That's all right. And, Liz...'

'Yes?'

'Don't let me down again.'

Was it just me, or did that sound like a threat?

'I won't.'

And, as I put the receiver back in its cradle, I honestly and sincerely meant it.

I went back to work the next day. Tom was delighted to have me back – none of the others would go drinking with him after work – and I assumed Helen was, too, but it was hard to tell, she was still so terribly down after her run-in with Philandering Phil.

And as for George – who knew? He sauntered in a little before lunchtime, as usual. It was his habit to look after his other business interests in the morning. I happened to know that these mainly involved property investment and development. He had always been on at me to buy my own place. ('Property investment is the way to go, Liz.' 'Is that so, George? Care to lend me twenty grand?')

'Morning, Mr Grainger.' The customary chorus.

'Morning, everyone.'

He was wearing his crombie draped across his shoulders, and he had a new haircut. He nodded and smiled at me enigmatically; then he disappeared into Helen's office. I analysed the smile for about five minutes before realising that somebody wanted to buy a book. I was stationed at the till beside the Mind, Body, Spirit section again, and I'd been plagued by weirdoes all morning. This particular weirdo wanted to buy *Advanced Numerology for Cats*. I refrained from commenting. I'd been warned about that in the past, and I had to be on my best behaviour, now that I'd been given a second chance. I'd wait until tomorrow, at least, before I started insulting customers.

I shifted around restlessly on my stool. I was bored and hungry, and Helen was taking her time; it was seven minutes past one already. I summoned over the girl who was to relieve me, and took myself and my bag off to the stockroom. I was sure I had a pear festering in there somewhere…yes. It had developed several brown patches since this morning, and a Biro that had also been lurking in the depths of my bag had gouged out a big blue hole in it, but it was still edible in my book.

Speaking of books, I scanned the shelves for something to carry me through the afternoon. I had just taken a particularly large and messy bite when the door opened and in walked Eric the Viking.

'I heard you were back,' he said, removing his headphones.

I nodded, my mouth still full. I rummaged around in my pockets, but I was all out of tissues; I had to resort to using the back of my hand to wipe away the pear juice that was dripping down my chin. How dignified. Luckily, it wasn't George who had just walked in.

'You took my advice, then.'

'I don't know what you mean.' I wasn't going to admit to Eric that a) I'd had an affair with my married boss and b) I'd all but threatened to tell his wife about us if he didn't give me my job back. I got up and aimed the remainder of the pear into the wastepaper basket, the one labelled 'Paper only'. I missed.

Eric didn't probe any further. I started to climb the stepladder; I had spotted *Love in the Time of Cholera* on the top shelf.

'I'll get that for you,' said Eric, reaching up effortlessly and lifting me down a copy. Sometimes I hated tall people.

I left the stockroom and knocked on Helen's door.

'Come in.'

I went in. Helen was putting up her hair, with the aid of a tortoiseshell grip and a hand-held mirror.

'Are you coming? It's twenty past already.'

'Sorry. I'll be with you now.'

I noticed she was puffy-eyed again. 'Helen, what's wrong?'

'Nothing.'

'But you've been crying.'

'No, I haven't. I just stuck my eyeliner into my eye by mistake. Come on, let's go. I'm starved.'

She stuck it into both eyes at the same time?

I also noticed that, even puffy-eyed, she was still beautiful. Not for the first time, I wondered if I'd feel better about myself if I didn't hang around with Helen.

16

When I look back now, the clues were legion. But I didn't know at the time that I was looking for clues.

First, there was the fact that Helen was popping indigestion tablets at the slightest provocation, for what seemed like weeks on end. Then there was that gorgeous day in May when we were sharing a pot of tea over lunch and she insisted that it had an odd, metallic tang to it; it tasted fine to me. Then, one afternoon at the start of June, I asked her if she had a spare tampon. She didn't – and she nearly took the head off me for asking. This was weird in itself, but I also happened to know that Helen always carried enough tampons in her bag to service a small army. (A female army, obviously. Imagine that: a whole army of women menstruating at the same time. Now that *would* be fierce.) But it wasn't until the last week of June, the day she fainted in work, that I copped. In fact, I didn't even cop straight away. She had to tell me that she was pregnant. Twelve weeks gone, to be exact.

Helen was pregnant. *Helen*. Up the duff, knocked up, up the pole, in the family way, in the club, a bun in the oven.

It was unthinkable. This was the type of thing that happened to *me*. It should have happened to me.

That dastardly mongrel, Phil. Needless to say, he hadn't turned up at any more of the flamenco classes. Doubtless he'd got what he wanted out of them. I thought he should be taken out and shot. And I was the one who had encouraged her to have a one-night stand in the first place. I had, however, expected her to use precautions.

'Are you going to tell Phil?' I asked her. We were on our coffee break, the day after the fainting incident.

'I can't. I have no way of contacting him.'

'But you have to tell him!'

'Can we not talk about this now, please?'

'OK, then. So what happened? Did the condom break?'

She didn't look up from her Palm Pilot, into which she was frantically typing a list.

'Helen. You did use a condom, didn't you?'

She muttered something.

'What?'

'He said he was allergic.'

'Allergic to condoms?'

'To latex.'

'What? You eejit! You can get latex-free condoms, you know.'

'Really?'

'Yes, really.'

Helen started to cry.

'I'm sorry.' I put an arm around her shoulders. 'But...did you just take your chances, then?'

'He withdrew.'

'Sounds to me like he made a deposit.'

She laughed for a second, and then began to cry again.

'Do your parents know yet?'

Helen shook her head, a picture of misery.

Helen came from a ridiculously functional family. One-point-four children – the point-four was a much younger brother who was away in boarding school, another rugger-bugger in the making. Her parents were nice. I sometimes pretended I was their daughter. Can you be adopted at the age of thirty-one? Helen was living at home while she saved up the deposit for a house of her own – and she'd almost managed it, too. I guessed those plans were scuppered for a while.

'How am I going to tell them I'm going to be an unmarried mother?'

'Lone parent,' I said. 'You're going to be a lone parent.' The truth was, if I had carried out a mental survey of all the single women I knew, I would have voted Helen the least likely to become either a lone parent *or* an unmarried mother.

And do you want to know the truth – the real, shocking, unmentionable, unpalatable truth? While I was sorry for my best friend – I really and truly was – there was some tiny corner of me that felt smug. Helen, perfect Helen, was going to be an unmarried mother, and I wasn't.

I was considering her plight the next day, feeling great rage towards Phil the Philanderer, when it occurred to me that his mother might still live in my area. I looked her up in the phone book – yes, still there. I took down the details on a slip of paper and gave it to Helen.

'What's this?'

'Phil's mother's address and telephone number.'

She let the slip of paper drop from her fingertips as if it were contaminated. 'What are you giving me that for?'

'So you can contact her and find out where he is. He deserves to know what he's done to you. You could call round to her house. I'll come with you if you like.'

'I'll do no such thing.'

'But, Helen—'

'For fuck's sake, this is none of your business! Now drop it.'

I was speechless, partly because Helen had used the F-word and partly because I'd seldom seen her so angry. Her cheeks were scarlet and her eyes had a wild look about them.

'All right. I'm sorry. I won't mention it again.'

I blamed the hormones.

The following day, I called around to Phil's mother's house. Yes, I knew I was interfering. But I honestly thought, at the time, that I was doing the right thing. I was determined that Phil should be held accountable for his actions. I wanted justice.

Mrs Gallagher was much as I remembered her. I, however, clearly wasn't as she remembered me; in fact, she didn't remember me at all.

'Hello, Mrs Gallagher.'

She frowned at me.

'I'm Elizabeth Clancy. I was in your son's class in school.'

Still the frown.

'You're in the ladies' club with my mother.'

'I don't know anyone in the ladies' club by the name of Clancy.'

The fact that I had a different surname from the rest of my family had caused confusion before. 'Róisín Murphy.'

'Oh, yes, Róisín. Of course. You don't look much like her, do you?'

'I'm told I favour my father.'

I waited to be invited in, but it wasn't happening. 'I need to speak to you about your son Phil.'

'What about Phil?'

'Mrs Gallagher, it's rather private. Do you mind if we step inside?'

She hesitated for a second or two before opening the door a few inches wider and stepping aside.

She brought me into the living room. I could tell by the feel of it that it was seldom used. It was less a room than a shrine to Phil – Phil in every musical or play in which he had ever starred, sung in a chorus or farted in a crowd scene. Pride of place had been given to a large photo of the pride and joy himself as Jesus Christ Superstar.

'What a lovely room,' I said.

Phil's mother – if memory served me, her name was Philomena – had a lot to answer for. She had enrolled Phil in the Biddy Bartley School for Precocious Little Wankers when he was just a tot. I remembered the day when that particular story had broken. We'd been in second year, and all the other boys in the class had beaten Phil up and called him a poof. In retrospect, it was to his credit that he'd remained undeterred in his quest for stardom.

I was remembering all manner of interesting little snippets, now that I was face to face with Philomena Gallagher once again. She had been a member of the PTA, right up until it came to light that she'd been having an affair with one of the teachers. The scandal had led to the sacking of said teacher and to the demise of Philomena's marriage. You could tell she'd been a handsome woman, but too many years of too many sunbed sessions and cigarettes had taken their toll.

'So what do you want with my Phil?'

'I met up with him recently.'

'Did you really?' Her features brightened momentarily.

'Yes. We took a dance class together – me and Phil and my friend Helen.'

'Oh, yes?'

'Yes. Well, you see, the thing is…Phil and my friend Helen had a kind of – fling. And…look, Mrs Gallagher, there's no nice way of putting this, so I'm just going to come out and say it.' Deep breath. 'Phil got Helen pregnant.'

'I beg your pardon!' Mrs Gallagher rose from the settee.

'And now Helen needs to find out where he is, so she can contact him and let him know he's going to be a father.'

'You must think I was born yesterday. Get out of my house this instant!'

What the hell?

'Come on – out!' She shooed me as if I were an errant pet.

'Mrs Gallagher—'

She stepped up so close to me that we were practically eyeball to eyeball and stabbed her forefinger intermittently into my face, making me blink repeatedly. 'If you are who you say you are – and I sincerely doubt it; coming here pretending to be Róisín Murphy's daughter, when you look nothing like her, and you don't even have the same name – you must think I'm really stupid.'

No, not stupid. Just mad.

'My Phil would never get a girl into trouble and desert her.'

'Well, he would, and he has.'

'What proof do you have that he's the father? This Helen could be the greatest slut going, for all I know. She could have had any number of men.'

'Helen isn't like that.'

'You know, this isn't the first time my son has been wrongly accused of fathering a child.'

'I wonder why?'

'I'll tell you why, will I?'

'Please do.'

'They're all after his money.'

'What money?'

'All those little scrubbers know he's going to be a big star one day, and they all want to jump on the bandwagon.'

I'd heard enough. 'I'll let myself out.'

Her words followed me down the garden path. 'This family has been persecuted for far too long. We won't tolerate it any more. Don't you darken this door again.' And she slammed said door behind me.

And I stood for a while in Philomena Gallagher's front garden, contemplating the phenomenon of Irish mothers and their sons.

That evening, I was still debating whether or not to tell Helen. I had been sitting for some time at the kitchen table. My decision-making process had been aided and abetted by countless fig rolls. Jim was at the kitchen counter, making himself a crisp-and-ketchup sandwich. He ate it standing up, as was his custom. Today he was wearing a black T-shirt with the words 'Nice One' emblazoned in red across the chest. It should have said 'Horrible One', I thought; but we must have been making some progress, because a few months earlier I would have said these words out loud. Jim and I had settled into an uneasy truce, which consisted largely of ignoring each other.

Speaking of uneasy truces, in walked my mother. The woman had a very accusing way about her.

'Hello,' she said accusingly.

I immediately felt guilty. Should I not be sitting at the kitchen table of an evening, eating fig rolls? Clearly not. I felt my body tense as she began opening and closing presses behind me.

'I had a very strange phone call this afternoon,' she said.

'Really? From who?'

'Philomena Gallagher.'

Shit, double shit and triple shit.

'Do you remember her?'

'Yes. Phil's mother. What did she have to say for herself?'

'Some very interesting things.' My mother sat down opposite me and, leaning forward in what I perceived to be a threatening manner, clasped her hands together like a quizmaster. 'She said she wanted to check whether or not I had a daughter. When I told her I did, she demanded a full physical description. So I described you, and she hung up.'

I was dying to know how she'd described me, but I was afraid to ask. 'That was weird,' was all I offered.

'Wasn't it just?'

A few moments' silence.

'What have you been up to, Libby?'

I sighed. 'You're going to find out sooner or later anyway. Helen's pregnant, and Phil Gallagher is the father.'

Watching my mother's jaw hit the linoleum was surprisingly satisfying.

'Helen!' she said finally. 'Your friend Helen? Helen Staunton?'

'That's the one.'

'And she's having it for Phil Gallagher?' She was incredulous. 'But he's an awful prick, that young fella.'

'Yeah, that's him. Phil the Prick. Literally.'

'Watch your language.'

'But you just said—'

'I got a shock. Was it planned?'

'God, no.'

'I didn't even know they knew each other.'

'They didn't. We met him at the flamenco-dancing classes. They had a fling, and now he's scarpered.'

'Well, my God. I would have thought the girl had better taste. Although he was quite a good-looking lad, wasn't he?'

'All right, I suppose.'

'Poor lamb. How far gone is she?'

'Almost thirteen weeks.'

'Is she keeping it?'

'I think so.'

'And how is she?'

'Devastated.'

My mother shook her head sadly. 'You know, she's the last person I ever would have expected to have an unplanned pregnancy.'

My mother had been expecting me to have an unplanned pregnancy since I was fifteen.

'You can't tell anyone,' I said. 'Her parents don't even know yet.'

'Do they not?' She shook her head again. 'That'll be a shock to them. You know, I just can't believe it – a lovely girl like that, with her whole future ahead of her. And she was doing so well in her career – manager of the shop at such a young age, and so ambitious, too… She'll have to forget all that now.'

'Not necessarily.'

'It's no joke bringing up a child on your own, you know.'

We looked at each other, then looked away. The elephant was in the room again.

'What hospital is she going to?'

'The Coombe.'

'Good. I've a friend who's a midwife there. You know Sheila? I'll give her a call and tell her to look out for Helen. And I'll find out who the best consultant is.' She shook her head again. 'Such a terrible thing to happen to such a lovely girl.'

I had always imagined that my mother thought of Helen as the daughter she should have had. Maybe Helen and I could swap parents – although it wouldn't really be fair on her, because I'd get two for the price of one.

17

What I'm about to write still fills me with shame. And anger.

I'm ashamed that I didn't have enough moral fibre to resist. I'm ashamed that I didn't have enough respect for myself to do the decent thing. I'm ashamed that I had so little regard for George's wife and children – his pregnant wife, his unborn child. And I'm angry with him – so angry; but not as angry as I am with myself.

It began innocently enough – or so I kidded myself. His daily visit to the shop became my daily highlight. He would wink at me on his way into Helen's office. At first I feigned indignation, then indifference. After a while, I would return his wink with a little smile – just a little one. I found myself taking extra-special care over my make-up and pretending that I was just doing it to make myself feel better.

What a crock.

The culmination of our furtive flirtation occurred one evening after work. It was late-night opening. George waited until everyone was gone before asking me to join him for a drink. For a chat. So along I went. For a chat.

One drink became two became too many. To make matters worse, he took me to 'our pub'. Although 'our pub' was no longer quite the way we remembered it. The original interior had been ripped out and replaced by an ultra-modern, ultra-trendy disco-bar-type effort. Gone were the comfy, maroon, cracked leather seats, and the snug where you could while away many a happy hour with only your pint and a newspaper for company, hidden away from the world behind the tacky frosted glass. And, worst of all, one of the few remaining pubs in Dublin in which you had been able to hear yourself think had gone and installed a wide-screen TV. Currently showing was the Real Madrid versus Juventus match. (Didn't Julio Iglesias used to be the goalie for Real Madrid?) But once George and I started talking and – crucially – got a few drinks inside us, we could have been anywhere.

It felt so bloody good. I told him all about meeting my father's mother. To his credit, he seemed genuinely interested.

'You know,' I said, feeling suddenly shy, 'some people might say that was why I was attracted to you before.'

'Why?'

'You know. The whole looking-for-a-father-figure thing.'

George grinned, a grin so full of confidence – no, arrogance – that I couldn't decide whether I wanted to hop on him or smack him one. 'And there was I, thinking it was my rugged good looks you were after.'

'Well, those too, obviously.'

'Obviously.'

To spare myself any further blushes, I deftly changed the subject. 'Shocking news about Helen, isn't it?'

'Yes, it is. Are you ready for another drink?'

'No, thanks. Did you know I was in school with the baby's father?'

'That I didn't know.'

'I went round to his mother's house recently. She lives near me.'

George was examining his whiskey glass as if it were made of the most intricately carved crystal. 'Does Helen know you did that?'

'God, no. She'd kill me.'

He nodded. 'Maybe you'd be better off leaving well enough alone. It's seldom a good idea to get involved in other people's relationships.'

'You're probably right. I won't be going around there again in a hurry, anyway; the daft old bat as good as threw me out of the house. But, seriously, what's Helen going to do? The bastard has left her completely in the lurch.'

'I agree. It's terrible. Now I have to take a whizz.'

On his way back, George purchased yet another vodka on my behalf. All part of his devious seduction plan. As if I needed to be seduced.

I shouldn't be doing this, I thought. But, through my deliberate, drunken haze, these words had no meaning. My actions were far louder.

From 'our pub' we adjourned to 'our hotel', to revisit several of 'our favourite positions'. When I woke up the next morning, I felt queasy from a combination of self-disgust and too much alcohol. I showered vigorously and left the room before George woke up. Yet, come the next late-night opening, I waited for him again.

I *was* George's late night opening.

Looking back, I felt alive, I felt exhilarated. I felt sick. I didn't tell anybody about my dirty little secret. Who could possibly approve? I knew I didn't.

I'd thought I'd felt guilty the last time I'd been with George. It turned out I hadn't known the meaning of the word. This time, I couldn't get the image of George's pregnant wife out of my head, except – ironically – when I was with George. The rest of the time was spent in mental torment, which made me even more desperate to see George… It was a vicious, vicious circle.

Four late-night openings later, I hung around at the back of the shop, as usual, but there was no sign of George. I checked my phone for messages, but it was blank. A surge of impotent fury rose up from my gut and into my throat.

'Bastard,' I spat, and kicked the nearest object, which happened to be a boxful of books. Several copies of *Lady Chatterley's Lover* clattered to the floor.

I might as well lock up, I thought. As I was doing the rounds, I noticed that somebody had left the light on in the stockroom. I opened the door to switch it off.

'Jesus Christ!' We both said it at the same time. I felt my hand fly up to my throat. Eric leapt to his feet; the foil-wrapped sandwich he had been munching fell to the dusty floor. I remember thinking, after I'd collected myself, *Isn't that sweet? His mammy must make him a packed lunch.*

'I thought I was alone,' he said.

'So did I.'

We laughed together.

'I nearly locked you in,' I told him. 'You would have had to spend the night here.'

'Wouldn't be the first time.'

This didn't surprise me. Eric was so quiet that you could easily forget that he was there. But he was – always there, ever watchful. There was a quality to his quietness that unnerved me. Some people were quiet because they were shy or lacking in confidence, whereas Eric's quietness could almost be interpreted as arrogance, as if he just couldn't be bothered wasting his words on you. And there was more: a stillness. It was all very mysterious. There was almost a Native American quality about him. He was, I decided, Dances with Books. Who was I? Dances with Words?

We left the shop together, which saved me from having to use the ladder to close the shutters. Eric really was very tall – well over six foot, and he looked even taller because he was so lean. He was going my way. I contemplated asking him for a piggyback.

We walked towards our respective bus stops on O'Connell

Street. I was faced with the dilemma of how to make small talk with a man who didn't do small talk – didn't do talk, really.

'Where are you headed?' I tried.

'Drumcondra.'

'Is that where you're from?'

'No. I rent there.'

So he didn't live with his parents, after all. I wondered how old he was. Eighteen or nineteen? I couldn't ask; that would be too direct. I'd check his employment file in Helen's office instead. Helen wouldn't mind, because Helen wouldn't know.

For the rest of the walk, I did what I always did with a very quiet person: I babbled. Eric didn't say a whole lot back. He merely glanced at me from time to time, an expression of detached amusement on his inscrutable features. Now why couldn't I do that – shut up and be all self-possessed? A boy of his age had no business being so self-possessed. Me, I was just possessed.

We reached the stop for the number 16 to Phibsboro first. 'This is me,' I said. 'Thanks for walking me. When are you working next?'

'Not till Tuesday.'

'See you then.'

'Do you ever go to gigs?' Eric asked.

'Sometimes.'

'We're playing in Whelan's this Saturday night. Why don't you come?'

'I might do.'

'Bring as many people as you like.'

'OK, I will. Looking forward to it.'

He nodded, and off he went. I watched him making mincemeat of the pavement with his long, rangy strides.

It had been ages since I'd been to Whelan's. It would probably be full of teenagers. But I was confident that I could still pass for twenty-eight.

Did you know that the second most successful mammal on the planet is the rat, largely due to its ability to adapt to almost any situation? I learnt this from a David Attenborough programme. And the most successful mammal of all? It's us – human beings, *Homo sapiens*. We'll eat anything, we'll live anywhere and we spread litter and pestilence wherever we go. We multiply at a staggering rate, overpopulating all our cities. We're a species, in fact, that could do with a good culling.

This was what I was thinking as I walked through Temple Bar that Saturday evening on my way to Whelan's. I was watching all the bodies spilling out of the bars and onto the pavements, shouting and roaring and discarding empty packets of bacon fries. Helen, Tom and Mindy accompanied me. Happily, the smoking ban meant that a four-months-gone Helen could join us without wanting to throw up every few minutes – although her sickness did appear to be on the wane. She was entering the radiant phase of her pregnancy. I was almost insanely jealous of her hair these days; it could have starred in its very own Pantene commercial. Her bump was just starting to reveal itself. Tonight, she had it hidden demurely under a black, floaty, empire-line top. She'd been far more relaxed since telling her parents about the baby. They, for their part, had handled the news beautifully.

Tom was wearing a cravat. I hated it when he did that, especially on a Saturday night, when we were going to a place like Whelan's. I was always afraid that he was going to get beaten up. This might have been why he had brought Mindy along: for protection. Mindy, for her part, had got a new haircut. Some women favour the just-out-of-bed look; Mindy favoured the just-out-of-prison look. Maternal granny was doing the honours with Clarissa. It had been ages since Tom and Mindy had had a night out together, and they were like prisoners on parole, giddy from a heady mixture of excitement and beer.

The pub wasn't packed, but it was getting there. We secured the last available table in the gig room and ordered a round. The crowd was a good mix – not all teenyboppers, as I had feared, and male and female in equal parts (a bit like Tom and Mindy). Tom laughed to himself from time to time. 'Eric and the Vikings?' he said. 'I don't believe it.'

We were seated beside a table full of women; there must have been about twelve of them, all twenty-somethings in various stages of undress. Even the mingers were done up to the knockers. I looked down critically at my own outfit. I clearly wasn't showing enough skin. Since when had it become mandatory to wear little more than a bikini on a night out in Dublin? OK, it was August, but it wasn't *that* warm.

The MC came on stage, wearing a battered brown leather jacket and a studiedly casual air. 'I'd like to introduce you to one of Dublin's most exciting up-and-coming bands. People...please give it up for Eric and the Vikings!'

He was far too old to get away with saying 'give it up', but everyone clapped regardless. Eric and the lads walked onto the stage, and the girls next to us rose to their feet and started to whistle.

'Go on, Eric, ya good thing!' yelled a girl with a crop top and multiple piercings. Helen and I looked at each other and giggled.

'Eric's got a groupie,' Helen said.

A few moments later, we discovered why.

110

Eric was dressed from head to toe in black. It made him look even taller and leaner; his white-blond hair had never looked more striking, and I swear I'd never before noticed how blue his eyes were. (Was that eyeliner he was wearing?) He also wore an electric guitar, which he had already started to strum before reaching the microphone.

'Howya,' was all he said, but it made the women erupt into rapturous applause once again. The other Vikings were a scruffy-looking bunch: a lead guitarist, a bass player and a drummer. If you'd asked me that afternoon whether I thought that Eric was a likely candidate to front a band, I'd have laughed in your face. Now I wasn't so sure.

'Our first song,' said Eric, 'is called "Mystic Lisa".' (Lisa? Lisa? Who the fuck is Lisa?)

Then he began to sing. I couldn't believe my ears; his voice was so gravelly and so sweet, in equal parts. Helen and I looked at each other again, this time in amazement. We hadn't actually expected Eric – our Eric, the lad who worked in the stockroom – to be any good. I was beginning to see him in a new light. The poster had said something about 'experimental rock', but I would have described the music – or rather Eric, who, let's face it, *was* the music – as a cross between Bowie and Cobain.

'How old is he, do you know?' I asked Helen.

'Twenty-six.'

He'd be gorgeous in another twenty years.

A few songs into the set, I couldn't help noticing that the attention of some of the girls at our neighbouring table had been diverted from Eric over to Tom. Tom wasn't as striking as Eric, nor was he as long and lean, but he was wearing a cravat and this gave him a certain rarity value. Furthermore, he had his legs crossed as elegantly as any young woman, and he was swinging his uppermost foot in time to the music, all the while examining his cuticles – the smoking ban had left his hands deprived of something to do, and he'd already ripped up every beer mat in sight.

Multiple Piercings was appraising him coldly. I feared that she might have had one too many alcopops. 'Here,' she said, punching her friend in the shoulder and gesturing towards Tom, 'look at the bleedin' state of yer man.'

Tom looked up from his nails. 'I beg your pardon, Miss. Are you referring to me?'

The two girls fell against each other, laughing.

'"Are you referring to me?"' mimicked Multiple Piercings. 'Yes, I am referring to you, you big, raving poofter. What were you thinking when you dressed yourself tonight?'

'Actually, sartorial elegance was what I had in mind. I'd imagine what you were thinking was, "How can I accentuate all my worst features and look like a cheap whore?"'

'What did you call me? Come over here and say that to me again, you fat fucker, and I'll bleedin' burst you.'

But Tom didn't need to, because by this time Mindy had risen to her feet and was advancing towards Super Groupie in an extremely threatening manner. 'Don't you talk to my husband like that, you fucking slapper.'

At this point, Helen fled, hands held protectively over her bump. I should have done the same, but I was transfixed – especially when Mindy smashed a bottle of Miller against the edge of our table and took another menacing step closer to the enemy.

Who knows what would have happened if a couple of bouncers hadn't come along and ejected our entire party – quite forcibly – from the premises? They even told Mindy that she was barred for life. So that put a bit of a damper on the evening.

18

I didn't bump into Eric again until the following week. I felt compelled to apologise for the fracas at his gig.

'No hassle,' he said. 'There's nothing like a good floor show.'

'Tom's wife got barred for life.'

'They always say that. There's this one guy who gets barred for life every week.'

'I'll tell her that. You were very good.'

'Thanks.' There was nothing coy about his response, no searching look to see whether I really meant it. He didn't need to search: he knew he was good. And he knew that I knew he was good.

'Can I ask you something?' I said.

Eric nodded cagily. I imagined he feared I was about to ask him something deeply personal, like how many brothers and sisters he had. Or maybe ask him out.

'I've been thinking about taking Spanish guitar lessons. Would you know how I'd go about it?'

'I didn't know you played the guitar.'

I frowned. 'I don't.'

He looked at me strangely. 'You do know that there's no such thing as a Spanish guitar, don't you? It's a style of playing, not an instrument.'

'Oh.' This I hadn't known. I blushed deeply.

'I do have a mate who gives guitar lessons to beginners,' Eric said. 'I'll give you his number if you like. But it'd be a long time before you'd be good enough to play flamenco-style.'

'That'd be great. Thanks.'

On my last visit to Granny's, she'd told me that my father had played the Spanish guitar. Maybe she didn't know the difference either. He'd had the guitar with him on the day he died. They had lain beside each other on Oxford Street, both mangled beyond recognition. He'd been busking around London, writing songs and trying to get a record deal. I'd had the bright idea that learning the 'Spanish guitar' would forge connections both with him and with my Spanish heritage; but if I was going to have to suffer years of 'Mary Had a Little Lamb' and 'Home on the Range', I didn't know if I could be bothered.

Furthermore, Eric now thought that I was an idiot. He wasn't the first, and I was sure he wouldn't be the last.

The following week, I heard a report on the radio that enraged me. Apparently, this report had come up with the 'finding' that girls who grew up without a stable father figure were a) more likely to develop unsuitable relationships with unsuitable men and b) more likely to have unplanned pregnancies. What a load of bull. Take Helen: her father figure was so stable that he was practically rooted to the ground, and look what had happened to her. Who came up with these reports, anyway? Did they actually pay people to do them? I felt like writing a letter, or making a phone call, or just shouting at someone in general. It was hard enough growing up without a father – through no fault of your own – without having such stereotypical crap foisted upon you.

I was being drawn ever deeper into my affair with George. Our 'dates' – which were invariably heavy on the sex and light on the romance – made me feel fantastic while I was on them, but increasingly sordid when I was not. I'd promise myself repeatedly that I'd end the affair, tomorrow; but the next night would find me, yet again, cradled under George's armpit, my head resting against his silver, hairy chest – the most comforting pillow I had ever known. I would nestle into that familiar George scent that made me feel so good while I smelt it, but so bereft when it was taken away from me again. And it was always being taken away – back to his wife, Judith, who grew more and more pregnant by the day. She was now eight months gone and counting. She was like a ticking time bomb in my life. I never mentioned her to George, and I never mentioned George to anyone. But my sense of foreboding grew along with his unborn child.

Helen's unborn child was growing too, causing unprecedented pressure upon her bladder and sphincter muscles. The previously tightly corked Helen found herself farting helplessly at inopportune moments, such as trade dinners and the like. And the other week, she had been standing innocently on Grafton Street, looking in at the new Brown Thomas window, when – for no apparent reason – she had weed herself. On the plus side, she was no longer popping Rennies. Instead, she took a family-sized bottle of Gaviscon with her wherever she went and gulped it down straight, like a wino with a bottle of meths. This pregnancy lark was not tempting.

Still, Helen seemed as content as anyone could be in her circumstances. She comforted herself by writing endless lists: 'Hospital Bag', 'Baby's First Week at Home', 'Foods for Optimum Nutrition'. I can't say I identified. I seldom felt the urge to write lists, not even when grocery shopping. I preferred to be inspired as I went – which was a sure-fire way to forget the broccoli and buy lots of biscuits. But who was I to begrudge Helen her lists? Her life was no longer perfection; she might as well be perfectly prepared for this baby.

So there I was, surrounded by all this fertility and creativity. It felt almost as if all these fecund women were mocking my own creative sterility. Because still there was no book three, not even an abortive attempt. I cast my mind back to the embryonic stirrings of book one. It was entirely possible that my memory had become dulled with the passing of time, but I was sure it had flowed from my pen like literary fine wine. And book two – I couldn't remember encountering any difficulties with that one, either. So what was so different this time? This thing with George? Not having a space of my own? The recent revelations about my father? Helen's pregnancy, which I sometimes felt I was experiencing right along with her? (Aside from the flatulence. Can you get sympathy flatulence? Do expectant fathers suffer from it?)

Whatever the reason for my writer's block, my six months were up. I tensed up horribly whenever the phone rang. It hadn't been Marian so far, but it was only a matter of time – and not much of it.

Then, one fateful day, the phone rang and Tim went to get it. I called out to him from the kitchen, 'If that's my editor, tell her I've gone to the moon.'

Tim picked up. 'Hello? I'll just check. Who's speaking? Oh, I'm very sorry, Marian, but she told me to tell you that she's gone to the—'

I managed to wrestle the receiver out of his grip before irrevocable damage was done. 'Marian! Great to hear from you.'

'You told him to tell me that you've gone where?'

'Upstairs to fetch the manuscript. I had this funny feeling it was you. Believe it or not, I was planning to ring you myself this afternoon.'

'Wow. That is pretty unbelievable. It seems that my timing is perfect, then.' Marian had heard it all before. 'So, Liz, you know why I'm calling. The six months are up. I can't wait to see what you've got for me. Something special, I hope.'

I could feel her anxiety. But it was nothing – I mean *nothing* – compared to my own.

'Well, I'd like to think so. I hope you think so too.'

'Sounds intriguing. Tell me more.'

'Well…it's a memoir. Basically, it's a fictionalised account of my family life.'

About five years earlier, I had started writing my memoirs – a fairly ambitious undertaking for a twenty-six-year-old. I had written about twenty chapters before giving it up as a bad job. I'd always felt it was way too personal to show to anybody. But what choice did I have? I had nothing else to offer Marian.

'Hmm,' she said. 'Interesting. I suppose memoirs are selling pretty well at the moment. How much have you got for me?'

'Well, I thought I'd send you ten chapters at first. I do have a lot more, but I'm revising at the moment.'

'Ten chapters?' she said sharply. 'I was expecting you to have a lot more for me at this stage.'

'Oh, I do – honestly, I do. I just want to perfect what I have before I show it to you.'

'All right, so. Send me the ten chapters and I'll have a look.'

'I'll have it to you by Friday.'

I put down the phone, leaned my back against the wall and slid slowly down until I was resting on my hunkers.

Once Marian read this, I'd be publishing history. My whole career was over before it had really begun. And I had no one to blame but myself.

Marian rang me the following Monday. The ice-cold fingers of fear closed tightly around my throat the moment I heard her voice. I could barely croak, 'Hello,' in response.

'Well, Liz, I read what you sent me.'

'Marian, I…'

'And I absolutely loved it.'

'You what?'

'It's brilliant. Arguably the best thing you've written so far.'

Was the woman taking the piss?

'And I showed it to Henry, and he loved it too. When can we see the next instalment?'

'Um…within the next couple of weeks.' I'd send her one chapter at a time, as a delaying tactic.

'Can't wait. I'll talk to you then. And, Liz…'

'Yes?'

'Well done.'

As I hung up, the icy fingers tightened once more. If that thing ever saw the light of day, nobody in my family would ever speak to me again.

I'd never told Helen about my visit to Phil's mother. I decided she had enough on her plate. Besides, she'd probably have killed me.

Helen had taken to visiting my own mother quite frequently. They would sit at the kitchen table, drinking pots of decaffeinated tea, discussing all things baby and milling into the good biscuits as if there were no such thing as cellulite. I would hover in the background, taking in snippets and feeling like the social outcast who wasn't allowed into the exclusive Mother Club. Because it *was* a club. Helen was in it, and my mother was a lifelong honorary member. What did I know of lochia (yuck!) and piles (yuck, yuck!) or of babies, for that matter – apart from the fact that I used to be one myself?

I had to admit – and it was really was in spite of myself – that my mother was being lovely to Helen. She did have the capacity to be quite a lovely person; it was just a pity she always squandered that loveliness on other people. Helen thought my mother was great, so easy to talk to, she could talk to her like she couldn't talk to her own mother, blah, blah, blah… Blah.

I just kept on taking more and more shifts in the bookshop, and kept on shifting the boss of the bookshop more and more. I knew I couldn't go on like this forever; and I was right.

I was lying in bed with George one afternoon. The nylon sheets on the hotel bed scratched my skin and made me sweat uncomfortably, but it was worth it for the feel of George – to be wrapped up in his strong, dark, hairy arms, to feel his hot breath against my bare skin. I wanted to stay like this forever, locked in his embrace, as if the rest of the world didn't exist.

It seemed so unfair that Judith should have the prior claim just because she had met him before I had. It didn't make her feelings more valid or intense than mine. In fact, I was convinced that she couldn't love him as much as I did. And she must know that he didn't really love her. That was why she'd had to trap him with a sprog… I can see now that I was addicted to the agony and the ecstasy of the situation. But, at the time, my twisted thinking made perfect sense to me.

On that fateful afternoon, our solitude was invaded by the grating harshness of George's mobile. (The ring tone was 'Sweet Child of Mine'.) He reached across my body to pick it up.

'Hello.' His voice was low and husky and, to me, unbearably sexy. I envied the person on the other end of that phone, the recipient of such a wonderful 'Hello'.

There were a few moments of silence while the other person

119

spoke. In that time, I felt George's shoulder tense beneath me. Then he sat up abruptly, as if I weren't there, causing me to roll off him and land clumsily on my side of the bed.

'OK. Calm down, love. I'll be there as soon as I can.'

Love.

I rolled onto my side, my face turned away from him. I heard him getting up and searching around for his clothes.

He came over to my side of the bed. He was still bare-chested, but he had his suit trousers on. 'Judith's gone into labour,' was all he said.

I stared up at him, and he stared back.

'I have to go,' he said.

I nodded.

It took him all of two minutes to vacate the room. But I lay there for – I don't know how long; an hour, maybe. Contemplating the wall. How it was such a putrid yellow colour. How it made me feel ill.

They had a girl. How lucky for her, I thought, that she'd grow up with the benefit of a stable father figure. Hopefully it would save her from making bad romantic decisions later in life.

19

'Would you mind if *I* sat down for a while?' My voice was terse and I knew it. Rachel gave me a sulky look before hopping down off the stool.

Two tills, one stool, two arses: therein lay the dilemma. Rachel was a new part-timer, twenty if she was a day, and yet she felt she had a God-given right to the one and only stool behind the cash desk. It'd be years before she'd have to start worrying about varicose veins – whereas an old broad like me needed her rest. Especially since Helen had asked me to be her – horror of horrors – 'birthing partner'.

Even the name, with its happy-clappy, American-self-help-guru connotations, filled me with dread. I'd refused point-blank at first. But when a heavily pregnant woman gets down on her hands and knees and begs – and needs a crane to get up afterwards...well, it's kind of hard to refuse. Besides, I still felt responsible, as I was the one who'd introduced her to Phil and encouraged her to have a one-night stand (although she was on her own when it came to the whole latex-allergy thing).

To make matters worse, she'd insisted on dragging me along to a few of her antenatal classes. *Anti*-natal, more like. Did they really think it was wise, telling pregnant women all that scary stuff? At the last class, they'd shown us a video of a live birth. A birth! Live! I'd seen less frightening Stephen King movies.

It was now two weeks before Helen's due date. Hard to believe. Equally hard for me to get my head around was the fact that I hadn't had any contact with George in the last four months. The night his wife had given birth to his daughter, our affair had ended. There had been no discussion and no argument – just a tacit agreement. Sure, I was devastated. But I accepted that devastation. I was, after all, getting my just deserts. There had been no doubt in my mind that, once the baby was born, our relationship would die. At first, I had felt George's lack like a gaping wound in my soul. This had closed over in part, but it was still exposed in places – like every time I saw him, and that terrible day when Judith had brought the baby into the shop to be admired. Luckily, I had been out the back, just about to return from a break, when I'd heard the commotion. I'd hidden in the stockroom until it was all over. Eric had made no comment when he found me huddled in the corner, pretending to read. And if anyone else had noticed my prolonged absence, they had kept it to themselves.

Every time Helen so much as coughed these days, I had a panic attack. Helen herself was either taking it all in her stride or putting on a very good show. She sailed serenely around the shop in a selection of billowy blouses, like the proud bow of a ship, handling pregnancy as efficiently as she handled everything else in her life. She'd had her hospital bag packed for so long that the high-energy muesli bars had had to be exchanged, as they'd passed their use-by date. Helen had two hospital bags, in fact, one at home and one in the shop, because she had no intention of quitting work until the baby's head and at least one of its shoulders had emerged. And she had to be physically restrained from lifting heavy boxes. She'd only stopped climbing up the ladders to get books when Tom pointed out that it made the customers uncomfortable.

It was a quiet enough afternoon in the shop. This had been good at first, because Tom and I had been able to have a really in-depth chat – I liked to have a good talk with him every now and then, if only to see how far up himself he'd managed to travel since our last proper talk; quite far, it seemed – but by now we were both quite bored. I was watching him stroll around the shelves with his hands behind his back, humming to himself.

The door of Helen's office opened. 'Liz? Can you come here a second, please?'

'Coming.'

No sooner had my toes touched the floor than Rachel's arse hit the stool again. She was an arse bandit.

Helen was sitting behind her desk. She had her face hidden in her hands so that only her eyes were showing. They were all I needed to see.

'What's wrong?'

'I'm bleeding.'

'What do you mean, you're bleeding?' I could feel all the little hairs on my face standing to attention.

'What do you think I mean? Blood is coming out of me.'

I relaxed momentarily. 'You know what that is, don't you? It's a show.' Thanks to the antenatal classes, I was far more knowledge-able about shows than I'd ever wanted to be.

'No. This is just blood.'

'Right, so.' *Stay nice and calm. Remember you're the birthing partner.* 'Have you had any contractions?'

'Yes. But I'd say they're only Braxton-Hicks.'

'How do you know?'

Helen started to shout. 'I *don't* bloody well know, do I? I've never done this before!'

I don't know which one of us was more terrified.

'Let's ring the hospital,' I said.

'I already have. They told me to come right in.'

'I'll call a taxi, then.'

123

'I already have. It's on its way.'

What did she need me for? This woman was capable of being her own birthing partner. I considered going home to bed. This was all too much for me.

'Can you call Tom in?' Helen said. 'I'll have to leave him in charge.'

Tom was agog. 'Can I come? I missed Clarissa being born, it was all over so quickly. I've always wanted to witness a birth.'

'I'm not a peep show,' Helen snapped.

'Oh, please. I'll stay at the top end.'

I told Tom in no uncertain terms to shut the hell up. I felt it was my duty as birthing partner.

Half an hour later, we were in the Coombe maternity hospital and Helen was attached to a foetal heart monitor. The consultant came in to see her. I hadn't met him before, but the dislike was instant. He looked at the readings on the monitor and made a face, which he made no attempt to hide from Helen. I felt her grip on my arm tighten.

'I'm going to induce you,' he said.

'What?' Helen looked around at me in a panic. 'But I don't want to be induced! I'm having a natural birth.'

The consultant snorted; presumably it was his idea of a laugh. 'I'm afraid that what you're having, my dear, is an induction.'

'Is there something wrong with the baby?'

'No, not yet. But it's best to get it out of there as quickly as possible.'

And off he went, merrily, on his rounds.

Helen was dumbstruck with fear. And who could blame her? 'Not yet'…what the hell did that mean?

I attempted to diffuse the situation with humour. 'Well, he's a right charmer, isn't he? That's not a bedside manner, that's a bedpan manner.'

'Oh, God, Liz. There's something wrong with the baby, I know there is.'

'Don't be daft. He's just being cautious. That's his job.'

'But there must be.'

'Not at all. He knows your dad's a lawyer, doesn't he?'

She nodded.

'Well, he'll just be covering himself in case you try and sue him.'

'But why would I sue him unless something went wrong?'

Oh, dear. Remind me to keep my mouth shut in future. I was saved from having to answer her by a brisk middle-aged woman whose job was to ferry us to the delivery suite. Sounds like quite a nice place, doesn't it? Well, it's not.

The next six hours may well have been the most arduous of Helen's life. As for me, I'd had more pleasant afternoons. First, we had the breaking of the waters. Which is almost an evocative expression, don't you think? Reminiscent of such phenomena as the meeting of the waters and the parting of the waves. Imagine our collective horror when we discovered that it was a most unpleasant procedure involving a utensil similar to a crochet hook. I'll spare you the grisly details of what happened next. Suffice to say, it involved a drip, a needle, a catheter, forceps, a pair of stirrups, another needle and several stitches – in that order. Poor Helen didn't even have the time to so much as nibble on one of her high-energy muesli bars.

I surprised myself by wanting to see the head coming out. Therefore, my first glimpse of Royston Staunton the First was of a wet black tangle, closely followed by a purplish, conical head. *His* first glimpse of this earth was of a blood-spattered hospital floor; then

125

he turned his head, as if to get a better look at whoever was subjecting him to this strange ordeal, and the rest of him slithered out.

'It's a boy!' I said, as soon as I was sure that the thing I was looking at wasn't the umbilical cord – which I declined to cut, by the way.

They took him off to do whatever they do with newborn, squalling infants.

'How do you feel?' I whispered to Helen, my face close to hers, her hand clasped in mine.

'Sick,' was all she said, before vomiting all over my left leg.

I could not understand why Helen insisted on calling him Royston. It didn't even go with her surname. Royston Staunton? Of course, Roy was better – although even that seemed like a funny thing to call a baby. No doubt he'd grow into it.

He regarded his mother with huge, china-blue eyes, and she regarded him. He reminded me of someone, but I couldn't quite figure out who it was. It was right on the tip of my mind.

'You know,' said Helen, 'I love him so much already.' It was a statement of fact, rather than a highly charged expression of emotion; it was the simple truth, and I believed her without a doubt.

Royston Staunton the First latched onto the nipple with all the enthusiasm of countless men before him. I stayed with the new family for about an hour, as befitted a good birthing partner; then the grandparents arrived in an almighty gush of emotion, and I graciously departed, promising to return the next morning bearing gifts. I was reeling. But it was a good feeling.

I overslept the following morning, exhausted by the overwhelming events of the previous day. I spared a thought for poor Helen, who

126

had doubtless been up half the night attempting to feed a tiny scrap of human – and with a sore bum, to boot.

So it was after eleven by the time the bus pulled up outside the hospital. I bought Helen *OK!* and *Hello!* magazines. Each sported a celebrity mum on the cover, along with promises of pages and pages of gush about 'my baby joy' on the inside. Of course, two nannies and a night nurse each probably contributed to their joy. I also bought her a large box of Milk Tray – to make sure she didn't get her figure back too quickly – and a blue helium balloon with 'Congratulations' written all over it in silver.

I felt a surge of excitement as I walked up the corridor towards Helen's ward. I couldn't wait to see my future godson again. I mean, who else could she ask to be his godmother? I'd seen her fanny, for God's sake. I almost giggled out loud in the lift. I had to stick the corner of *Hello!* into my mouth to stop myself.

I could see Helen from the corridor. She was sitting up, smiling and talking to someone – probably the proud granny and granddad again; I wouldn't have been surprised to learn that they'd camped there overnight. She saw me, and her face did something very strange that I couldn't quite fathom. Then I turned the corner and saw that George was sitting by her bed.

I got quite a shock. I hadn't seen him in close proximity for a while. He would just nod at me, from time to time, when he came into the shop. Sometimes I nodded back and sometimes I didn't.

My first thought was that it was very nice of him to take the trouble of visiting his employee in hospital. Then I reached the door and saw that he was cradling Royston in his arms. That was very familiar, wasn't it? Then he saw me, and his face developed the same look that Helen's wore. Something was making me feel nauseated, but I couldn't work out what it was.

Then I realised who the baby reminded me of.

'What's going on?' I had to clear my throat a couple of times before the words would come out properly.

'Liz, I've been wanting to tell you for ages.' Helen was looking at me imploringly, her hand held out.

I didn't move. 'Is this what I think it is?'

'Please don't be angry with us. We're so very happy. And it ended with you two such a long time ago now.'

Us. We're. 'Not as long ago as you think,' I said between gritted teeth. George was looking at me fearfully.

'What?' said Helen. But I appeared to have lost the power of speech.

'You'll get used to the idea in time,' she continued. 'I know this must be a shock – but we really love each other, and we both want you to be a part of this child's life. Don't we, George?' And again the 'we'.

'Yes,' said George, unconvincingly.

Not knowing what else to do, I ran out of the ward, into the nearest toilet, and threw my ring up.

Outside the hospital, I sat in the bus shelter and considered the bombshell that had just exploded all over my world. The bus came and went, but I didn't get on it. I found that I didn't want to go home. My mother would only bombard me with questions: How was Helen? How was the baby? What did he look like? Well, Mother, he looks just like the married man with whom we've both been having an affair for – goodness knew how long, in Helen's case. I still had so many unanswered questions myself.

I got up and slowly began to walk. I turned the collar of my long black coat up around my ears and dug my hands deep into the pockets, grateful for the comfort this afforded me. A few minutes passed before I registered that I was headed in the direction of Granny's. I rang the doorbell and waited for her distorted image to appear behind the frosted glass.

The image drew closer and closer, and my grandmother opened the door. 'Ah, hello, love. What a lovely surprise. How have you been?'

I think the fit of uncontrollable sobbing may have answered her question.

20

I'd never thought I'd be so grateful to be in such an ugly room. A strange peace enfolded me, as did the gigantic floral armchair into which I was sinking. I was holding a large mug of hot, sweet tea in both hands and I was still wearing my coat – I kept meaning to take it off, but I couldn't muster up the energy.

Granny sat down opposite me, her face grave. 'What's wrong, love?'

'I can't tell you. I'm too ashamed,' I said, two great rivers of snot flowing from my nostrils.

'You needn't be ashamed in front of me, love. You can tell me anything.'

'I can't tell you this. You'll hate me.' God knows, I hated myself.

'Now you're being silly. I could never hate you – me own flesh and blood – not in a million years. Not even if you committed mass murder.'

I was silent, apart from the sniffs.

'You haven't, have you?'

'What?'

'Committed mass murder.'

'No! Of course not.'

'Well, there you are, now. Things can't be that bad after all.'

I shook my head, and Granny's face blurred anew as fresh tears gushed onto my cheeks.

'Ah, here. This is getting us nowhere. Dry your eyes and blow your nose like a good girl.' Granny thrust a toilet roll at me. Judging by the length of time it took to disintegrate – several nanoseconds – I guessed that it came from Kit's stall.

By the time I managed to stop crying, I had a mound of sodden white pulp, like wet papier-mâché, on my lap.

'That's better,' she said. 'Now, tell your granny all about it – and remember, I've lived on God's good earth for over eighty years now. There's not much I haven't already heard.'

That did sound reasonable. I took a deep breath. 'I've been having an affair with a married man.'

I waited for her disapproval, but she was merely nodding her head. 'You're not the first and you won't be the last. Your own Auntie Aggie, God rest her soul' – she paused to bless herself – 'never married herself, but she had two childer for a married man, a boy and a girl.'

'No!' Not Auntie Aggie, of all people. 'How did she cope? It must have been very difficult, in those days.'

'Ah, it was. Terrible hard on her.'

'What happened to the kids?'

'They both live in England now. They've done very well for themselves. Gwen married an accountant and John is an executive engineer.'

Executive! Excuse me… But I had stopped thinking about my own predicament for a few brief moments – which, I guessed, was the whole idea. I realised I was breathing more freely, and the words began to tumble out.

'This married man…he was having an affair with my best friend all along – you know, Helen, you've heard me talking about her. Only I didn't know, and she didn't know either, and now she's had a baby and I've only just found out it's his, and – and I don't know what to do…'

'Hush, child, hush. You're going to be grand.' Granny stroked

131

my shoulder rhythmically, somehow preventing my voice from rising another few octaves.

I told her my story in fits and starts, stopping every so often for sob breaks. I told her stuff that I hadn't told anyone – stuff about George and the sordid, humiliating months leading up to the birth of his child with Judith. Two children in the past few months: that was pretty good going – oh most potent, most virile of men... I wondered if he was spreading his seed on purpose.

'I feel so betrayed,' I wailed. 'The two people I loved most in the world...'

'What about your family?' Granny asked.

'What about them?'

She just looked at me.

'Why do I keep getting myself into these messes?' I started to cry again. 'What's wrong with me?' It was a genuine question. I really felt that there was something wrong with me. I wasn't just fishing for comfort – which was just as well, because, instead of replying, Granny left the room. I listened to her slow ascent upstairs, then to the sound of creaking floorboards overhead, followed by her equally slow descent. She came back in and held her hand out to me.

'Here,' she said. 'I was going to leave you this when I died, but maybe you could use it now.'

I hated it when old people talked about dying. I held out my upturned palm, and into it Granny dropped a delicate piece of gold jewellery. It was a locket, shaped like a heart.

'Go on, open it,' she urged.

I unclasped the locket. On the left-hand side was a photo of my father. He was wearing the same moustache he had worn on his wedding day. On the right was a lock of jet-black hair.

'Is this...?'

She nodded. 'I took that from his head the day he was born. And that's the last photo ever taken of him.'

If she was trying to stop me from crying, she wasn't doing a very good job. The tears were flowing down my cheeks in two constant streams. I'd stopped bothering to wipe them away.

'I can't take this from you. You're his mother.'

'And you're his daughter, and you've had little enough of him in your life. At least I had him for twenty years.'

That was true. The man had abandoned me when I was a baby, becoming the first in a long line of men to do so.

In an instant, I was furious. 'I don't want it,' I said, thrusting the locket back at Granny.

'But I want you to have it.'

'I said I don't want it. He didn't want me, and I don't want him.' I glared at the poor woman as if it were all her fault.

'What do you know about your father leaving?' Granny said softly.

'That he left me and my mother so he could pursue his *music career*.' I spat out the last two words.

'It wasn't as simple as that.'

'It seems fairly cut and dried to me.'

Granny ignored my hostility. 'Your daddy – my Robert – wanted a career in music. That much is true. But he wanted you and your mother to go with him to London. Your mammy wouldn't go because she wanted to stay living close to her own mother, and she didn't think London was the right place to bring up a child. Is she still with us, your mother's mother?'

'She died when I was ten.'

Granny blessed herself. 'Your parents argued about it a lot. After a really bad row, your mammy threw Robert out of the house, and he went to London in a rage. He was only there a few months

133

before he died.' I could see that she was starting to get teary-eyed herself. 'He rang me, you know, just a few minutes before he got knocked down, to tell me he was coming home. He said he wanted to give it another go with Róisín – your mammy. He missed the two of you too much to stay in London another week. He was on his way to the travel agent's, to book his ticket home. He'd tried ringing Róisín just before he spoke to me, but she hung up on him.'

I was staring at the pattern on the carpet. Each word dropped like a clanger in my brain. I didn't know what to think. The reality upon which my whole existence was based was shifting beneath me. I experienced a strange, disorientating sensation, like those times when you look at yourself in the mirror and you don't recognise the person staring back at you. I felt as if I'd been given the road map of my life on the day my father left me, and it had turned out to be the wrong map.

'Does my mother know any of this?' I said eventually.

'Not the part about him coming back, no. I wrote her a long letter after he died – I felt it was my duty, even though she didn't come to the funeral – but she sent it back unopened. I rang her a few times, but she wouldn't speak to me.'

'Why not? It wasn't your fault.'

'She felt betrayed, love.'

Betrayed. I knew how that felt. I stared hard at my grandmother. There was one question to which I ached to know the answer, and I wondered if I had the guts to ask. The winter sun shone weakly through the net curtains and onto her face, illuminating her great age. *If not now, when?*

'Why didn't you ever try and contact me?'

'I sent a card with money on each of your first five birthdays, but your mother sent them all back. So I stopped. I always hoped you'd look me up one day, when you were ready. And here you are.' She leant over, squeezed my arm and smiled at me. I saw that her face was nearly as wet as mine. 'Can you imagine how I felt – losing my son and then losing my granddaughter?'

I couldn't. But it was probably a damn sight worse than I was feeling.

'You sit there, Granny, and I'll get you a hot drop.'

We were still ensconced there one hour and one fresh pot of tea later. We'd been flicking through the old photo albums again. I must have worn Granny out, asking questions about the family tree, but she didn't seem to mind.

There was one picture of my mother, on the day she got engaged. She was leaning against the front wall of Granny's house, squinting into the sunlight, looking self-conscious in an impossibly mini mini-skirt. If I'd ever worn anything that indecent, she'd have had me excommunicated.

'What did you think of her?' I said.

'Who – your mammy?'

'Yes.'

Granny laughed her gravelly laugh. 'Well, love. To tell the truth, I thought she was a bit of a consequence.'

'A what?'

She laughed again. 'She thought a lot of herself. Although I did think she'd be a good influence on your father. She was a good, solid, sensible girl. Robert...' She shook her head. 'Well, he always had his head in the clouds. And he was flighty. My own mother used to say there was a bit of a gypsy in that lad.'

Interesting. And I liked that word, 'consequence'. I knew a few of those myself. 'So you didn't disapprove of her, then.'

'Not at all. Sure, what good would that have done, anyways?

135

Anyone with eyes in their head could see he had a right smack for her.'

'A what?'

'A smack. He fancied her something rotten.'

'Oh.'

Granny had her own lingo. She was like a rapper. M.C. Granny.

'I hope you don't mind me asking you all these questions.'

'No. I'm glad to answer them, love. You need to know your history. You've been rootless for far too long. That's why you've been buffeted around all your life: you didn't have any roots. It's high time you learnt that you're not a blade of grass, you're a mighty oak tree.' She raised her arms above her head, no doubt attempting to emulate a mighty oak but failing miserably.

'You need to stand tall now,' she continued, 'and remember you're a Clancy. Your father didn't die on the streets of London, trying to make a better life for his family, just for you to give up. And your ancestor didn't crawl onto that beach in Sligo, half drownded, and go on the run in fear of his life, just for you to throw in your hand when the going gets tough. It's up to you to live a life that'll make them look down and be proud of you. A life that makes their struggles worthwhile.'

I'd like to tell you that these words instantly changed my life. In fact, they did change my life – eventually; but first they had to sink in. And that took a while.

When it was nearly teatime, I reluctantly closed the album that was resting across my knees and uncurled my legs out from under me. 'I suppose I'd better go home.'

'You can stay if you like.'

'For my tea?'

136

'For your tea, and for the night if you like. I'll get Kit to make up the bed in the spare room.'

'I'd love that,' I said, realising that I really would. 'I'll just call home and let them know.'

The phone rang twice before my mother picked up. *Shit!* I'd been hoping that one of the others would answer.

'Hi, it's me.'

'Where have you been? I've been dying to hear about Helen and the baby. Are you still in the hospital?'

I drew a deep breath. I'd had enough lies. 'I'm in my grandmother's house. I'm going to stay the night.'

When my mother finally answered, the ice in her voice chilled me. 'Right, so,' she said.

Then she hung up.

I don't know whether it was the tears, the tea or the nostalgia, but I woke up the next morning feeling remarkably refreshed – cleansed, even. Kit brought me my breakfast in bed, which made me feel better still. It was mid-morning when I said my goodbyes and squeezed my way out the front door, past the boxes of toilet rolls and tights for Kit's stall.

I turned on my mobile: six missed calls, all from Helen. I deleted them all. Then, in a fit of anger, I deleted Helen's name and number from my address book.

I'd been so absorbed with thoughts of my father that I'd almost managed to forget about Helen. But now I was confronted with the hurt afresh – not to mention the practical difficulties. How could I go on working in Grainger's? Even while Helen was on maternity leave, I'd still have to deal with himself coming in and out. Speaking of whom, were they a couple now? Was he going to leave his wife for her – her and Royston? Fucking stupid name, although it did sound better with Grainger. Royston Grainger. Roy Grainger. Would he have his father's surname? And how long, exactly, had Helen and George been seeing each other? Did he impregnate her before or after she'd slept with Phil? Had she slept with Phil at all? All that crap about an allergy to latex... My head began to spin. I had known that something had got into Helen. What I hadn't known was that that something was George.

When I thought of her pious clap-trap about how I should leave George alone, how I should consider his wife and children...my God! By the time the bus came, I'd worked myself up into a complete rage. The bus driver looked at me fearfully as I stomped on board. *How dare she? How dare he?* But I decided I couldn't help my anger. It wasn't that I was a bad-tempered cow. It was my Latin temperament coming through.

21

I did go back to Grainger's – the very next day, to be precise. I held my head up, made like a mighty oak and remembered I was a Clancy. The shop looked empty at first, devoid not just of customers but of staff.

'Hello?' I called out. No reply.

They were all down the back, having a confab: Tom, Rachel, another young girl by the name of Annalise... Even Eric, who never indulged in idle gossip, was leaning against the back wall, headphones about his neck, arms folded across his chest. He was the first to see me. He nodded without smiling. Then the rest of them turned around to have a good look. Tom's eyes fairly popped with surprise.

'I didn't think you'd be coming in today,' he said.

'Why not? My name's on the roster, isn't it?'

'Well – yes, it is.'

'I didn't like to leave you in the lurch, what with Helen out of commission and everything.'

'Thank you,' Tom said, still looking amazed.

From the way the two girls were looking at me, I could tell that they had recently discovered not only that George had fathered Helen's child, but that it was only by the grace of God and Durex that he hadn't fathered mine. *Thanks, Tom. You and your notorious big mouth*. Doubtless they'd been discussing the juicy details when I interrupted them.

I straightened my shoulders and thought hard about mighty

oaks. I was horribly aware of the weight of Eric's stare. When I met his gaze, he looked away quickly and returned to the stockroom. The Viking couldn't even look at me. This made me feel worst of all.

I made it through the morning thanks to a combination of willpower, Polo mints and *Memoirs of a Geisha*. Tom offered to treat me to lunch – out of guilt, I think – and I was planning to order something really expensive.

Eric was in the stockroom when I went to collect my coat. He looked up but said nothing, just kept emptying his boxful of books.

'I suppose you think I'm an idiot.' I knew I should just shut up, but I couldn't help myself.

Eric stopped what he was doing and stood up, hands on hips. 'No. I don't think you're an idiot. But I do think he's a shit.'

Oh.

'You're right. He is a shit.'

'A big, steaming pile of dog turd.'

I giggled. 'I couldn't have put it better myself.' I felt instantly better. 'Thanks, Eric.'

'Any time, Liz.'

Tom – bless him – did his damnedest to keep my spirits up in the couple of months following Royston's birth. He kept ringing me up and dragging me out for drinks and dinners. I must have cost him a small fortune. On this particular occasion, he was trying to convince me to accompany him to some concert or other.

'These guys are fantastic. They've got rave reviews wherever they go.'

'I don't care, Tom. I don't feel up to it.'

'There'll be alcohol.'

'Lots of it?'

'The place will be swimming.'

'I don't know. Maybe.'

'They're Spanish.'

'What time does it start?'

The opportunity to explore my Spanish roots had me quite excited. I fidgeted as I watched the other audience members take their seats. Tonight, I would hear guitar played flamenco-style.

My own attempts at guitar-playing had come to a sad end. I hadn't even mastered the first chord – C – when an unsightly callus had appeared on my left index finger. When I complained to my sadistic teacher, he seemed delighted: he informed me not only that I could expect to develop calluses on the remaining fingers of my left hand, but that they would most likely bleed in due course. It was only then that I would know I was making progress. Thinking that his idea of progress and mine were probably two very different things, I gave the lessons up as a bad job. I might have inherited my father's looks, but the musical gene had obviously skipped a generation.

Tom seemed preoccupied.

'Is everything all right?' I said.

'Fine. Why do you ask?'

'You seem a little quiet, that's all.'

'Is that not allowed?'

'Of course it's allowed. It's just so out of character.'

'Well. There is something.' He gave me a doubtful, sidelong glance. 'But I don't know if I should tell you or not.'

'I hate that. Now you have to tell me.'

'It's about Helen and George.'

Oh, dear.

'Go on,' I said.

'You won't like it.'

'Just tell me.'

'He's left his wife and they've moved in together.'

A blow to the stomach would have had a similar effect. Luckily for both of us, the band chose that moment to take to the stage. I clapped my hands together like an automaton. I felt like getting up and going home, but I was damned if I was going to let George and Helen wreck yet another night for me.

I didn't really take in the first couple of songs. The music was good – that I registered: a more hard-core version of the Gypsy Kings. But my vision was blurred by salt water. I managed to contain it, except for one big, fat tear that travelled down my cheek and my neck before disappearing down the front of my top. I blinked back the rest and focused on what was in front of me.

We were in the front row. I could practically see up the nostrils of the five-piece band, and every time the lead singer gave it socks, little showers of spittle were rendered visible by the stage lights. Maybe there was such a thing as too close to the stage. We were right beneath the man who appeared to be the principal guitarist – although he was a dab hand at the accordion too.

From the top down: his long, black, wavy hair was drawn back into a ponytail. He was good-looking in a rough sort of way – a kind of pockmarked Antonio Banderas. He wore a black denim shirt, lots of chunky silver rings and a silver sleeper in one of his ears. He also had several plasters on his fingers. *Bleeding calluses,* I thought knowingly. He was wearing blue denim jeans and black pointy boots. But the things that struck me most were his hands: brown, strong and heavily veined, with long, elegant fingers.

He was sitting it out for this song, just tapping his foot. As if aware that he was under scrutiny, he looked straight at me and smiled. Then he ran the tip of one of his long fingers down the side of his face, from his eye to his chin, as if tracing the track of a tear. Then he shrugged and smiled again. *Why are you crying, little girl?* He got a watery smile back.

In the next song, he and his guitar played a pivotal role. I was entranced. I know it was silly, but I felt as if my father was reaching out and comforting me through the music. I reached up and stroked the locket at my throat. The news about George and Helen didn't seem so bad – not now. Tomorrow it would probably hurt like hell again; but for now, while the music washed over me, soothing me like a balm, all was well.

At the interval, there was plenty of alcohol, as promised by Tom. I did my best to deplete the reserves of a small vineyard in Southern Spain.

'Glad you came?' asked Tom.

'Very glad. Thanks for forcing me.'

'I was trying to think of a good place to break the news. I didn't want you to hear it from anyone else.'

'How long have you known?'

'A couple of days. Helen rang me.'

I nodded.

'Don't you want to know how she is?'

'No, I do not. She can rot in hell for all I care.'

'Now, you don't mean that.'

'Oh, don't I? Do you know how many lectures I had to put up with from that sanctimonious cow?'

'I'm guessing a lot.'

'Shitloads. She kept going on about how wrong it was of me to have an affair with a married man – and all the time she just wanted him for herself. I can't believe he left his wife for that bitch. He wouldn't leave his wife for me. Why wouldn't he leave her for me, Tom?'

Tom laid his hands on my shoulders and said gently, 'I don't know. The man is clearly mad. Now, you need to calm yourself down. Remember you're in a public place.'

I nodded and sighed. I was beginning to feel utterly miserable again. I needed more music – nice, soothing, calming music.

'Where are they living?' I asked.

'Ranelagh.'

'Well, fuck him! He knew that's where I wanted us to live.'

'Liz, Liz – nice and calm, remember? Forget about him. Plenty more sharks in the sea.'

'I think I've already met all the sharks. And I think they must have eaten all the decent fish. That's why there aren't any left.'

'That's just not true,' said Tom. 'You know what? I'm going to make it my mission to find you a lovely new man.'

'You're not going to try and set me up, are you?'

'Well, I might have a couple of friends in mind.'

'I've met your friends, and they're all idiots – apart from me, that is.'

'All right, then, we'll find you somebody new. Is there anyone you like?'

'The guitarist in the band isn't half bad.'

'The guy with the ponytail?' Tom sounded incredulous.

'Yes. What's wrong with him?'

'Hello? Ponytail.'

'Hello? Cravat.'

'We're not talking about me. We're talking about Mr Ponytail.'

'So what? He's allowed to have one. He's in a band. It's not like it's an eighties power-ponytail.'

'But he's old.'

144

'How old would you say he is?'

'Too old for you.'

'Mid-forties?' I said hopefully.

'At least. God, there's no hope for you. Lock up your fathers, she's single again.'

The second half of the concert made the first sound like a warm-up – although, mind you, that could have been the wine. There was a space at the back of the hall, and before long audience members began to gather there and dance.

'May I have the pleasure?' Tom held out his hand. I didn't take much convincing. Trying to recall my flamenco lessons, and no doubt making a complete mockery of them, I set up my imaginary gypsy campfire and danced around it once again. Not until the concert drew to a close did we return to our seats, breathless.

Two encores later, the crowd were still clapping and shouting for more. But the band had had enough. We were gathering up our coats, and I was starting to wonder how I was going to make it through the rest of the night, when I felt a tap on my shoulder.

It was the guitarist. He was standing behind me and grinning.

'Would you like to join the band for a drink?'

No, I don't know what I was thinking either. It was complete madness, going off with a total stranger and contemplating a one-night stand – something I'd sworn off years before. And make no mistake: that was exactly what I was contemplating. But there was a kind of wildness to my logic. I had been feeling so bad about myself since the George-and-Helen revelations, and the guitarist – Carlos – was heaping compliments upon me as if they were going out of style. And, to cap it all, he was Spanish – and he played Spanish guitar, just like Dad. That made me feel safe, somehow.

Carlos and I took a cab back to his hotel and ordered yet more drinks in the bar. It wasn't long before he suggested bringing them upstairs.

What are you doing? said the little voice inside my head, as he clasped my hand in the lift. *Shut up,* I told it. *I'm enjoying myself. I'm young(ish), free and single, we're two consenting adults and we're not hurting anyone.* To the best of my knowledge, Carlos was single too; his ring finger was bare, in any case. *So what's the problem?*

As soon as we entered the hotel room (standard: a bed, a TV and tea- and coffee-making facilities), I felt hideously awkward. I stood just inside the door and watched Carlos as he sat down on the bed and began taking off his watch. I didn't know where to put myself. Suddenly, my clothes felt as if they didn't fit right and I couldn't work out how to arrange my features. I made a brave attempt at a smile, but it felt fake, more like a grimace. I resorted to playing with the straps of my handbag.

Carlos patted the patch of bedspread beside him. 'Come. Sit.'

Then I did what I always did at those critical moments in my life. I ignored what my gut – my eloquent gut – was telling me. I sat down beside Carlos on the bed.

I watched in fascination as he loosened his ponytail and shook back his head like a proud stallion. Hair cascaded down past his shoulders; it was longer and blacker than mine, though shot through with silver. He was quite exotic, all the same, what with all the hair and the silver jewellery (what *was* it with me and men who wore jewellery?). Next he unbuttoned his shirt, his eyes fixed on mine. There was one nervous person in that hotel room, and it wasn't him. He took off his shirt and grinned at me. He stroked the tender skin on my throat with those long, elegant fingers of his and pulled me in for a kiss. It felt OK.

146

Knowing that I could put it off no longer, and feeling like it was the last thing in the world that I wanted to do, I unbuttoned my blouse and let it fall off my shoulders. This wasn't as quick and easy as it sounds: I fumbled around with the buttons for what seemed like an age, and in the end Carlos had to help me. I felt like a moron, sitting there in my slightly off-white Dunne's Stores bra. But this was OK, I thought foolishly. He wouldn't know this, as they didn't have Dunne's Stores in Spain.

Finally disrobed, we lay beneath the sheets and fiddled with each other's bits. Some of it even felt vaguely nice. But I might as well have been floating somewhere around the ceiling and looking down at myself, for all the involvement I felt. I went through the motions, acting excited at the right moments and making all the appropriate noises. Sometimes a self-absorbed man can be quite handy.

When it was all over, Carlos lit a cigarette and handed it to me, before lighting one for himself. I smoked it, even though I didn't really want to. It made my mouth feel as disgusting as the rest of me. I was just contemplating how to make my departure as graciously as possible when Carlos sat up in bed, pulled the phone towards him and dialled. He started talking in rapid-fire Spanish. I could only make out the odd word. Ordering room service, perhaps? Most hotel receptionists spoke several languages. I decided that this would probably be a good time to get up and get dressed. I started to get out of bed, but he pulled me back in against him. Fair enough. If he wanted to snuggle, I could snuggle. I was an accomplished snuggler. Half the time, that was all I really wanted from a man in bed.

I'd only been nestling against his hairy chest for a few minutes when there was a knock on the door. He must have been ordering food after all. I watched his naked arse, which was considerably whiter than the rest of him, as he padded to the door.

Then two of the other band members – the lead singer and the drummer, to be exact – walked into the room. They all started talking loudly in Spanish, and one of them slammed a six-pack down on the bedside table. I let out a strangled cry that didn't sound like me and pulled the sheet up so that only my eyes were visible. Prior to that, at least one nipple had been exposed. What had Carlos been thinking, letting them in without warning me first?

Then it became all too clear what he was thinking – what they were all thinking. My eyes widened with fear as the drummer sat down on the bed beside me and ran his finger along my bare arm, the only part of my skin that was still exposed.

I leapt up as if scalded. I yanked the sheet out from under the drummer's backside and wrapped it around my body like a toga. 'Get your fucking hands off me!' I heard myself screaming. I felt like a cornered animal, and it appeared that I was behaving like one too.

The drummer raised his hands in the air and started shouting at me in Spanish. I could smell the booze from the other side of the bed. With my free hand, I scooped up as many items of my discarded clothing as I could find and backed towards the door, holding the heel of one of my shoes out in front of me in a threatening manner. 'Get away from me!' I kept screeching, over and over.

Miraculously, I had the presence of mind to grab my bag, which I'd left on a table just inside the door. Unfortunately, I couldn't manage this without letting go of my protective sheet. But at least I was out. I sprinted down the corridor, naked as the day I was born. In my haste to find an exit, I tripped over a tray that had been left outside a bedroom door and bashed my head against the wall; not even stopping to register the pain, I scrambled to my feet and started running again. But I couldn't find a way out.

On the verge of complete meltdown, I spied a door that was

partially ajar and stumbled into a kind of storage area for cleaning equipment. Narrowly avoiding tripping over a Hoover, I began to dress myself, my hands shaking as if I had a bad case of the DTs. My breath came in short, rapid bursts and I found that I couldn't stop whimpering. I felt tempted to stay in there all night, crouched in a corner, until the hotel came to life again and it was light and safe to leave. But the urge to put as much distance between Carlos, his colleagues and myself was even stronger.

I'd left my knickers in the hotel room. I was hardly going back to get them.

I inched the door open, my eyes darting from side to side. The coast was clear. Having managed to calm myself down slightly, I spotted an exit sign and followed it, all the while checking over my shoulder for rogue musicians. I took the stairs three at a time. I was too afraid to take the lift; what if I got trapped in there with one of them?

Once I reached the reception area, I allowed myself to breathe more normally. There was just one man at the desk.

'Can you call me a cab, please?'

He barely nodded. He looked me up and down, and I could read his mind: *Common tart.*

I can't describe my feeling of relief as the taxi pulled up outside my front door. I let myself in, fingers still trembling. I discarded my clothing once again, climbed into the sofa-bed, curled up into a ball and willed death to come.

It wasn't until the next morning that I realised I'd lost my locket.

149

22

I didn't go into work the next day. I just stayed curled up in my ball. For the exorbitant sum of ten euro, Tim rang in sick for me. He was saving for some model fortress or other. So I was encouraging my impressionable little brother to lie *and* to accept bribes. What a positive influence I was.

Well after eleven, I was finally forced up by my bladder. I emerged from under the covers and stumbled blearily into the bathroom. I couldn't work out why my head hurt like it did. Then I remembered tripping over the tray whilst running naked through the hotel corridor. I winced at the memory. Then I winced afresh as I pressed the mound of raised, purplish flesh on the side of my forehead. I examined it minutely in the mirror.

I avoided looking into my own eyes at first; I was frightened of what I might find. When I finally worked up the courage, I was shocked by the pain I saw. They were large, dark, wild, fearful eyes – too large, too dark; eyes that took in too much, absorbed too much. Like a greedy man eating more than his stomach can cope with, my eyes had seen more than they could handle.

I felt marginally better after I'd showered, but only marginally. That was when I noticed my locket was gone. I searched my bag and the bedroom-*cum*-sitting-room; but, with a growing sense of dread, I acknowledged that I must have lost it in the hotel. I'd vowed never to set foot in that place again. But I had to – just had to – find that locket.

So I rang the hotel. Thankfully, the man who'd been on the

reception desk the night before must have gone off duty. He had been replaced by a much less judgmental-sounding girl. I gave her the room number – which was indelibly imprinted on my mind – and my own details, before describing the locket in heartbreaking detail. As I replaced the receiver, I uttered a silent prayer. *Please, God, I've already lost my father once. Don't let me lose him again.*

I'd thought I was alone in the house – Tim had long since gone to school – but, alas, I was wrong. My mother was working nights that week. I virtually spilled my coffee all over myself when she walked into the kitchen.

'I thought you were in work today,' she said.

'I rang in sick.'

'Why? What's wrong with you?'

'I don't know, Mam. I just feel crap.'

She took my chin in her hand and tilted my face up so that she could look into it properly, as if I were eight years old. I swiped ineffectually at her hand, but she didn't let go.

'Hmm,' she said, in her nurse's voice. 'You're looking a bit washed out, all right.' I hoped against hope that the lump on my head was covered by my hair. 'Do you have any pain?'

'My head hurts.'

'Right, so. I'll give you a couple of Ponstan and it's back to bed with you, my dear.'

I didn't argue. It felt quite pleasant to be treated like a sick child and to have my mammy looking after me. In fact, she seemed particularly well disposed towards me today...

'Mam?'

'Yes, love?'

'You know when I stayed over with my grandmother that time?'

She stopped what she was doing for a couple of seconds, but she didn't look at me. Then she went back to unloading the dishwasher. 'What about it?'

'Well. She told me some very interesting things.'

No response.

'Stuff about Dad that I think you should know.'

This time Mam looked at me. I wished she hadn't. 'If it's about your father,' she said, 'I don't want to know.'

'But—'

'I don't see the use in opening up old wounds.'

'But, Mam—'

'That's enough, Libby. I don't want to hear another word about it.'

There was nothing else for it. I went back to bed. As per nurse's orders. I meant to get up again that evening, but when it came to it, I just couldn't muster up the energy.

The next day was, mercifully, my day off. I wouldn't have gone in anyway. There was no way I was going to face Tom's incessant questioning. I kept my mobile switched resolutely off.

When I arrived at Granny's place that afternoon, unannounced, she was having a conniption. She didn't seem remotely surprised to see me; she just brandished a postcard in my face. 'Would you ever look at what I'm after getting in the post!'

'A postcard? That's nice.'

'Nice! Here – you read it.'

The postcard – which was from Helsinki – read as follows:

> *Dear Mrs Clancy,*
>
> *I've been kidnapped and only you can rescue me. If you want to see me again, please send one hundred euro to the Gnome Liberation Front.*
>
> *Gnobby the Gnome*

I began to laugh.

'It's not funny, Elizabeth. I paid good money for that gnome, and these hooligans robbed him on me. And now they want a ransom!'

'It's just a joke, Granny. Do you not think it's just a little bit funny?'

'I do not.' She drew her lips tight and pulled herself up to her full height. 'He was my favourite gnome, too. I'll be getting on to the Guards about this, so I will.'

I could imagine the hilarity down at the cop shop.

'In my day, you wouldn't get young fellas behaving like this. We had respect for our elders, so we did. This town has gone to the dogs. Only last week, Mrs Jacobs from number 10 got mugged on Francis Street. And then you have those laptop-dancing clubs springing up all over the place—'

'It's lap-dancing, Granny. Not laptop-dancing.'

'Well, whatever you call it, I think it's a disgrace. Now, are you coming in for a cup of tea, or are you going to stand out here on the side of the street all evening?'

'A cup of tea would be lovely.'

Now that I'd become a regular visitor, I no longer qualified for a china cup and saucer. I was given a mug – unchipped, if I was lucky. Somehow, it made me feel more special. And I had to wait for the wrestling to finish before I got Granny's undivided attention. It wasn't the American World Wrestling Federation type that she watched; it was the good old-fashioned English kind, where the sporting descendants of Big Daddy, Giant Haystacks and their ilk butted one another with their gigantic bellies. By the time it was over, Granny had managed to calm herself down.

'You don't look yourself, love,' she said.

I shrugged. When did I ever look myself? I sometimes felt as if I was a much messier, more dishevelled version of the person I was meant to be, and that someday the real me would emerge out of all the crap, like a butterfly emerging from its chrysalis. But ninety-nine per cent of the time I didn't feel remotely like a butterfly. I didn't even feel like a caterpillar. I was the chrysalis itself: an ugly, dried-up shell. Something to be discarded.

'I suppose it's that thing with your friend and your boss that's bothering you again.'

I nodded. Actually, I was currently miserable about a different disaster in my life, but I wouldn't have dreamed of telling Granny about the other night. I desperately wanted to tell someone, but it had to be the right person – somebody like Helen. I felt a terrible pang as it hit me afresh how much I missed Helen. But how could I forgive her, after what she'd done to me?

'I'm only after remembering,' said Granny, breaking into my thoughts. 'I have something for you.'

She went over to the bureau, unlocked it and took out a book. 'There you go.' She handed it to me.

'*The Journey of Francisco de Cuellar*,' I read. 'What's this?'

'He was with your ancestor, the one that got shipwrecked. Now you can read all about their journey.'

'Thanks, Granny.' *I think.*

23

I did not know what to do, nor what means to adopt, as I did not know how to swim, and the waves and storm were very great; and on the other hand, the land and shore were full of enemies, who went jumping and dancing with delight at our misfortunes; and when one of our people reached the beach, two hundred savages and other enemies fell upon him and stripped him of what he had on until he was left in his naked skin. Such they maltreated and wounded without pity, all of which was plainly visible from the battered ships, and it did not seem to me that there was anything good happening on any side.

– from the City of Antwerp, 4 October 1589, signed Francisco de Cuellar

Talk about being caught between a rock and a hard place. My ancestor must have faced a similar dilemma. I tried hard to imagine what it must have been like for him. And I amazed myself by reading the book from cover to cover. It even spurred me into visiting the Berkeley Library in Trinity, a few weeks later, to do some background research.

I stopped off briefly in the college shop to buy a chocolate bar. The shop hadn't changed much since the days when I used to buy a chocolate bar nearly every day for my lunch. I usually couldn't afford much else, having already spent my weekly allowance on beer served in plastic pint glasses. To stop myself from feeling deprived, I would pick a different bar every day: a Snickers on Monday (or were they still Marathon bars back then?), a dark chocolate Bounty on Tuesday, a Dairy Milk on Wednesday; Thursdays were generally Turkish Delight day, and on Friday, what else but a Crunchie? I could have brought in my own packed lunch, but that just wouldn't have been cool.

I came out of the shop and considered the cobblestones. In my Doc Marten days, I hadn't given them a second thought, but today I was wearing stupid girly shoes. I was wobbling along, feeling like something out of *Educating Rita*, when I experienced one of those illuminating moments that stay with you forever.

Two young girls – students – were ahead of me. They were both slender and slight, wearing faded denims and light, casual tops. They both had long, hippyish hair. They were the type of girl I had longed to be when I was a student. One of them was standing up; the other was sitting on a low chain railing, rocking back and forth, sunlight trickling through her honey-gold hair. Without warning, she began to sing 'I Want to Be Seduced' in the style of Mary Coughlan. She called to mind young girls with long hair, being seduced by long-haired men on long, hot summer nights. And this from me, who had sworn off men for life only days previously.

With a start, I realised it was spring again. A year ago, almost to the day, I had walked past Trinity College one evening at the end of March, full of excitement: I had been on my way to meet George, thinking that he would leave his wife for me and we would set up home together... It all seemed so ludicrous now. But the crucial thing was that I had survived the long, dark winter.

I inhaled. Yes, there it was: fresh-cut grass. The same inspired person as last year had cut the lawn at the front of the college – possibly for the first time that spring. It seemed obvious to me that those girls, too, had inhaled the scent of freshly mown grass and had been infected by spring madness. They, too, could feel the sap rising in their loins. I reflected that it's no coincidence that so many babies are born around Christmas.

I think that moment will stay with me for the rest of my life. Even when I'm a little, grey old woman, I'll evoke that image as an embodiment of everything it means to be full of youth, beauty, promise and endless possibility.

And on that spring day, for the first time in what seemed like an aeon, possibilities were awoken in my soul – not least the possibility of new love. George hadn't ruined me for other men after all.

I was ready.

Breaking out of my spell, I advanced towards the library as quickly as the cobbles would allow. Once inside, I experienced that all-too-familiar heavy feeling that I used to get when I tried to study. It was like being transported back a decade.

The Berkeley had that stuffy atmosphere peculiar to most libraries, as if it were weighted down by years of academia, ancient dust and too many people thinking too hard. This library needed to lighten up. Undeterred, I found the History section. It was in the same place I'd left it. I even recognised some of the older librarians, their faces now looking even more like dusty old books. After much searching, I found the section I was looking for. I gathered up several books on Ireland and the Spanish Armada, and I was about to go and sit down with them when I became aware of a presence behind me. I turned around.

'Hello,' said Eric the Viking.

'Hello. What are you doing here?'

'Studying. What are you doing here?'

'Um…research. For my latest novel.'

'What's it about?'

I paused. 'If you don't mind, I don't like discussing a book while I'm still writing it.'

'Fine by me.'

'What are you studying – if you don't mind me asking?' I vaguely remembered Helen telling me once that Eric was a part-time student, which was one of the reasons I had assumed that he was younger than he actually was.

'I'm working on my PhD. It's on the Spanish Armada in Ireland.'

Well what do you know?

'Can I buy you a coffee?' I asked.

'All right, then.'

I must admit that my motives for inviting Eric for coffee weren't entirely pure. I knew a brain ripe for picking when I saw one. Who would have guessed there was such a lot going on underneath all that white-blond hair?

With Eric, there was no need for idle chit-chat. I went straight in for the kill. I asked him if he'd heard of Streedagh Strand, the beach where my great-great-et-cetera-grandfather had been washed up (although I didn't tell him that part – not yet). He had; not only that, but he'd even visited it as part of his research. I couldn't believe my good fortune. Now I wouldn't have to bother reading any of those dry-shite books. They were way too thick, anyway, suitable only for use as paperweights or doorstops, or for hitting nasty people.

I wasn't, however, to get my information entirely gratis.

'Are you really writing a novel about this stuff?' Eric asked.

I evaluated his enquiring look. He'd been incredibly generous with his information, and his time; I was sure he had better things to do than hang around drinking coffee with the likes of me. 'No, not really. I'm just researching my family history. I found out I'm descended from a survivor of one of the Armada shipwrecks.'

'I often wondered that about you.'

Really? As far as I'd been aware, Eric never wasted a second wondering anything about me – except, perhaps, why that idiot woman kept dumping her coat on the boxes of books he was trying to unload.

'You're so dark for an Irish person. And that day I met you in town with your little brother – he was red-headed. I assumed you must be a throwback.'

I'd been described in prettier terms. 'Not necessarily. We have different fathers.'

'Oh, right. Are your parents separated?'

'No. My dad died when I was small.'

'Right. Is that why you go for old codgers like Grainger?'

'No, it is not!' *For fuck's sake.* That was a little close to the bone. What was wrong with small talk?

'I've insulted you, haven't I?' Eric peered at me intently, his light-blue eyes narrowed.

'No.'

'I have. I'm sorry. I know I'm too direct sometimes, but I'm working on it.'

He did seem genuinely concerned that he'd upset me.

'Forget it, Eric. I already have.'

This seemed to satisfy him. 'Sorry about your dad.'

'Thanks.'

We were silent for several seconds, sipping our coffees. Then he said, 'Can I ask you one more thing?'

'Go on, then.'

'Where did you get that coat?'

'Oxfam.'

'Yeah? I love it. I've been looking all over for a coat like that.'

My coat's very first compliment!

159

'Are you hungry?' Eric asked.

'A bit,' I said, expecting him to suggest a muffin or two.

'Do you want to get some dinner?'

'Oh. All right.' I still had loads of questions I wanted to ask him.

One hour later, we were sharing a gigantic pizza in Little Caesar's and I'd succeeded in getting a ton more information out of Eric. If only I'd thought of wearing a concealed recording device under my clothes when I'd got dressed that morning… I'd never known him to talk so much. It seemed that, when you got Eric away from the shop and onto a pet topic, he had plenty to say for himself. It wasn't that I was subjected to any boring monologues; he answered my questions succinctly, telling me exactly what I wanted to know, no more, no less. Unlike a lot of men I could mention, he didn't try to impress me with the depth and breadth of his knowledge. It struck me that Eric never tried to impress, full stop. This in itself was impressive.

'You know, you should teach this stuff,' I told him.

'I do teach this stuff. I give tutorials to undergrads twice a week.'

So Eric was part-time student, part-time teacher, part-time book-stocker and part-time rocker – a man of many parts. He must have had more than twenty-four hours in each of his days.

He caught me smiling to myself. 'What?'

'I was just thinking…it's not very rock-star, is it – a PhD in history?'

He grinned – a rare gem – and leaned back in his chair. 'You don't think the Viking fans would appreciate it?'

'Let's just say I wouldn't put it on the posters if I were you.'

He laughed. 'I think you're underestimating our fans.'

'I don't think so. I've had experience of them, remember?'

'How could I forget? How come you never came to any more of our gigs?'

160

'I was too embarrassed about getting kicked out of the first one.'

I was starting to think that the Eric I'd thought I knew – well, semi-knew – bore little resemblance to the man himself. 'Do you mind if I ask you something?' I said.

'No.'

'How did you come up with the name of your band?'

'It was Tom who gave me the idea.'

'What, my Tom? Bookshop Tom?'

'Yes. He's always called me "the Viking" behind my back, so I thought, "That's not a bad idea."'

I felt myself blush. 'You knew about that?'

'I'm not deaf.' Eric wasn't smiling, but I could tell by his eyes that he was amused – by my discomfort, probably. I could also tell that he knew I called him 'the Viking' behind his back, too.

'I'm sorry for calling you that,' I said softly, staring at my mozzarella.

'That's all right.'

Suddenly I had a thought. 'Can I tell Tom?'

'Be my guest.'

'I can't wait to see the look on his face.'

I couldn't believe I'd never taken this man seriously – hadn't even thought of him as a man, really. It turned out that the Viking – Eric – was a force to be reckoned with.

'Do you want dessert?' he asked.

'No, I'm stuffed.'

'Let's go for a drink, then.'

I watched Eric up at the bar, and it was like I was seeing him for the very first time. Of course, I'd seen him many times before, and I knew how tall and how broad he was; but the latent power he seemed to possess was a revelation. He reminded me of a big cat in repose – a snow leopard, maybe, but a snow leopard that had had his dinner and was nice and lazy and relaxed. And as for those cheekbones...you could have sliced bread on them, you really could.

He handed me a drink and squeezed in beside me on the bench. His knees barely fit under the table. He couldn't possibly have been comfortable.

'My turn,' he said.

'To do what?'

'To ask you questions. You've been pumping me for information all night.'

I felt myself blush again. Had I been that obvious? I supposed it was only fair. I just hoped he wasn't going to ask about George or Helen.

It was worse than that. 'So this famous novel you're writing – what's it about, really?'

Oh, God. I looked directly into his unflinching gaze. 'It's not about anything. I have writer's block.'

He raised his blond brows. 'A serious case?'

'You could say that. I haven't written anything in over a year.'

It was the first time I'd admitted it to anyone – or, indeed, said it out loud. Instead of terrifying the bejasus out of me, as I'd thought it would, it actually made me feel better.

'You don't know what a relief it is to tell someone,' I said. 'I've been so worried, I don't know what I'm going to do. I gave my editor this memoir that I wrote a few years ago; I thought she'd reject it, but she loves it. She actually wants to publish it.'

'That doesn't sound so bad.'

'Well, you see, it is. It's all about my family – really personal stuff that can't possibly be let out into the public domain. If they publish

162

it, my mother will disown me. I'm telling you, I can't let it happen. I have to come up with something else – something better, and less personal – so that my editor will drop it. But I've been racking my brains for months, practically bashing my head against my laptop, and I've come up with zilch.'

'Well, this might help,' Eric said.

'What?'

'Getting it off your chest.'

'Don't tell me you're a part-time counsellor too.'

'No. But I do write songs, and I know that when you bottle everything up inside, it doesn't exactly help the creative process.'

I nodded.

'And another thing: you've had a lot of crap to deal with in the last year. That can't have helped.'

I just nodded again. What was the point in denying it? He knew exactly what had gone on.

'You could probably do with a change of scene, too.'

'I agree. The Bahamas would be nice.'

Eric smiled, but didn't say anything more.

'I guess you're sorry you asked,' I said.

'No. I'm genuinely interested. I read your first two books, and I was wondering when I'd get a chance to read a third.'

I was mortified, as I always was when I heard that somebody I knew had read one of my books – let alone two. I know that's the whole point – you write books, and somebody out there reads them – but I still found it excruciating to think that somebody I knew was privy to my innermost thoughts. I'd always been this way. I'd even found it difficult to hand up English essays in school. The teacher practically had to prise them out of my vice-like grip.

'I loved them,' Eric said.

'Pardon?'

'Your books. I loved them. You're a very good writer.'

For the umpteenth time that night, I felt my colour deepen. Eric liked my books. And I knew I might be mistaken, but I wondered if it was possible that maybe he liked me too – just a teeny, weeny little bit.

Eric insisted on taking the same bus as me and walking me right to my front gate. He'd never seemed worried that I might get attacked before. We sat on the garden wall for ages, just talking. I had the distinct impression that I was being watched. I turned and looked back at the house every now and then, suddenly and without warning, but I could spy no discernable twitch of a curtain. Yet the windows all appeared to have eyes.

Eric seemed incapable of shutting up. It was as if he'd opened the floodgates and didn't know how to close them again; as if he'd finally been given permission to speak, after years of holding it all in. No, that wasn't quite it, I realised. What he was actually doing was babbling. And there I was, casually sitting on the wall, being all quiet and self-possessed.

Abruptly, Eric stopped talking and stood up. For a fleeting second, I anticipated a little doorstep awkwardness; but he just said, 'See you tomorrow,' swivelled on his heel and disappeared off into the night.

As I let myself into the house, I caught the sound of scurrying footsteps and a bedroom door closing. I frowned to myself as I stood at the bottom of the stairs. Had I just been on a *date*?

24

I couldn't deny the frisson of excitement I felt as I walked into Grainger's the next day. But Eric had brought his shutters down again; it was as if our 'date' had never happened. Granted, he wasn't alone when I went to leave my belongings in the stockroom – but he could have at least *smiled*, in recognition of the evening we'd spent together. All I got was his usual curt nod. Well, fuck that for a game of soldiers. Clearly our 'connection' had all been in my head.

And the morning had even more unpleasantness in store for me. As I headed back out to the shop floor, I heard voices – high-pitched, girly voices, gushing and making googly sounds. It could mean only one thing: there was a baby on the premises. Oh, well – a welcome distraction. Then I heard Helen's voice.

I stood stock-still. I hadn't seen Helen since that horrendous day in the hospital. I'd seen her 'partner', all right. He still came into the shop for his daily visits and gave Tom – the acting manager – a hard time, but we completely ignored each other these days. I quickly constructed an emotional wall when I saw him coming; and I could almost hear him asking himself why I didn't just do the decent thing and resign. *Well, you're not getting rid of me that easily, Georgie Boy. You've made your beds – all three of them – and you can damn well lie in them all.*

I wondered if Helen had known I'd be in the shop. But of course she had. Knowing her, she would have rung ahead and checked; this was no accidental encounter. I steeled myself and walked onto the

165

shop floor. Not only did I have Helen and her brat to contend with, I also had to deal with the rest of the staff's expectant stares, which varied from pitying to incredulous to downright voracious.

I walked calmly to my till, feeling the weight of their collective gaze, and stared straight ahead of me. I could hear them all making fools of themselves over the baby in the background. Idiots.

At last, Helen approached me, babe in arms. 'Hello, Liz.'

'Helen.'

'It's good to see you again.'

She didn't seriously expect me to respond to that.

'How have you been?' she asked.

I looked at her then for the first time. Her eyes were so full of hope that I almost caved in. Then I concentrated on her hair, which was as vibrant as ever, and that strengthened my resolve.

'Fine, thank you.'

'I brought Royston in. I thought it was high time I showed him off. He's almost three months now, you know.'

Which was my cue, I supposed, to admire the little blighter. Reluctantly, I peered down at him. Helen had him in one of those papoose things; he was strapped to her chest, facing forwards, his limbs dangling freely. Royston Staunton – or should I say Royston Grainger – the First stared right back up at me. You could tell that his once-blue eyes were midway to turning brown, and he'd lost his voluminous, black baby hair; it was now nut-brown and wispy. In other circumstances – namely, any circumstance other than this one – I would have been forced to admit that he was a stunning baby. I thought of the words of the song, 'Summertime'. Then I changed them to *Your daddy's a three-timing turd and your mamma's a hypocritical cow.*

'He's lovely.' My tone was as neutral as I could possibly make it.

'He'd love to see more of his Auntie Liz.'

'Oh, give me a fucking break, Helen.'

Helen drew back as if stung. I thought she'd go then. I saw her considering it, but she wasn't to be deterred that easily.

'You know,' she said, 'we really appreciate you staying on here, after everything that's happened.'

We. Was she trying to piss me off? I glanced at her and realised that she wasn't.

'Not a problem,' I said coolly. 'I need the dosh.'

'Even so…it can't be easy for you.'

'Spare me the tired clichés, Helen. And will you please stop patronising me?'

'I'm sorry. I don't mean to. Look…I won't be coming back to work for another three months, at least. Could we please meet up sometime soon?'

'What would you like me to do? Call around to your little love nest in Ranelagh?'

'No, of course not. We could go somewhere neutral – meet in town, maybe?'

Her smile was bright and her voice chirpy; anyone else would have thought she was perfectly together. But I knew Helen better than family, and I knew she was close to losing it.

'No,' I said, relishing the effect this had on her expression. I know this was hardly a laudable way to treat a nursing mother – and I was positive that uber-mamma would still be breast-feeding – but I still felt so very hurt and betrayed. And I wasn't my mother's daughter for nothing.

Helen left shortly after that. My back, which I'd kept ramrod-straight throughout her visit, collapsed back into its usual slump, and I had difficulty maintaining an even vaguely pleasant expression for the benefit of customers and certain staff members, who were still agog, having witnessed our altercation. At long last, lunchtime rolled around – surely it was at least knocking-off time already – and I made my weary way out to the back of the shop. I declined Tom's kind offer to bring me to the Gotham Café. I felt the urgent need to be by myself.

The day was mild and pleasant, so I decided on St Stephen's Green. And so, unfortunately, had half the population of Dublin. The private little cry that I'd been promising myself all morning would have to wait. I hadn't a hope in hell of securing an empty bench, so instead I claimed a decent-looking patch of grass, half-secluded behind a bush. This meant that I could watch the world go by, but that the world couldn't necessarily see me. But did I want to see the world? That was the question. Because, today of all days, the world seemed to be entirely comprised of couples, either entwined blissfully together or wheeling buggies with expressions of benign contentment on their faces. It was like some cosmic game of torment. Maybe I would have just a little cry…

I had to ask myself: had I been too hard on Helen? She hadn't, after all, known that I'd got back together with George. I'd kept it a secret from everyone. But she had known that I was still in love with him. No. It was unforgivable. The harridan deserved it.

I finished eating my prawn-cocktail sandwich and bequeathed the crusts to the ducks. I had a habit – a hangover from childhood – of leaving my crusts, which drove my mother potty. It was a worse crime, apparently, than getting bits of butter in the marmalade, or toast crumbs in the butter.

I walked back to the shop – or, as I referred to it these days, hell on earth. I tried to work out whether I felt lousier about seeing Helen again, or about Eric all but ignoring me. Helen won, hands down. If something didn't give soon, I was in serious danger of sliding down into a dark, bottomless pit from which there was little hope of escape.

The day droned on, devoid of incident. But, at four o'clock, something unexpected occurred: Eric came out onto the shop floor. Eric *never* came out onto the shop floor. He hid in the back, like some sort of hobbit. It was probably just as well; I couldn't imagine that customer relations would be his strong suit. He came right up to me and proffered a book – not an unusual thing to do, in a bookshop, except that this was a book of his own.

'I thought you might be interested in this,' he said, handing it to me. 'It's not too long, and it's very accessible. Lots of interesting background information about the Spanish in Ireland.'

'Thanks, Eric. That's very good—'

'I'm knocking off early today, so I'll see you whenever.'

'Oh. All right, then. Bye.'

'Bye.'

And that was that. 'Whenever'? When was that? Still, at least he was speaking to me. And it had been considerate of him to bring in the book.

Tom had been watching this exchange like a beady-eyed little bird. He shot over to me as soon as Eric had gone.

'What was that about?' he demanded.

'Eric's helping me out with some research.'

'Can I see?'

'Course.' I handed the book to him. Tom read the front and back covers; then, satisfied that my story held up under scrutiny, he handed it back to me.

'Is that research for the mysterious, long-awaited novel?'

'Yes.' I was afraid he was going to start questioning me about it, but he had other matters on his mind.

'He fancies you, you know,' he said smugly.

'Who? What?'

'"Who? What?" Listen to her. You know exactly who and what I mean. The Viking.'

'He knows you call him that,' I said, in a desperate attempt to change the subject.

'Does he really? Is he pissed off?'

'Well...no. In fact, that's how he came up with the name of his band.'

'Are you serious? I'm flattered.' It would be nice, I thought, to be so easily flattered. 'Anyway,' Tom continued, 'we're not talking about me – more's the pity. You and Eric – what's the deal?'

'There is no deal.'

'He hasn't pillaged your village yet?'

'God, no.'

'What's he lending you books for, then?'

'Please. Have you slept with every person who's ever lent you a book?'

Tom considered this. 'I'd have to give that a resounding "yes".'

'Well, we're not all like you, thank God.'

'Do you know how I know he fancies you?'

'Enlighten me.'

'It's all in the body language, my dear. My first clue was the headphones. He always takes them off when he talks to you. With the rest of us, he just turns down the volume a bit.'

I thought about this. Was it true?

'And just now he came out onto the shop floor – and we all know he never, *ever* does that – just on the pretext of lending you a book. And his body language was all awkward and shy. It's quite sweet, really. Oh, yes: the Viking has the hots, all right.'

'You're delusional,' I said.

'I'm not, you know. So...' Tom leaned right over the cash desk, scrutinising my features. 'Would you do him?'

'Tom! Please!'

'It's a perfectly legitimate question. He's a fine figure of a man.'

'Oh, you think so, do you?'

'Don't start that again. We're focusing on you, darling.'

'Leave me alone, Tom. I'm really not in the mood.'

'Aha! I note that you're not denying it.'

'Look,' I said, 'I really don't know whether he fancies me or not. And it's too dangerous for me even to think about it right now. I'd be much better off just forgetting all about men for the time being. Frankly, the way I feel about myself at the moment, I'd be amazed if anyone was ever attracted to me again.'

'That's only because you've been attracted to the wrong type of man for far too long. What you need in your life right now is a nice big piece of Scandinavian salami.'

'Right. That's it. This conversation is now officially over.'

25

I decided to test out Eric's theory. Had talking about my writer's block helped clear my writer's block?

I stared at the dreaded blank screen of my laptop. Then I stared at it some more. I continued to stare until I felt the familiar sensation of panic rising in my throat. This was no good. I'd surf the Net for a while and then go back to it.

I typed 'ancestor' into Google – just for divilment – and scrolled down through the start of a list containing thousands of hits. One phrase kept catching my eye. I'd scroll by it but, lo and behold, up it cropped again. OK, I'll mega-bite: what was 'ancestral healing' when it was at home? I clicked onto a site.

The theory, it turned out, was that, when problems had occurred in the lives of forebears, the negative energy from those experiences got passed on to future generations. Not only that – you could actually be liable for the unwholesome actions of your ancestors and, unbeknownst to yourself, be experiencing all manner of bad karma because of them. How depressing. I was paying not only for my own past mistakes and misdemeanours, but also for those of people I'd never met and, in some cases, never even heard of. I wouldn't be buying into that particular theory.

The next day in work, I found myself placed, yet again, at the till close to the Mind, Body, Spirit section. I was staring vacantly at the books, as I often did, not really taking anything in, when one of them caught my attention. It was a book on ancestral healing. Now, there was a coincidence – or, as a religious friend of mine used to say, a God-incidence. I carried out a quick visual check: nobody around. I swiftly left my post, grabbed up the book and returned with it. With practised ease, I flicked adroitly through it, in such a way that nobody could tell I was reading. Not that I cared, at this stage, if I got caught reading; but I did care if I got caught reading shite like this.

I spent most of the morning dug into the book – save when I was interrupted by pesky customers. It honestly was very interesting shite. I found one story especially appealing: the story of a woman who had developed a phobia of water, only to discover that one of her ancestors had been a passenger on the *Titanic*. By sending him 'healing energy', she had rid herself of her fear.

My ancestors must have been a right bunch of bad bastards, I decided, if my sorry excuse for a life was anything to go by. It occurred to me that it might be no harm to have somebody else to blame for a change. They were already dead anyway, so what harm could it do them?

I had just reached the chapter containing exercises on how to heal your ancestral pain when a shadow fell across my soul.

'Is the book good?'

'Not bad.'

'Can I speak to you in the office, please?'

'You mean *Helen's* office?'

'I don't want any trouble, Liz. Come with me, please.'

I followed George into the back office, my brain frantically trying to keep up with the situation. What could this mean? He hadn't so much as looked at me since that dreadful day in the hospital – and now he wanted to talk? Maybe he'd finally come up with a legitimate way to sack me.

He closed the door and sat down behind the desk, no doubt to assert his authority. I continued to stand, in an effort to assert my own – my moral authority, that is. Because, bad as I was, I wasn't as bad as him.

'What did you say to Helen when she was in here the other day?' he demanded.

'That's between me and Helen.'

'Not when she comes home in tears, it isn't. She's been in bits ever since.'

'Your concern for your mistress is touching.'

'Cut the hostile crap, Elizabeth. You're skating on thin ice as it is.'

'That wouldn't be a threat, George, would it? Because I really don't think you're in a position to make threats – seeing as your girlfriend doesn't know you were seeing me nearly the whole time she was pregnant. I didn't say anything before, because of the baby; but Helen's dying to meet up with me, and you know how these things can sometimes slip out.'

George didn't reply, but I could see the muscle in his jaw working overtime. Feeling as if I had the advantage – temporarily, at least – I sat down opposite him and crossed my legs. I must admit I felt empowered. I'd never spoken to George like this before. Was it possible that I was starting to get over him?

'What would it take to get you out of our lives for good?' he said eventually. 'Do you want money?'

I tried to hide it as best I could, but this really stung. Did he hate me that much? 'Helen doesn't want me out of her life. She wants us to be friends again.'

This time he looked as if his head was about to explode. 'You'll stay away from her if you know what's good for you.'

'My, my, George. You're going to have to learn to control

yourself a bit better, because that sounded very much like another threat to me.'

I'd been doing well so far, but I didn't know how much longer I could keep this up. I got up to leave. 'Will that be all?'

'No, that will not be all. Sit back down.'

'I will not. And kindly don't bark orders at me. I'm not a dog.'

'No. You're a bitch. I don't know what the fuck I ever saw in you.'

'I think you'll find it was the sex, George. Now, must dash; it wouldn't do to leave my post unattended for too long. Tell Helen I'll give her a call.'

'You'll do no such thing!' This time his voice was a yell. Before I could even reach the door, he'd come around from his side of the desk – as if he were on wheels or something – and blocked my exit. Then, to my horror, he shoved me up against the wall, his forearm pressed against my throat. I was absolutely rigid. His face was right up against mine, eyes wide and bloodshot, mouth curled into a snarl, spittle at the corners of his lips.

'Don't you go anywhere near her,' he hissed.

I didn't have time to formulate a response, because at that moment the door flew open. I didn't see who it was at first, but I felt the weight of George being dragged off me. By the time I realised it was Eric, he had given George an almighty whack in the face. George collapsed on the floor, groaning and clutching his bleeding nose.

'Are you all right?' Eric said to me.

'Fine,' I said to Eric.

'You're fired,' George said to Eric.

'Fine by me,' Eric said to George.

'In that case, I resign,' I said to George.

'Thank fuck for that,' George said to me.

I sighed. I should have done that a long time ago. I glanced across at Eric, who was rubbing his knuckles. I didn't fancy his chances in the unfair dismissals tribunal this time around.

My mother had barely spoken to me for the best part of two months. First, there was the small matter of my resignation – a resignation to which I felt peculiarly resigned. The last time I'd lost my job in Grainger's, it had felt like the end of the world; this time, it felt like a beginning. This time, it was on my own terms. This time, it was the right time. Time to move on.

The second reason my mother wasn't speaking to me was the less-than-pristine state in which I was keeping the sitting room. I couldn't argue with her there. My domestic habits would have had my old home economics teacher spinning in her own spin cycle. To my knowledge – and my mother's – there had been a slightly used black sock lurking behind the sofa for at least three weeks. We both refused to remove it, Mam because it wasn't her sock, and neither was it her duty to pick up after her grown-up daughter, me because she'd gone on about it so much that she'd totally pissed me off and now I was refusing to remove it as a point of principle. This was utterly stupid, of course – if I had just picked up the offending item and placed it in the laundry basket, she'd probably have started speaking to me again; but, quite frankly, I was enjoying the peace and quiet.

That afternoon, I was flirting with my laptop as usual when the phone rang.

'Get that, Libby, I'm in the bath,' called my mother. This was our first communication of the day.

'Hello,' I said.

'Is that you, Liz?'

'Auntie Kit?' It couldn't be. *What on God's earth are you doing ringing me here?* I felt like adding.

'It's me mother. She's after having a nasty turn. I thought you should know.'

The medical term for 'a nasty turn' was a heart attack – and it wasn't Granny's first, as I learned when I got to the hospital. When I asked Aunt Kit what else they'd been keeping from me, she told me about the medication, and the angina. The guilt! That day I'd walked back into Granny's life, unannounced, it was only by the grace of God that I hadn't brought on an attack.

'Granny? Can you hear me, Granny?' Kit had gone to get coffee – neither of us really wanted any, but it gave her something to do, made her feel a little less helpless. I could relate to that. We were all alone: just me, my grandmother and enough tubing to stretch from here to Belfast. Of course she couldn't hear me. The woman was unconscious.

I could scarcely bear to look at her face. Her dentures had been removed, and all her features seemed to have caved in on one another. Her skin was the colour and texture of leftover dough, except for the purple pits that her eye sockets had become. The veins on her hands were purple too. I stroked her fingers delicately. I was relieved that they were still soft and warm to the touch, not waxy, as I had feared they would be – like the skin of my other grandmother, that time I'd touched her hand as she lay in the funeral parlour. So cold. Not how skin was meant to feel.

This couldn't be happening. It was too cruel. We were only getting to know each other, Granny and I. A wave of fury at my mother threatened to sweep me away. If it hadn't been for that confounded woman and her stupid bitterness and stubbornness, I could have had a proper, lifelong relationship with my grand-mother, instead of a few measly months. She couldn't die now. I still had so many questions I wanted to ask – things about my father that only she would know; things about her that only she would know.

Suddenly overcome, I decided I couldn't wait for Kit's return. I'd ring her later and explain. Right now I just wanted to be on my own.

As I walked down the monotonous hospital corridors, towards the lift, I wondered what all the other people were doing there – what tragedies had befallen their loved ones. What a depressing place... Of course, for some people, it was just another day at the office – people like my mother, for instance. As luck would have it, she was standing on the other side of the lift doors as they slid open. I was getting off; she was getting on.

'Libby. What are you doing here?'

She was just coming on duty; this was evident from her brisk appearance. I couldn't think of a lie quickly enough, so I had no option but to tell the truth.

'I'm here to visit my grandmother.'

The silence echoed in my ears as if someone was sounding a large gong over and over. I watched my mother's pupils dilate.

'What's wrong with her?' she said finally.

'Heart attack.'

'Serious?'

'Yes. It's not her first.'

'I'm sorry to hear that, Libby. I really am.'

'Why don't you go and see her?'

'Is she conscious?'

'No.'

'Well, then there's very little point, is there?'

And with that, she stepped into the lift, just as the doors slid shut again. I wanted to say something else, but it was too late. Always too late.

Then it occurred to me that, if I didn't sit down and have a proper talk with my mother soon, it would be too late for us – if it wasn't already.

26

I decided to enlist the help of Graham, the original silent partner. He might not say much, but he sure had an uncanny knack of handling his wife. I knew I would do well to take a leaf or two out of his book and keep my mouth shut once in a while, but unfortunately this didn't seem to be in my nature.

I found him at the kitchen table, as usual. It was his favourite haunt since he'd been ousted from the sitting room by all my paraphernalia. I felt somewhat guilty about this, especially since he was the only one who never complained about my presence. He just treated it with the same benign acceptance that he applied to everything else in his life: to the job he didn't like very much but attended, day in, day out, so that the mortgage could be paid; to his eldest son, the biggest pain in the arse in the Western world; and to his wife's volatile daughter, who drifted in and out of his life like some useless piece of flotsam.

Graham had married my mother when I was a very opinionated, incredibly annoying eleven-year-old. I had made up my mind that there was no way he was going to tell me what to do. Sensing this, he had never tried. As a result, I hadn't gained a father so much as a friend. I suddenly wondered whether I'd ever truly understood the value of that before.

The aforementioned eldest son was in the kitchen too, wearing a T-shirt that said, 'Never Mind the Bollocks'. I tried not to, I really did, but it was hard. He had his head buried deep in the fridge; I couldn't see much of the top part of his body, but I could hear munching and slurping noises from time to time.

'Jim,' I said.

No reply.

'Jim,' I said, louder.

Still nothing. As usual, he was less vocal than his own clothing. I gave up and sat down opposite Graham.

'Can I talk to you?' I said.

Graham looked up from filling in an application form out of his gun-club magazine – clearly ordering another murderous weapon to add to his massive collection. Graham had what I was sure was an extremely impressive selection of guns (all fully licensed) and knives, which he kept in a heavily padlocked shed at the end of the back garden. I was sure he had never shot so much as a rabbit; mostly he just liked to admire and polish them. He spent many a happy hour in his shed, at times when my mother was driving even him to distraction. I couldn't help thinking that this was Graham's way of releasing his pent-up aggression, his means of pounding the punch-bag or the pillow. And he was such a gentle, inoffensive soul. I just hoped he wouldn't go postal one day. It was always the quiet ones…

He placed the magazine, the pen and the application form precisely to one side and clasped his hands in front of him, letting me know that I had his undivided attention.

'It's about Mam,' I said.

'You two haven't had another falling-out, have you?'

'No, nothing like that. Not yet, anyhow.'

Graham raised his eyebrows.

'It's just that I have to talk to her about something,' I continued swiftly, 'and I could use your advice on how to go about it.'

'Go on.'

I hesitated. 'It's about my father.'

'Oh.'

I looked at him uncertainly, and he looked back – well, I couldn't quite interpret how he was looking back at me.

'Maybe I shouldn't be asking…' I began.

'Libby,' Graham interrupted, his tone firm, 'you have every right to ask me or your mam anything you like about your father – or about anything else, for that matter.'

There was a slamming sound behind me and I was aware of Jim once again. He stood beside me, wiping his mouth with the back of his hand. 'You're not going to start stirring the shit again, are you?' he said.

'No, Jim, I'm not. I just need to tell Mam a few things. My father's mother is very ill—'

'You are, aren't you? Why do you always have to do this? I thought you were only staying for a few months. We were doing fine before you came back and ruined everything. You always put her in a bad mood, and we all have to suffer for it.'

And, with that, Jim slammed out of the room. *Oh, God,* I thought. *Does my whole family hate me?* I felt Graham looking at me and knew that the pain must be written all over my face.

'Don't mind him,' he said softly. 'He's at a difficult age.'

'He's having a difficult decade, if you ask me.'

Graham smiled at me, and I managed a weak smile back.

'What do you need to tell your mam?'

I drew a deep breath. 'You know how she's always said that my father abandoned her?'

He nodded.

'Well, I've found out that's not true. He'd decided to come back to us. He was on his way to buy a ticket when he got knocked down.'

'How did you find this out?'

'I managed to track down my grandmother – his mother. I've been meeting up with her for quite a while now.'

Graham nodded. 'I thought as much.'

'Why? Did Mam say something?'

'She might have done.'

I could well imagine. I respected his tact and didn't delve any further.

'The thing is,' I said, 'my grandmother's very sick. It might be too late already, but if she gains consciousness again, I really think it's important that Mam speaks to her. I think she needs to hear it from the horse's mouth. What do you think?'

I waited for him to speak. As usual, his response was slow and measured and well thought out. 'If you think it's the right thing, Libby, I've no doubt that it is. Leave it with me. I'll have a word.'

'Oh, would you really? That'd be brilliant, Graham. Thank you so much.'

'Not a bother.'

He pulled the form towards him again and resumed filling in boxes. I took that as my cue to leave.

When I was halfway out the kitchen door, I looked back at Graham's balding auburn head, bent over the form in rapt concentration. I wondered then how I had ever doubted the existence of a strong father figure in my life.

So what was my excuse, then?

A few days later, Granny opened her eyes and spoke her first words since the attack. I believe they were something along the lines of 'Get me out of here,' only less polite. So, against all medical advice, she left the hospital the moment they disconnected the last tube. I went along to help bring her home; but when I got there, I found I was superfluous to requirements.

My Uncle Martin – my father's elder brother – had just arrived from Australia. He had thick white hair, a black moustache and vivid blue eyes, which he must have inherited from the other side of the family. He stopped packing Granny's bags and stared at me unabashedly as I walked into the ward.

'Jaysus,' he said. Thirty-odd years of living in Melbourne hadn't dulled his Dublin accent one iota. 'Look at the cut of her. She's her father's daughter, all right.'

You could say he made a good first impression.

That night, I was still in a good mood. I even removed the sock from behind the sofa, and no, I didn't put it into the laundry basket; straight into the washing machine it went. There's efficiency for you!

I was in bed, re-reading *The Journey of Francisco de Cuellar*. I'd got to the part where he'd reached the safety of the castle of McClancy.

> *They helped me the best they could with a blanket of the kind they use, and I remained there three months, acting as a real savage like themselves. The wife of my master was very beautiful in the extreme, and showed me much kindness. One day we were sitting in the sun with some of her female friends and relatives, and they asked me about Spanish matters and of other parts, and in the end it came to be suggested that I should examine their hands and tell them their fortunes. Giving thanks to God that it had not gone even worse for me than to be gypsy among savages, I began to look at the hands of each, and to say to them a hundred thousand absurdities, which pleased them so much that there was no other Spaniard better than I.*

Had my ancestor also read the palms of the savages? Had he predicted that Mary McClancy would be left up the pole while he hot-footed it back to Spain?

184

My musings were interrupted by a knock on the sitting-room door. 'Come in,' I called.

It was my mother, looking uncharacteristically subdued. She came and sat on the edge of my sofa-bed. I didn't know what to make of this unprecedented behaviour.

'I see your granny's been discharged from the hospital,' she said.

'How—'

'I stopped in to her ward today, but she'd already left.' I sat up straighter. Did this mean... 'When are you visiting her next?'

'I was going to go over to her house tomorrow night.'

'I'll go over with you,' Mam said, 'if that's all right.'

Dumbstruck wasn't the word.

'It is all right, isn't it?'

'Yes, yes. Of course it is.'

'After tea, so.'

'That'd be fine.'

'Good night, Libby.'

'Good night.' I wanted her to tell me not to let the bedbugs bite, like she used to.

I couldn't imagine what Graham had said to her – but, by God, it had certainly done the trick. I rang Auntie Kit the next morning to break the news.

Her initial reaction was, 'Oh my God, the house is in bits.'

'Don't worry about it, Kit. She's coming to see Granny, not the house.'

'Are you joking me? I remember what that one was like – no offence, love. But, Jesus, I'll have to scrub the house from top to bottom before she comes. I'd better take the day off from the stall.'

So it wasn't just me, then.

Mam and I drove to Granny's house in silence. You'd think that a profound conversation – maybe even an apology – would have been in order, but no: we'd never known what to say to each other, and today was no exception. The radio eased the tension somewhat, but even then, we wanted to listen to different stations. It was as if we were permanently tuned to different frequencies.

'You don't seem to have much to do with Helen these days,' Mam was saying. I'm sure the poor woman was just trying to relieve the silence – and if it had been any other topic, I would have been with her all the way. Now I longed for the silence again.

'No,' I said.

Not exactly an encouraging response, but she was undeterred. 'Any particular reason?'

'No.'

'I hope you haven't had a falling-out.'

'Mam, I really don't want to talk about it, if you don't mind.'

She gave me a look; but, thankfully, we had reached my grandmother's road, and my relationship with Helen – or lack thereof – was spared any further scrutiny.

The journey was familiar and yet unfamiliar. I was accustomed to travelling this route by bus and by foot; my mother's 98D Toyota Corolla was the lap of luxury in comparison. We both got out of the car and slammed our doors. The only other sound in the cul-de-sac was that of the birds settling down for the night, twittering away gently. I was consumed by a strange, eerie feeling; I found myself transported back to that day, a little over a year ago, when I had visited my grandmother for the very first time. Mrs Clancy, fortune-teller extraordinaire. Tonight there was no queue of hopeful young women. She wasn't really up to it.

Kit opened the door to us, and I saw that her hair was newly dyed a matt ebony. She was wearing her good earrings, too – solid gold hoops normally reserved for high days and holidays. 'Róisín.' She nodded.

'Kit.' My mother nodded back.

'Come in.' Her voice – her entire demeanour – was hushed.

I noticed that the boxes of tights and toilet rolls had been removed from the front hall. We were ushered into the good room – a riot of bad taste, as usual. My Uncle Martin (I loved saying that) was drinking tea out of a china cup (fancy, with flowers on the inside) with an old woman whom I recognised as Mrs Baxter from number 14. She got up from her seat as we walked in.

'Ah, hello to you,' she said. 'I'm sorry for your trouble.'

For a terrible couple of seconds I felt a whizzing sensation in my ears, because I thought she meant my grandmother was dead. With an effort, I managed to calm myself: surely this was something Kit would have mentioned as soon as we arrived.

Introductions were made and cups of tea offered. Martin got up and gave my mother his seat. I perched on the arm of her chair.

'I'll just go and see if she's up to visitors,' said Kit, leaving the room. We four sat in awkward silence.

'Lovely weather we're having,' said Mrs Baxter, to no one in particular.

'Yes, lovely,' replied my mother.

'Very good for this time of year.'

'Very.'

We silently willed Kit to return. Thankfully, we didn't have long to wait.

'She'll see you first, Róisín,' she said, coming back into the room.

'What – now?' My mother set down her cup and saucer with a clatter and looked uncharacteristically unsure of herself.

'Well, she's waited long enough.' I was sure Kit didn't mean to snap.

Giving me one last baleful glance, Róisín Murphy followed Kit Clancy out of the room.

I slid down into her seat. Then I changed my mind and went and stood beside the mantelpiece. I was right beside all the postcards that Granny had been getting, on a regular basis, from Gnobby the Gnome. (Unfortunately, the Gardaí's inquiries had proved fruitless so far.) That gnome sure got around. Making sure that nobody was looking, I snuck a couple of postcards into my pocket.

'How is she today?' I asked Martin, who was leaning against the dresser (a capital offence) having a cigarette. He held it like the boys in school used to hold their cigarettes, fag concealed by the palm, only a thin plume of smoke showing.

'Ah, all right, considering. If you ask me, she should still be in the hospital. She's not out of the woods yet – not by any means.'

'Mmm,' concurred Mrs Baxter, nodding her head several times, thus emphasising her triple chin. 'She's terrible shook-looking.'

'The sisters are coming home next week,' Martin said.

I wasn't sure how I felt about this. On the one hand, I was dying to meet them. On the other, their return could mean only one thing: they feared that their mother was dying. It was bad enough coping with my own fear, without being confronted with other people's.

'It's a shocking business,' said Mrs Baxter. 'A shocking business altogether.'

Talk about stating the bleeding obvious. She was starting to get on my nerves. What was she doing here anyway? She wasn't family.

'You know,' she said suddenly, to me, 'I knew your daddy when he was a lad.'

'Really.'

'Indeed and I did. A gorgeous young fella, he was. He'd light up

188

a room just by walking into it, so he would. And he was the apple of his mammy's eye. You don't know how happy you made her, coming back into her life the way you did.'

'Would you like another cup of tea, Mrs Baxter? A Mikado?' I offered her the plate.

'No, thanks, love. I'd better be getting back to my Frank. He'll be wanting his supper. Useless as the day he was born, that oul' fella.'

She hauled herself to her swollen feet. For a fleeting second, I was reminded of Helen in the final days of her pregnancy. I walked her to the front door.

'Bye, love. You look after your granny, now, and your Auntie Kit.'

'I will, Mrs Baxter.' Impulsively, I kissed her on the cheek. Her expression as she walked out the door was one of both pleasure and surprise.

No sooner had I walked back in than the door of Granny's room opened, and my mother and Kit came out. My mother was holding a handkerchief up to her nose. I was shocked to realise that she was crying.

'I'll wait for you in the car, Libby,' she said in muffled tones.

I looked up questioningly at Kit.

'She'll see you now, Elizabeth.'

'OK, then,' I said uncertainly. This was becoming uncomfortably like the death scene in a B-movie. Would somebody please pass the popcorn?

My grandmother's room smelt of Milton sterilising fluid and rose-scented talc. Granny had her teeth in, thanks be to God, which meant that she looked more like her old self, and her eyes had emerged to some extent from their sunken pits. But Mrs Baxter had been right: she was still awful shook-looking.

'Elizabeth!' She stretched out her hand. 'Come here to me till I

189

have a look at you. I never thought I'd see you again.' In the badly lit gloom, I saw that her eyes were shiny with unshed tears. *Oh, God, don't do this,* I thought. I hated it when old people talked about dying – especially when the words had the whiff of truth about them.

'Don't be silly, Granny. Why wouldn't you be seeing me again? I'm not going anywhere.'

She smiled and patted my hand. 'Thank you for bringing your mammy to see me.'

'It wasn't really my doing. Graham – my stepdad – convinced her to come.'

'All the same, she wouldn't have come if it wasn't for you. It was good to talk to her. Set the record straight.'

'Did you tell her, then – all about my dad?'

'I did.'

'And did she believe you?'

'Sure, why wouldn't she, and me not long for this world? Why would I be lying?'

'Granny! Stop talking like that. You're going to be fine.'

Granny patted my hand again, examining my face. Then her eyes travelled down to my neck.

'Where's that locket I gave you? I haven't seen you wearing it this long time.'

I froze. 'It's in the jewellers'. I didn't think the clasp was secure enough, so I left it in to be fixed.'

'Good girl. It'd be terrible if you lost it.'

'Yes, it would.'

'And it would break my heart.'

'I know it would, Granny.'

There was a short silence.

'I want you to do something for me,' she said.

'Anything.'

'I want you to go to Streedagh Strand – the place where our ancestor was shipwrecked. I've always meant to go myself, but it doesn't look like I'm going to make it now.'

'Don't be talking—'

She cut me off. 'I want you to go there for me and come back and tell me exactly what it's like – the colour of the sand, the size of the rocks, everything. As if I was seeing it for myself. Will you do that for me?'

'Of course I will.'

'And do it for yourself, too. To know where you're going in this life, you have to know where you've been. Now I'm getting tired. Be a good girl and tell your Auntie Kit I'll be needing one of me pills before I go to sleep.'

'All right. Good night, Granny.' I kissed her warm, flaccid cheek.

'Good night, love. And remember: I want to know everything.' She closed her eyes as I closed the door.

I took out the postcards as soon as I got home. One was from Stockholm:

> *Dear Mrs Clancy,*
>
> *I am very disappointed that you have failed to pay the ransom money. I thought you cared. The kidnappers are threatening to cut the bell off my hat if you don't pay up soon. Please don't let me down.*
>
> *Yours imploringly,*
> *Gnobby the Gnome*

The other was from Amsterdam:

Dear Mrs Clancy,
Shame on you. The kidnappers have now cut off my bell.
They are threatening to cut off my toes next, one by one.
Have a heart, Mrs Clancy. Don't let this happen.
Gnobby the Gnome

Sellotaped to the bottom of this card was what could only have been a half-smoked joint. How on earth had that made it through the postal system? I presumed that 'Gnobby' had smoked the rest of the joint prior to writing the postcard. It would explain a lot.

I found pen and paper.

The Gnome Liberation Front
P.O. Box 42
Dublin

To Whom It May Concern
I am writing on behalf of my grandmother, Elizabeth Clancy. I believe that your 'gang' was responsible for the heinous abduction of Gnobby the Gnome from the garden that he had called home for many a long and happy year.
I was horrified to discover that you had cut off his bell. What kind of people are you, to do such a thing to an innocent gnome? This has to stop. Gnobby deserves to be returned to his rightful owner forthwith. I plead with you not to cut off any more of his body parts.
Your members are probably unaware that the aforementioned Mrs Elizabeth Clancy recently suffered a serious heart attack, for which she had to be hospitalised. I'm

quite sure that her recovery could only be hastened by the
prompt return of her favourite gnome.

   I beg of you, please do the honourable thing and release
Gnobby immediately.

   Yours most sincerely,
   Elizabeth Clancy Jr

I giggled to myself as I sealed the envelope. That should do the trick.

27

I knew exactly whom to ask for directions to Streedagh Strand. But, seeing as Eric lived in rented accommodation, I was unlikely to find his number or address in the phone directory. The way I saw it, I had two options: I could hire a private investigator, or I could return to the scene of the crime – Grainger's – and wrangle his address out of acting manager Tom. The latter was distinctly unappealing. Tom wouldn't let that one go lightly. But, since I was strapped for cash, I didn't have much of a choice – unless I fancied hanging around the Berkeley library all day, or scouring the walls of every alleyway in Dublin for Eric and the Vikings posters to tell me where their next gig was going to be. That would take time – and that was something I feared Granny didn't have.

I lurked outside the shop for a good ten minutes, checking for signs of that mongrel George, before I judged it safe to enter. I approached Rachel, who was stationed at the till nearest the door. 'Tom around?' I asked.

I allowed several seconds for her eyes to pop out of her head.

'Out the back,' she said finally.

I rapped on the office door.

'Come in,' said Tom's voice, loud and imperious. He didn't look up as I entered; he continued shuffling a mound of papers in a super-busy fashion, his reading glasses perched low on the bridge of his nose. Finally, he looked up over them, and his eyes widened.

'Oh, it's you! I thought it was the first applicant.'

'For what?'

'I'm interviewing for Eric's old job.' Tom visibly swelled with self-importance. This was right up his street. He loved sitting in judgement on people.

'Funny you should mention Eric…' I began.

'No! You two haven't got it together?'

'No. Nothing like that. I need his address or phone number, that's all.'

'Oh, is that all? Why, pray tell?'

'Because I just do. Can't you just give it to me?'

'Much as I'd love to, I'm afraid that's confidential employee information.'

'But he's not an employee any more.'

'I'm afraid the rule still applies. How would Eric like it if I divulged his personal details to all and sundry?'

'Do I look like all and sundry to you?'

'You think he'd like to hear from you, do you?'

'Jesus, Tom. You're such a pain in the arse.'

I sat down in the chair opposite him. I was immediately and uncomfortably carried back to that day, in the not-too-distant past, when I had sat in that same chair in front of another, even more arrogant man.

'Well, my dear,' said Tom, 'if you're going to be all secretive about it, how can you expect me to be any different?'

'Fine. I can tell you the truth.'

He leant forward hungrily. 'Great. And just know: if you're telling porkies, I'll be able to spot it a mile off.'

I told him the truth – about my distant Spanish ancestor being washed up on Streedagh Strand, and about Eric's expertise in the area. I even threw in the part about my sick – and possibly dying – grandmother.

'Hmm.' Tom leaned back into his swivelly executive chair and folded his arms across his barrel chest. He looked unconvinced. 'Why can't you just buy a map?'

'I'm useless at reading maps. Besides, he's been there before. He can give me insider advice on where to stay, where to eat – stuff like that.'

'Why can't you ring the tourist office?'

I sighed heavily. 'Because it's not the same as talking to someone who's actually been there.'

'You have an answer for everything, don't you?'

I shrugged.

'Well,' Tom announced, 'I have reached a decision.'

'Oh, have you now?'

'Indeed I have. I've decided to give you his details, but only because of your outrageous and shameless mention of your sick grandmother.'

'Well, I am doing it for her.'

'Handy to have an excuse, isn't it?'

'Just give me the damn details.'

'So gracious.'

'So pompous.'

Tom pushed himself off the side of the desk and launched the executive chair towards the filing cabinet at the other side of the room. He opened the employee file and rifled around; he launched himself back and transcribed Eric's phone number and address onto a Post-it. He handed it to me.

'Now, that wasn't so very hard, was it?' I said.

'No. But I want it on record that it was done against my better judgement, and that you owe me several large gin and tonics.'

'How are you fixed tonight after work?'

'Whose work?'

'Yours, smart-arse.'

'Meet me in Neary's at half six.' Where, I suspected, the interrogation would continue.

As I closed the office door behind me, I got quite a shock. Sitting quietly in a chair outside Tom's door was my hero – the man who had accosted my mugger and retrieved my mobile phone, with a rugby tackle that would have put Brian O'Driscoll to shame. I hadn't had the heart to tell him that that particular model of phone wasn't really worth the trouble.

I smiled at him. 'Hello.'

He smiled and nodded at me, but there was no recognition in his eyes. Perhaps he rescued damsels in distress on a daily basis and couldn't keep track of them all. I was about to say something to him, but I changed my mind at the last minute; I merely nodded and went back into the office, failing to knock this time.

'Tom, you'll never guess.'

Tom's impressive brows knitted together. 'Is it half six already?' he said, glancing at his wristwatch. 'Doesn't time fly when you're having fun?'

'The first job applicant. Guess who he is?'

'Colin Farrell's younger and better-looking brother.'

'Remember that time I got mugged on Thomas Street?'

'Entirely your own fault for wandering around there alone in the dark, if you ask me.'

'Well, it's him.'

'The mugger?'

'No! The rescuer.'

'Oh. You were right: I never would have guessed.'

'What's his name?'

Tom consulted a piece of paper on the desk in front of him. 'Deji…something or other. I can't even attempt to pronounce it. He must be African.'

'Yes, I think he is. Tom, you have to give him the job.'

'I have to do no such thing. What I have to do is give the job to the best applicant. It's my duty as acting manager.'

'Which you take very seriously at all times.'

'Enough of the sarcasm, please.'

'But, Tom, how could there possibly be a better applicant? The man is a hero. You already know he has courage and integrity and morality and…and athleticism.'

'All the qualities I'm looking for in a stockroom employee.'

'Come on, Tom. Give him a break. Who knows what heartless regime he's escaped from? Maybe he was starving. Maybe his whole family was massacred. Maybe—'

'All right, all right! I can't take any more. I'll see what I can do.'

'Thanks, Tom.' I let out a deep breath and realised I'd allowed myself to get quite worked up.

'But I'm not promising anything.'

'Fine. I'll see you later.'

Later on, in Neary's, Tom confided that Deji had indeed been successful in securing the position. What he neglected to tell me, until I'd expressed my gratitude profusely and bought him copious drinks, was that Deji had been the only applicant for the job.

I tried the phone number on the Post-it several times, but I kept getting an incomprehensible beeping. Damn! I'd have to go around to Eric's house unannounced.

It had been lashing out of the heavens for what seemed like two days solid; but, in the last hour, the deluge had come to an end and the wind had blown the clouds over to somebody else's sky. Having secured my favourite spot at the very front of the top deck of the bus, I looked up gratefully at the blue expanse. Every time the bus

198

wheezed to a halt, I could hear the extra-loud twittering of the birds, making up for lost time now that the flood had ended. They must always be there, I thought, going about their daily business; it just wasn't possible to hear them normally, over the din of the weekday traffic. I was willing to bet you could hear the birds in Streedagh.

I got off the bus somewhat reluctantly. Now that I was actually doing this, I felt more nervous than I had expected. Eric might not even be in, I told myself. It was a Sunday afternoon; he might be at his mother's house, having roast beef and gravy. Or the address might be as defunct as his phone number.

The bus dropped me off on the main street in Drumcondra. There was only a scattering of people about, mainly buying newspapers or walking off their Sunday dinner. I set off onto the narrow side-streets lined with rows of terraced, red-brick houses. The rented buildings stood out like sore thumbs against the owner-occupied ones with their window boxes and glass porches. And everywhere you looked loomed the new, improved Croke Park, like something out of *Close Encounters of the Third Kind*.

After only a couple of wrong turns, I found myself on Eric's street. My footsteps slowing down somewhat, I scanned the houses for number 22. I heard it before I saw it: what sounded like someone hammering metal to the accompaniment of muted heavy-metal music. I stood outside the gate.

The house was clearly rented. In the front driveway, a bottle-green, wheelless, fifteen-year-old car rested on four stacks of breeze-blocks. A large pair of feet stuck out from underneath. They could have belonged to Eric, but there was no guarantee.

'Hello,' I said, at the first break in the hammering.

The hammering resumed.

'Hello!' This time I shouted.

The hammering stopped. The feet developed ankles, shins, knees, thighs – until the entire overalled body of Eric slid out from underneath the car. His hair was considerably darker than usual, due to the addition of Castrol GTX, and a broad streak of oil traversed his right cheekbone like war paint. He'd never looked so much like a Viking. He stood up and brushed himself off. I must admit that it did occur to me that he'd have been more comfortable, on what had turned out to be a lovely mild day, working without his shirt on.

'What are you doing here?' Eric said.

'Lovely to see you too.'

When he failed to return my smile, I continued quickly, 'I wanted to return your book.'

'You'd better come in.'

Without further ceremony, he turned his back on me and walked towards the front door, wiping his hands on an oily rag as he went. I followed him indoors. *I knew it*, I thought: *I shouldn't have come.*

He led me into the kitchen. It was sparse but relatively clean-looking; he'd probably grown out of the phase where you leave the washing-up until the only thing left to eat off is the dog's dish, then scrape the green stuff off the plates, have a mammoth washing-up session and start the cycle all over again. I sat on a kitchen chair, as directed, and watched his back again as he scrubbed his hands at the sink.

'I hope you don't mind me coming here like this.' I had to raise my voice over the gushing of the water.

Eric looked back at me briefly. 'No. I'm just surprised.'

I would have been, too, if he'd turned up at my gaff unexpectedly. He wiped his hands on a tea towel. 'Drink?' he said.

'Tea would be nice.'

'I've only got beer.'

'Which would be equally nice.'

He took two cans of Foster's out of the fridge, cracked one open and handed it to me. 'What did you think of it?' he asked, sitting down across from me and opening his own can.

I frowned. 'What did I think of what?'

'The book.'

'Oh, the book! Of course.' My one and only reason for being there. 'It was very good. Excellent, in fact.'

Eric nodded and took a swig of beer. I could see I was going to have to do all the work here.

'How have you been?' I asked. Lame, I know.

'You mean since I got the sack?'

'Well...yes, I suppose I do. I'm very sorry about that, by the way. I feel kind of responsible.'

'Why?'

I looked at Eric carefully. 'Well. It was sort of because of me that you hit George.'

'He'd had that coming for a long time.'

'You think?'

'Oh, yeah. It was well worth getting the sack for.'

Well, that was OK, then. An embarrassing silence would have followed, if it hadn't been for the thunderous sound of someone thudding down the stairs. The kitchen door flew open and a blonde, ponytailed girl burst in. She reminded me of one of the lady tennis darlings of the seventies and eighties – a young Sue Barker, or Chris Evert before she became Lloyd.

'I'm going down the shops. Do you want... Oh, hello.' She smiled at me and looked at Eric expectantly.

'Liz, this is my sister, Zeta.'

The breath I'd been holding on to escaped from my body like a valve being released. For a fleeting second there I'd thought... Well,

201

let's just say that the presence of a live-in girlfriend in Eric's life would have made me feel distinctly awkward, not to mention foolish, at that particular moment.

'Nice to meet you, Zeta,' I said enthusiastically. Zeta? She was far too old to have been named after Catherine Zeta Jones, and the family certainly didn't look Indian.

She came further into the kitchen and leaned against the counter. 'Liz,' she said. 'You didn't work in the bookshop, by any chance?'

'Yes – well, I used to—'

'I thought you were going to the shops,' said Eric.

'I am. Do you want anything?'

'We're out of tea bags.'

'Right. Won't be long.'

'Take your time.'

Zeta grinned at Eric, then at me. 'Nice to meet you, Liz. Have fun, kids.' And she was gone.

'She seems nice,' I said.

'She is. Another beer?'

'No, thanks.' I'd only taken a couple of sips. Eric had made short work of his. Thirsty work, fixing up a car – and quite manly, as well.

He got a second can out of the fridge and remained standing. He seemed uneasy. As usual, small talk was out of the question.

'Look, Eric,' I said, 'I have a confession to make. I didn't really come here because of the book – well, I did, but that wasn't the only reason.'

The way he was staring at me made me babble a bit. 'The thing is, I need to go to Streedagh, and I wanted to ask your advice about it.'

He was still looking at me in a most unnerving way. I felt I had no option but to continue. 'I thought you might be able to tell me how to get there, and where to stay when I do actually make it there – that kind of thing…'

At last he spoke. 'How were you thinking of travelling?'

'I guess a train from Dublin to Sligo, and…I'm not sure after that.'

'Can you drive?'

'No.' I hung my head in shame: a woman of my advanced years, not able to drive… But there didn't seem to be any point in learning, in a city where a car was more of a hindrance than a help.

I was about to make some such excuse when Eric said, 'I'll take you there.'

'What?'

'I'll take you to Streedagh if you like.'

'How? You mean in that car outside?'

'What's wrong with it?'

'Well – no offence, but it's hardly greased lightning, is it?'

He laughed then for the first time. 'I will be putting the wheels back on, you know.'

'Fair enough. But do you really think it can make it as far as Sligo?'

'Sure. It'll be good for her, anyway, to get a nice long run.'

Men are forever saying things like that. It made no sense whatsoever to me; the heap of junk didn't look as if it could reach the end of the street. Still, if he thought it could make it to Sligo… 'That'd be great, Eric – if you have the time, of course.'

'I've plenty of time since I got the boot.' How could I have forgotten? 'How's next week?'

'Perfect.'

'I'll pick you up from your house Tuesday lunchtime.'

My work here was done.

28

The car that pulled up outside my house that Tuesday was barely recognisable. I think it was the wheels that did it. It was considerably cleaner, too; it turned out to be light green, rather than dark.

I was still making last-minute preparations in the bathroom when I heard a car horn being beeped twice. I ran over to the landing window and looked out onto the street below. Sure enough, there Eric was, bang on time. He was leaning casually against the side of the car, one foot on the pavement, the other up against the back wheel. He was wearing a dark-blue baseball cap pulled down low over his eyes. If he was trying to look cool, he was doing beautifully. I felt a thrill of excitement. I was going on a road trip, just like Thelma and Louise – except that neither of us was wearing a headscarf, and hopefully we wouldn't end up driving off the side of a cliff. And Eric was a man.

I'd had difficulty packing, primarily because we hadn't actually discussed how long we'd be away. Ridiculous as it sounds, I didn't even know if we were staying overnight or not. I'd asked Graham how long it took to drive from Dublin to Sligo, and he'd told me four hours. We were hardly going to drive there, look at the beach for five minutes and drive straight back again – although anything was possible when it came to Eric. And you could be sure that I wouldn't be the first to bring it up.

So down the stairs and straight out the front door I bounded, my overnight bag – which was trying very hard not to look like an overnight bag – slung across my shoulder. Thankfully, no other members of the household were around and I was able to make a quick getaway.

'Hi, Eric,' I said breezily, closing the front gate behind me in an effort to prevent errant terriers from pissing all over my mother's lupins. I couldn't see his eyes at first, shaded as they were by the peak of his baseball cap; but then he took it off and I saw that they were smiling, deep-set and light blue, the colour of the sky.

He took my bag from me. 'Jesus. What've you got in here? Gold bars?'

'Just a few essentials.' (Beauty products. Don't leave home without them.)

He threw the bag in the boot and climbed into the driver's seat. The interior of the car smelled of leather and the cleaning product formerly known as Jif. I sat there happily, my sunglasses perched on top of my head, in preparation for the sunshine that was sure to be on its way. As yet, the sun had done no more than play peek-a-boo with the clouds, but the day was still young.

Eric turned the key in the ignition – and, to my immense surprise and relief, the engine revved into action. The sound seemed to please Eric, too; he smiled at me like a proud father. I decided this car wasn't half bad after all. In fact, it was almost old enough to be vintage – like some of my outfits.

We were barely out of Phibsboro when Eric handed me something. It was a pear.

'What's this?' I said.

'It's a pear.'

'I know that. Why are you giving me a pear?'

'Because I know you like them. You used to eat them all the time in the stockroom. I was always fishing the cores out of the "paper only" bin. I could always tell when you'd been in there.'

'Oh. Thanks very much.'

As soon as I'd consumed the pear and wiped the juice from my hands, Eric handed me what appeared to be some type of booklet.

'What's this?'

'It's a map. You're going to be navigating.'

'I thought you'd been there before.'

'I have, but I've never driven before. You're going to have to help.'

'How did you get there the last time?'

'The university hired a minibus.'

I gave him a look.

'What's wrong?'

'Have you never read the book, *Why Men Don't Listen and Women Can't Read Maps*?'

'No. But I've unpacked it often enough.'

'Well, then. Need I say more?'

'Don't worry about it. I'll help.'

'Good.' I opened the map; I thought I should at least look as if I was making some kind of effort. It was the type that folds out into a gigantic sheet and is almost impossible to fold back up again. I was aware that Eric was watching me struggle, so I left it open on my lap in a nonchalant fashion.

It wasn't until Mullingar that Eric actually needed directions. 'Can you see what road we need to take out of the town?'

I felt some panic as I furrowed my brow and tried hard to look as if I was concentrating on the incomprehensible coloured lines and squiggles before me.

'Liz, why are you holding the map upside down?'

'I'm not – am I?'

Eric pulled the car over. 'Here. Let me have a look.'

Feeling vaguely humiliated, I handed him the map and crossed my arms sulkily.

'Yes, I think we're going the right way. Here.' He thrust the map back at me. 'I might need your help again soon, so keep it open.' As if I had any choice. I'd have had a better chance of completing all the sides of a Rubik cube than of folding that map again.

A few minutes later we were zooming along a wide national road, doing about eighty. The day had turned out bright and breezy, and I'd put my sunglasses on and wound the window right down. The wind was whipping through my hair, catching my breath and making me feel exhilarated.

Then the unimaginable happened. A massive gust of wind wrenched the map from my hands and whipped it right out of the car window. I twisted around in my seat and watched in horror as the map took flight, like a whirling dervish, and landed squarely on the windscreen of the car behind us.

'Ohmigod!' I gasped, and clamped my hands over my mouth. I looked, wild-eyed, at Eric, expecting him to be angry with me – but no: he was shaking with laughter. He was laughing so hard that he had to pull over.

The driver behind us, who had somehow managed to dislodge the map – who knew where it was headed now? – sounded his horn angrily as he overtook us.

'Save it for your wife!' Eric shouted after him, before dissolving into laughter once again. It was infectious. It was a good couple of minutes before either of us had the capacity to speak again.

'What are we going to do now?' I finally said.

Eric grinned at me. 'Maybe we should just follow the road signs.'

'Do you hear a rattling sound?' Eric asked me.

'For the third time, no, I don't.'

I didn't claim to know much about cars, but I did know

something about the men who drove them. They were *always* hearing imaginary rattles in their beloved rust-buckets. Graham and George were both exactly the same.

We were in Longford. In fact, we had been in Longford for a suspiciously long time.

'Eric,' I said, 'are we lost?'

'No.'

'Then why have we just gone past the same McDonald's for the second time?'

'We haven't. All McDonald's look alike, that's all.'

'But, Eric, the same family is sitting in the window.'

He didn't say anything.

After a couple more minutes, I suggested, 'Why don't we ask that man for directions?'

'We don't need to. We're not lost.'

'If you say so.'

This was getting ridiculous. If only I'd known him a bit better, I wouldn't have had to be so polite. But it turned out that our lack of direction was the least of our problems.

'Do I smell burning?' I looked at him in alarm.

'You do. I didn't like to tell you before, but we're having a slight mechanical problem.'

'What sort of a problem?'

'The brakes have gone.'

'What?' I shrieked, gripping the dashboard. 'Stop the car!'

Eric *laughed*. 'I'd love to, but the brakes have gone.'

'Shit. What are we going to do?'

'Don't panic. They've been gone for the last ten miles or so. I'm just circling while I come up with a plan.'

'Ring the AA. They'll know what to do.'

He didn't say anything.

208

'You are in the AA – aren't you?'

Again, he didn't answer. I took this to be a bad sign.

'How would you feel about staying in Longford for the night?' he asked me.

'Do we have a choice?'

'Not really.'

'Then I'd love to stay in Longford for the night.'

'Good. There's a B&B over there. How about it?'

'You mean the one with the pillars that we've passed four times already?'

'That's the one.'

'Eric, anything stationary looks wonderful to me right now.'

'OK, then. The next time we pass it, I'll slow right down and you can jump out.'

I whipped my head around to look at him. 'You *are* kidding.'

'Yes.'

'Bastard.'

Eric laughed – laughed! – again.

'Seriously,' I said. 'What are we going to do?'

'Leave it to me. I have an idea.'

And he swung into the driveway of the B&B. 'Oh, Christ!' I clapped my hands over my eyes and braced myself for the impact, but it never came. Instead, the car fizzled to a halt, accompanied by a large puff of smoke, like something out of a magic trick.

My legs nearly buckled under me when my feet touched terra firma. Our trip was turning out to be nearly as exciting as Thelma and Louise's after all.

As Eric handed me my now-very-definitely-overnight bag, I thanked God I'd brought all my lotions and potions (not to mention spare pairs of knickers). I felt the familiar excitement of staying overnight in a strange new place – even if it was the B&B that taste

209

forgot – intermingled with nervousness and an odd sense of displacement. I certainly hadn't expected to wind up here tonight.

Eric had opened the bonnet of the car and was peering into it anxiously.

'So,' I said. 'Break it to me gently. How long are we going to have to stay here? Couple of weeks?'

'Don't worry, I know how to fix it. This has happened before.'

'It's *what*?'

'Well, I didn't think it would happen this time.'

'Clearly not.'

Men were such idiots when it came to their cars. Even Eric the Enigma wasn't immune.

He slammed the bonnet back down, wiped his hands on his back pockets and rang the doorbell. There was a sliding glass porch door with a matching china dog on either side. *Granny would love it here,* I thought. *Would have loved it here.*

Then I thought, *He needn't assume we're sharing a room.*

The door opened to reveal a small, dumpy, floral woman.

'Hi, there. Would you happen to have two single rooms?' said Eric.

That was all right, then.

'You're in luck,' the floral woman said. 'I do. Come on in.'

Fancy that: such a tastefully designed establishment, and in Longford of all places, having rooms to spare. We stepped inside. Eric had to duck to avoid colliding with what I can only describe as a plastic chandelier that was hanging from the hall ceiling. Ducking must become a habit when you're that tall.

'What brings you to Longford?' the floral woman asked me. She had obviously guessed – correctly – that I was going to be the more forthcoming of the two of us.

'Car trouble, actually. We were on our way to Sligo.'

'Go 'way. That's terrible altogether. I have a brother who's a mechanic, living down the town. I'll give him a tinkle if you like.'

'That's all right,' said Eric. 'There won't be any need.'

Fucking eejit, I thought. I'd get the number off her when Eric was out of earshot.

'Right, so. I'm Freda, by the way.'

'Nice to meet you, Freda,' I said. 'I'm Liz.'

'This will be your room, Liz.' Freda opened the door on a floral explosion. 'And this will be yours…'

'Thanks.' I saw Eric recoil as she opened door number 7 for him, and I guessed that his décor must be similar to mine.

My duvet cover was seventies-inspired psychedelic floral, blue, yellow and white. I pulled it back to reveal matching sheets and pillowcases. The curtains, however, did not match, and neither did the carpet; this may have been a blessing in disguise. No TV, no tea- or coffee-making facilities. I unpacked in a desultory fashion. As soon as I heard Eric's door opening, I went out to the corridor.

'How's your room?' I said.

'Flowery.'

'Mine too. What'll we do now?'

'I don't know about you,' said Eric, 'but I have to fix the car.'

'How long will that take?'

'A few hours, tops.'

My face must have fallen.

'Why don't you go and explore the town?' he suggested.

I was sure I'd find many fascinating things to do and see. I was in Longford, after all.

'A few hours, tops,' my arse – or should I say my *numb* arse, after all the sitting around I did in what must have been every coffee shop in Longford. It was almost midnight by the time Eric had finished

211

fixing the car. ('Why don't you give Freda's brother a call?' 'There's no need. I can do it myself.') Dinner was a takeaway, consumed on the front doorstep of the B&B, a china dog behind each of us like an overly attentive waiter. Eric seemed glad of the company. But it was hardly my idea of eating out.

The death-trap did appear to be working again, however. The only remaining glitch seemed to be that the CD player was holding the Rolling Stones' *Forty Licks* CD for ransom and insisted on playing that song about not waiting for a lady, on a constant loop.

We set out at around eleven the next morning, after a hearty breakfast, which we ate to the accompaniment of the water feature in the breakfast room – I think it was meant to be a miniature version of the Trevi Fountain. The sunglasses perched on top of my head didn't seem quite so jaunty any more. I wouldn't be needing them for a while, by the looks of things. The grey sky weighed down upon us, oppressive and heavy, making me feel headachy.

We'd been driving in silence for a while when I sensed I was being looked at. I turned my head. Eric was glancing over at me.

'What?' I was immediately self-conscious.

'You look really nice.'

I reacted the way I normally reacted to a compliment: with total loss of self-control. I felt myself grow hot, and just managed to prevent myself from winding down the window. Then I remembered what I'd read about the correct way to receive compliments: just smile graciously and say, 'Thank you.' Good advice, which I chose to ignore.

'Don't be mad,' I said. 'I look a right state this morning.'

'Well, you are a bit dishevelled-looking; but, then again, you always are.'

He thought I looked dishevelled – *always* looked dishevelled. Hell, at least this was more my kind of compliment.

'You don't think very highly of yourself, do you?' he said.

'Are you surprised, with compliments like that?'

'Sorry. Maybe it came out wrong.'

'No. I'd say it came out exactly the way you meant it.' I was feigning indignation, but I wasn't really indignant.

There was an almighty rumble overhead, as if a giant dog was growling in the sky.

'What was that?' I said.

'Thunder.'

Before long, lightning joined it. The car crawled along, windscreen wipers working overtime.

'Don't worry,' said Eric. 'The rubber in the tyres will insulate us from the shock if we get hit.'

'Lucky you put them back on again, then, isn't it?'

I wasn't worried, not remotely. If there was one thing I loved, it was a great big fuck-off electric storm. I loved the frisson, the sense of electricity in the air. It made me feel so alive.

It seemed that the car, however, liked wet conditions even less than it liked dry ones. We had to make frequent stops, to allow Eric to fiddle mysteriously under the bonnet. I did my bit – and showed admirable restraint – by managing not to criticise the clapped-out old banger. Love me, love my car; insult my car, insult me.

The result of all this stopping and starting was that it was late afternoon by the time we reached Sligo. The county greeted us with a sky of such brilliant azure that, if you looked heavenward, you could fantasise that you were in the Caribbean rather than the north-west of Ireland. But, weirdly enough, at that moment there was nowhere I would rather have been.

Everywhere you looked, Ben Bulben rose up out of the earth like a green colossus, different from every angle and endlessly fascinating. Every now and then, a cloud cast its shadow across the craggy surface and changed it anew. We rounded the corner of the mountain – the angle reminded me of the Flatiron building in New York – and headed towards the village of Grange.

Before long, we came to a bungalow with a bonfire burning in the front garden. I assumed that someone was burning garden debris, but when we came to another house with a fire blazing out front, and then a third, I realised there must be something more to it.

'What's with all the bonfires?'

'Midsummer's Eve,' said Eric. 'It's an ancient custom to light bonfires on this night. It goes back to pagan times.'

'I never heard of that before.'

'Oh, yes. It's a really big thing in Scandinavia. In the old days, they'd light the bonfires at the summer solstice to ward away evil spirits. Some people believe the custom was brought over here by the Vikings.'

You had to love those Vikings. And you had to love the custom – although, in my own head, I chose to imagine that the people had lit the bonfires for me. To welcome me back to my ancestral home.

29

This B&B was an improvement on the last. And where it was lacking, the view more than made up for it. The B&B was a bungalow – they were ubiquitous in these parts – slap bang on top of a hill, with landscaped gardens sweeping all the way up to the front door. The car spluttered to a grateful halt. We got out and took in the full magnificence of the stunning vista before us: first the gardens; then acres of lush, green vegetation; then the still, blue expanse of the sea; and, finally, the hazy mountains beyond.

'Good choice, Eric,' I said.

He inclined his head in acknowledgement. 'See that section of strand, just past the clump of trees?' He pointed to our right.

'Over there?'

'No. The second clump.'

He took my hand and adjusted its direction. The remnants of the electric storm still lingered in his fingertips.

'I see it, yes. What about it?'

'That's Streedagh Strand.'

I was so close, I could practically smell the ozone.

There must be a great big factory somewhere where they manufacture B&B landladies. For a split second, when this one opened the door, I thought Freda had followed us all the way from Longford. It wouldn't have been hard to get here before us.

'Would you have any spare rooms?' I said.

'I've the one room left,' she said. 'It's a twin, if that's any good to you.'

Eric and I looked at each other.

'What do you think?' I said.

'Fine with me, but I'll leave the decision up to you.'

I pretended to think about it. 'Well, I'm pretty tired, and the views are spectacular... We'll take it, please.'

'Right you are,' the landlady said. 'I'm Maura.'

'Pleased to meet you, Maura. I'm Tallulah Jones and this is my husband, Eric.'

'What brings you to Grange?'

'I'm doing some research on the history of the Spanish Armada in the area.'

'Oh. Are you a historian, then?'

'No, a novelist. I'm writing a book about it.'

Was I?

'A novelist! Really? I love to read. What are the names of your books? Maybe I've heard of them.'

I duly reeled off the titles of my books, and Maura looked at me blankly – something I had grown to expect. But she was a nice woman, and I could see her really wanting to have heard of them. She insisted on writing down the titles – probably more out of politeness than anything – and swore that she'd ask for them in her local bookshop.

'There's just one thing,' I said. 'I write under a pseudonym – Elizabeth Clancy.' Maura took this down.

She glanced at Eric from time to time as she led us to the room. 'Have you stayed here before?' she finally asked him.

'Yes. About eighteen months ago.'

'I thought so. You were with – someone different. Anyhow, here's your key. Breakfast is at nine sharp. Enjoy your stay.'

Maura left the room, and I sat down on the nearest bed.

'What did you say that for?' asked Eric.

'What?'

'Tallulah? Your *husband*?'

'Oh, that. So she'd think we were married, of course. They don't allow two people of the opposite sex to share a room in a B&B in Ireland unless they're married.'

'Who's "they"?'

'The Association of B&B Landladies, of course.'

'Of course.' He smiled and shook his head slightly.

'Is that not the case?'

'Maybe fifteen or twenty years ago, but not any more – not in this B&B, anyway.'

'Oh, yes. She said you'd been here before—'

'Let's go down to the strand while it's still bright,' Eric said.

Topic closed.

I couldn't believe I'd finally made it to Streedagh Strand, where it had all begun – where the founder of my particular dynasty had crawled, half drowned, onto the inhospitable shores of Sligo, in the shadow of Ben Bulben and the gunman. I pictured him wriggling on his belly, dodging the bullets fired by the English soldiers who lay in wait for the survivors, only to be beaten and stripped naked by the Irish of a thousand welcomes. *Céad míle fáilte*, lads. You'll hardly be needing those trousers any more, sure you won't.

Strolling along the strand that evening, it was hard to imagine that the beach had ever been the site of unimaginable carnage, that hundreds of Spanish soldiers and sailors had lain dying there. The evening was mild and clear. The tide was out, revealing acres of pale golden sand. Several old men sat in their cars, overlooking the sea and reading their newspapers. Why did they do that? Why did they never get out?

The beach was sparsely populated. There was a man with a horse and drey cart, and a family with three young children and a demented dog – he came up to me and Eric, at one stage, and rolled ecstatically on the body of a dead seagull – and there was us. We took off our shoes, rolled up our trouser legs and walked along the edge of the Atlantic.

Eric didn't say much, and I was grateful for this. I was concentrating. I was trying to visualise that day, back in September 1588, when a ferocious storm blew up and dashed three Spanish galleons against the black rocks of Streedagh Strand, pummelling them and the hapless Spaniards on board into oblivion. I looked back at the dunes, sparsely covered with bits of coarse grass, like so many balding heads. I imagined the English soldiers and their muskets hiding there, and I was overcome by a terrible wave of sadness, far more overwhelming than any of the waves that lapped against the shore. I felt my eyes fill with salt water, and I squatted down at the water's edge in an effort to hide it. I stayed like that for a couple of minutes, ankle-deep, picking up handfuls of underwater sand and letting it trickle back through my fingers again. When I eventually stood up, Eric took me by the hand and led me back to the car.

On our journey back, I stared out my window and attempted to memorise every stone and blade of grass along the way, so I could take it all back to Granny. The yellow flag irises in the marshy fields; the foxgloves, elderflower and ox-eye daisies in the hedgerows; and everywhere the sycamore and the ash. That tree over there – had it been a sapling in 1588? Had my Spanish ancestor sought shelter under its branches, naked and shivering, on his way to the Castle of McClancy at Rossclogher, where he was later to impregnate one of the Clancy women? Did he tell fortunes to the women of the clan, like his fellow survivor Captain Francisco de Cuellar, whose story Granny had given me?

After a while, it occurred to me that we were no longer travelling in the direction of the B&B.

'Where are we going?' I asked.

'I'm taking you out for dinner,' Eric said.

'There's no need.'

'There's every need. To thank you for your patience last night – it can't have been much fun for you – and to apologise on behalf of my car.'

I laughed. 'I think you should make your car apologise for itself.'

'She would if she could.'

'Do you have to call it "she"?'

'Sorry. See, there I go again, apologising.'

We smiled at each other. My sadness had passed, and I felt suddenly happy – renewed, or something.

'We're going to this great seafood restaurant I know in a place called Mullaghmore. You do like seafood, don't you?' Eric looked suddenly very worried.

'Oh, yes. I love seafood.' I see food, I eat it. 'Have you eaten there many times?' I asked innocently.

'Just the once.'

I see. No doubt with the mysterious person with whom he'd stayed in the B&B. I was going to have to get to the bottom of that one.

30

I lied. I didn't like seafood at all. It was just that Eric had seemed so enthusiastic about the restaurant, like it was a great treat. Fish was all right, I supposed; but all that shellfish – salty, squidgy stuff – and anything with tentacles... Most of it didn't even look like food. I didn't know if it tasted like food, because I'd never had the nerve to try it. You wouldn't catch me sliding one of those oyster yokes down my throat. Fish fingers were OK; they didn't look like fish, what with being square and psychedelic orange. I wondered if the restaurant had fish fingers on the menu...

It didn't. I ordered Thai fish cakes (round, didn't look much like fish, disguised by much sauce and salad) for the starter, and for the main course the John Dory – whatever the hell that was. It certainly sounded reassuringly normal; you couldn't go wrong with a name like John. I fervently hoped that the desserts wouldn't involve fish in any form. Eric ordered a bowl of mussels to start with and a whole lobster for the main course. I watched in fascination at the practised ease with which he polished off the mussels, one by one, like a true connoisseur.

As we waited for our main courses, I watched plates of food being carried to the other tables. My interest turned to abject fear as the man at the next table received an entire creature – intact, head and all, glassy eye gazing forever upwards. I swallowed. I was no veggie, but that didn't mean I liked the poor unfortunate animal to look at me while I ate it. There was no way I would be able to convince Eric I was enjoying my food if it came out with a face.

'I'm just going to the toilet,' I said.

I disappeared around the corner and apprehended our waitress. 'Excuse me. I've ordered the John Dory. Could you please ask the chef – no offence meant to him, or her – to take the head off before you bring it to the table, if you don't mind?'

'Don't worry,' said the young waitress kindly, placing her hand on my arm. 'They remove the head before they cook it.'

'Oh, thank God for that. Thank you. Thank you very much.' What an eejit. I'd shown myself up as a food philistine for no good reason.

I went to the loo, to make my excuse look convincing. Once inside the ladies', I exhaled deeply and leant heavily against the counter in front of the mirror. I looked hard at myself. Was that really me? My eyes were glowing with an almost unnatural light. I'd have to lay off the wine a little. I re-applied my red lipstick; it brought up my tan and made my teeth look whiter. I ran a brush through my hair, more times than I really needed to; it was soothing. As a finishing touch, I dabbed Opium on my bare wrists and behind my earlobes. I was stuck in a perfume rut, as well as everything else.

I peered more closely at myself. Was it just my imagination, or did Eric like me? He was treating me to dinner – and he had offered to bring me to Sligo in the first place. It couldn't have been only to give the car a good long run – could it? I was so unsure of myself these days. And Eric was the lead singer of a band; he could have had any number of dreadlocked, multi-pierced young ones. I was five years older than him, for pity's sake. But we were sharing a room tonight – albeit a room with two separate beds... Would they stay separate?

I returned to the table before I drove myself mad. As I sat down, the main courses arrived. My kindly waitress winked at me as she laid the headless John Dory before me. I tried not to show my disgust at the giant, pink, fleshy sea-insect that she placed in front of Eric. He began to attack it, with the aid of many strange instruments. You shouldn't need so many tools to eat your dinner; it isn't natural.

I regarded my fish. The head might have been gone, but the tail and ribcage remained. I began to dissect it respectfully, as if I were carrying out a post-mortem.

'Here. Let me,' said Eric. He gently took the cutlery from my hands and cut the tail and the fin away from John Dory's body. (Would I have felt less guilty if it had had a less human name?) Then he removed all the visible bones.

'There. Is that better?' He handed me back my knife and fork and covered the discarded fishy remains with a giant lettuce leaf, as if he were burying them. I found this oddly touching.

'You're not a fishmonger, are you?' I said. 'As well as a student, a tutor, a rock star and an ex-bookshop employee?'

He laughed. 'No. I just love my seafood.'

He certainly did. I watched as he polished off his lobster with consummate professionalism – almost as if he were a sea creature himself.

'Here,' he said. 'You try some.'

He held a soft, pink piece of flesh to my lips. I took it, my lower lip brushing his thumb.

'Nice – isn't it?'

'Yes, it is.'

Eric went back to eating, his fingers dripping with butter. It came to me that eating in a seafood restaurant was, possibly, more romantic than dining at a normal restaurant. It was more tactile – picking up the food and eating it with your bare hands – and the meat from the sea was softer and more delicate, somehow. Or maybe it was just me, and the night that was in it.

The crème brulée more than made up for the tribulations of my main course. Eric didn't have dessert; he just watched me as I ate mine, nibbling from the outside in, savouring every tiny mouthful, letting it melt on my tongue. I'd never had a meal that was so much like foreplay. But would there be any afterplay?

'What do you want to do now?' Eric asked me as we stood outside the restaurant. The sun had gone down, but the evening was still clear and bright. I put on my cardigan for the first time that day. 'Drink?' he suggested.

'You know what I'd really like to do?' I said slowly, carefully.

'What?'

'Go back to Streedagh.'

'Walk along the strand again?'

'No. Not exactly.' He was looking at me expectantly. This was awkward. 'The thing is...' I began. 'Have you ever heard of ancestral healing?'

'Yes.'

'Have you really?'

'Yes.' He was so knowledgeable. My – whatever he was. 'What about it?'

'I wanted to try it out. On the strand. For my Spanish ancestor.'

Now he'd really think I was nuts. He sat on the wall overlooking the harbour and I waited for him to speak, for what seemed like a really long time.

Finally he looked up at me. 'Will you need candles?'

'I beg your pardon?'

'Candles. Zeta's always doing that kind of thing – spells, shit like that – and she always lights a ton of candles.'

'Well, I hadn't really thought about it...'

'There's a Spar in the village. They might have night-lights.'

'OK, then. If you're sure you don't mind.'

'Why would I mind?'

'You'd probably prefer to go for a pint.'

'I can do that any night of the week.'

True. Whereas ancestral healing…well, that was something of a rarity.

Tragically, the local Spar was all out of night-lights. I liked to imagine that, all around Sligo that night, people were indulging in their own private pagan rituals. I wasn't that bothered, but Eric looked bitterly disappointed. Then his expression brightened.

'I know,' he said. 'I'll build you a bonfire.'

'Eric, there's no need—'

'Come on. It'll be fun. For the night that's in it. That's what they do in Denmark: build bonfires on the beach.'

'Eric…no offence, but this is something I wanted to do on my own.'

'Oh, I know. Don't worry. I'll totally respect your privacy. I'll build you a fire; then I'll go and wait for you in the car.'

'You don't have to wait for me.'

'I'm not leaving you on your own on a beach at night.'

'OK. Thanks. Only you have to promise not to look. I won't be able to do it properly if I think I'm being watched.'

So we got back in the car and drove to Streedagh strand. I had all the requisite equipment in my bag: the copy of the family tree, the crystal pendulum, and the notebook into which I had transcribed the ancestral-healing instructions from my laptop. I was good to go.

It was still bright when we got there, but the old men had folded up their newspapers and driven home, without ever feeling the sand between their arthritic toes. Unfortunately, a gang of youths (as in

224

'Gang of Youths Had Fight Outside Local Chipper and Appeared in District Court on Monday Morning') had decided to have a cider party right in the centre of the strand.

'Oh, for Christ's sake. There's no way I'm doing it now.' I turned angrily and stomped – no mean feat on a sandy surface – back to the car.

Eric followed me. 'You know,' he said, 'I do know of another place, if you're interested.'

'Go on.'

'It's a little cove not far from here. It's still part of the same beach, really.'

'Lead the way.'

It was the little cove that time forgot. It would have looked the same, I remember thinking, whether it had been 1588, 1888 or 2088. It was a little horseshoe-shaped beach, the same light-golden sand as at Streedagh. Large pebbles in varying shades of grey congregated in groups at the shoreline, worn perfectly spherical by the persistent waves and the passage of time. Fronds of bladder-wrack floated on the tide, and the surrounding sand dunes lent the cove a secluded air.

I watched Eric collecting twigs and pieces of driftwood. I'd offered to help, but he'd insisted that I should instead prepare myself for 'the ceremony'. Since I had no idea what such preparation would entail, I took off my sandals and walked along the verge of the Atlantic Ocean. Surely it would be beneficial to get in touch with the elements. Its iciness put paid to my Caribbean fantasies. Still…who needed the Caribbean when you had this?

Eric finished constructing his little pyre and lit it. I don't know where he got the matches.

'Right,' he said. 'You know where I am if you need me. Good luck.'

'Thanks.'

He really was taking this incredibly seriously.

I waited until his entire form had disappeared beyond the sand dunes. I was alone, on a beach in County Sligo, on midsummer night. What would be my dream?

I sat cross-legged a short distance from the fire. I laid my notebook and my pendulum beside me, and I spread my family tree out before me. There I was: a late addition, right at the tip of the nearest branch.

I tried to relax – to become aware of my body, to connect to my spiritual self. I attempted to recall ancient, long-abandoned yoga classes. Sadly, the only thing I could remember was how bad I was at meditation. Concentrating on my breathing merely made me hyperventilate. I calmed myself down again and began counting my breaths. This seemed to work.

Then I tried to imagine a golden light shining on the family tree. I tried to shine it on my ancestor, tell him I had come to heal his trauma at long last.

Nothing.

I tried again. I meditated so hard that I almost cracked a rib. But could I visualise so much as a speck of golden light? Could I heck. In desperation, I picked up the crystal pendulum. It couldn't hurt. I held it aloft over the family tree, not expecting anything much and beginning to feel quite stupid.

But then it began to move – all by itself. *What the...?* The pendulum swung in ever-widening arcs. Before long, it became obvious that it was moving in the direction of the Spaniard... But no, hold on – not the Spaniard: Mary McClancy, the woman he had knocked up. It was definitely focusing on her. Well, what did you know? No wonder it hadn't worked before. I'd been focusing on the wrong ancestor.

Of course she needed my healing energy. He'd fecked off back to Spain and left her holding the dark-skinned, dark-eyed baby. And in those days they didn't even have the mickey money to ease the pain.

All right, Mary. Here goes.

Focusing as hard as I possibly could, I tried to sense what Mary needed me to heal. Then I sent her out all the healing energy I could muster up. Then I imagined the new healing pattern flowing from my ancestor to me – whatever that meant – and I saw our energies intertwining. It really did feel as if I was making some weird connection with her, although I couldn't describe the feeling, not even to myself.

When it was all over, I thanked Mary McClancy and opened my eyes. I blinked several times. The bonfire was still blazing away, as before, but the sky had darkened considerably. There was, however, still a bright turquoise streak on the horizon.

I stood up and brushed the sand from my skirt. I was glad it was the longest day of the year. I wanted it to last forever.

31

At first I thought Eric was asleep, but when I tapped gently on the side window, his eyes opened instantly. He wound the window down. 'Finished?'

'Yes.'

'How did it go?'

'Well, I think. Yes, very well.'

'I'm glad.'

I moved aside to let him get out of the car. 'What do you want to do now?' My question rose and expanded until it filled the air above our heads.

'Well, it seems like a shame to waste a good bonfire.'

I walked back down to the cove, sandals in my hand, heart in my mouth. Eric followed, bearing a guitar that he'd got out of the boot and a six-pack he'd got from goodness knows where. We were like the lads on Streedagh Strand with their cider party.

I sat back down beside the dwindling flames and watched Eric as he collected more driftwood. I knew by now that I wasn't expected to help. He returned and re-kindled the flames.

'What's with the guitar?' I said, more out of nervousness than anything else.

He smiled, picked up the instrument and strummed gently. 'I'm going to serenade you.'

'Isn't that a Spanish word?' I said. I was starting to babble again. 'Is it?'

'I don't know. It sounds Spanish, though, doesn't it?'

'I suppose it does. Like señorita.'

'Fernando.'

'Is that a request?' Eric raised one eyebrow.

'What? Oh. No. Well, play it if you like.'

'You're all right. I don't really like Abba.'

'You don't like Abba? Everyone likes Abba.'

'What would you like me to play for you?'

'I don't know.' I thought for a moment. 'Something – apt.'

'Something apt.' Eric considered this, still strumming, a faraway expression on his face. A stray gust of wind blew across the beach, causing the smoke from the fire to veer sideways and causing me to draw my cardigan tighter across my shoulders.

Then Eric began to sing 'Wuthering Heights' – one of my all-time favourite songs, but one I wouldn't have considered requesting in a zillion years. It was strange to hear a man sing that song, with nothing to accompany him but the waves and an acoustic guitar. The combined effect of the song, the location – yielding sand, clear night sky, crisp breeze, waves rolling over one another – and the company was quite overwhelming. My emotions were already frazzled, on account of my stint of ancestral healing – but this, this song… I was mesmerized, intoxicated, as I listened to this man singing words that were so full of longing, words about a passion that had endured even beyond the grave. I wondered whether that was why he'd picked this song. Or had the sudden gust merely reminded him of windswept moors?

Inevitably, the song ended. I wasn't sure what to do. A round of applause seemed inappropriate.

'That was beautiful,' I said at last. And, to diffuse the tension that I felt growing between us: 'I'd definitely buy your CD.'

His lips curved upward. 'Funny you should mention that. I have a few copies of my new CD in the back of the car.'

'So all this has been a gigantic sales ploy?'

'No.' He started strumming again, saving me from having to answer.

He seemed to go off into his own world for a little while, just him and his guitar. I didn't mind at first; but, after a few minutes, I felt anxious to pull him back into mine.

'So tell me more about this tradition of burning fires at midsummer,' I said.

'It dates all the way back to Neolithic times. The summer solstice was considered to be sacred. Then, later on, people built bonfires to protect themselves against the evil spirits they believed roamed free on midsummer night – witches on their way to meetings with other witches, shit like that.' He didn't sound as if he thought it was shit.

'And you said that the Scandinavians still celebrate it?'

'Yes, they do. In Denmark they've celebrated the summer solstice since the time of the Vikings. They have bonfires on the beach, for instance.'

'Like this?' I nodded at our little bonfire.

'Just like this.'

'What else?'

'Well, in Sweden they dance around a maypole. Traditionally it's a fertility ritual. Single men and women drink, dance and... procreate.'

'Really?'

'Yes.'

'Would you like another beer?'

'Don't mind if I do.'

Eric was an intriguing man. He knew so much about so much. But it wasn't really his extensive knowledge of historical custom that I was interested in.

He started to play his guitar in what I now knew to be flamenco style. A horrible image of my naked self, running down that hotel corridor, flashed in front of my mind's eye. Determined to banish this picture forever, I got up and started to dance.

My bare feet stirred up the sand, and the fire crackled and popped. The music, the fire and the night sky transformed me into a raven-haired temptress with a flaming red dress, clicking my imaginary castanets and dancing around the gypsy campfire. In a strange way, I felt as if I'd been born for this moment, as if my whole life had been leading up to it, like a wave gathering force as it went. I was part of that beach, part of the music, part of that very night – and Eric was part of it, too. As his playing became more frenzied, so did my dancing – until the final crescendo, when I collapsed onto my knees into the sand. I threw my head back and laughed, acutely aware of the sensation of my hair cascading back over my bare shoulders – my cardigan having long since fallen to the sand.

Eric stood up. I raised my eyes to his. I felt like a tiny, insignificant dot, sitting there in the sand, almost as small as a grain of the sand itself in comparison to his hulking frame.

'Do you know what else the Vikings used to do on midsummer's eve?' he said.

'No.'

'They swam naked in the sea.'

He held out his hand. I took it without hesitation, and he pulled me to my feet with apparent lack of effort. Without another word, he walked me to the water's edge. He let go of my hand and pulled his top over his head; then off came his trousers, then the rest. I heard the sharp intake of breath as he took his first step into the sea. Undeterred, he kept going, until he was thigh-deep in the water. Only then did he turn back to me.

'Come on!' he called.

'I don't know. It must be freezing in there.'

'It isn't.'

I could tell he was lying by the look of what Danielle Steele might have called his throbbing manhood. I was trying not to look, but it was proving almost impossible.

Eric shrugged, turned his back to me and waded further into the sea, until he was far enough to dive right in. I watched, fascinated, as his head disappeared intermittently, only to reappear several seconds later in a new location. With his hair slicked back and darkened by wetness, he reminded me of a seal. I thought, for the first time in many years, of the ancient Irish belief that seals were the souls of drowned fishermen.

I looked around nervously. There was nobody around; or, if there was, I couldn't see them. And they'd have difficulty seeing me – as would Eric. The dark could be quite flattering. Part of me didn't want to go in. I was afraid. But I was even more afraid that, if I didn't take the plunge, I'd ruin the whole night – and I was damned if I was going to let that happen.

Before I could think myself out of it, I tore the clothes from my body, leaving them in a little warm heap on the cold sand, and walked into the waves. Bloody hell, it was cold. Following Eric's lead, I waded in. The desire to cover up my private parts was quite a large incentive. Soon enough, I was waist-deep in the water and all but numb from the waist down. Did I mention it was cold? At least it made the breasts look pert and the nipples nice and erect – which was good, because Eric was watching me now, submerged apart from his head, neck and shoulders. He smiled and held out his arms.

'I can't,' I shouted. 'I'll be out of my depth, and I'm not a good swimmer.'

'Don't worry,' he shouted back. 'I am.' He stretched out his arms again.

Here goes. I lunged forward, then experienced a moment of pure, blind panic when I could no longer feel the sea bed beneath my feet. Just as this feeling threatened to overwhelm me, something warm and strong enveloped me and pulled me towards it, and I found myself encircled in Eric's arms. He was grinning at me. He looked the same yet strangely different, with his hair plastered dark and close on his head.

'Are you all right?' I heard him say.

'Yes, but cold,' I replied.

'You need to put your head underwater.'

I stared at him. 'You must be joking.'

'I'm serious. You'll feel warm if you do that.'

'Promise?'

'Promise.'

'OK, then.' I took a massive breath and ducked my head right in, and everything went dark and quiet. I emerged seconds later coughing and spluttering and spitting out water. I hated getting my face wet. Truth be told, I'd never been this far out in the sea before. Even in the local swimming pool, I was a shallow-end dweller, splashing about for the sake of it and getting out before the full hour was up. But this was different.

I recovered my composure and smoothed my hair back away from my forehead.

'Is that better?' Eric asked.

I laughed. 'I'm not sure yet.'

'You can wrap your legs around my waist if you like.'

I like.

I was no longer numb from the waist down. And then he was kissing me – or was it me who was kissing him? Either way, I was experiencing the kiss that reached the places that other kisses could not reach, had never reached before. I didn't know if it was Eric or the sea or the night that was in it, but it was definitely something.

We certainly frightened all the little fishies that night. And when it was all over – half an hour, an hour later – we emerged out of the sea hand in hand, like the man from Atlantis and his missus. We shook out our clothes and dressed rapidly, our skin still damp underneath. I huddled beside the dying embers of the fire, reluctant to leave this hallowed place.

'Come on,' said Eric, pulling me to my feet. 'Let's go back. You'll catch your death.' Now he was worried.

But before we left, he took a charred stick of wood out of the fire and drew a huge love-heart in the sand. Then he wrote inside it, 'Eric and Tallulah forever.'

That night we pushed the two single beds together. Some hours later, I lay wide awake, listening to Eric breathing, thinking how it was the most comforting, happiness-inducing sound in the world. After a while, I carefully – so as not to wake him – untangled my limbs from his. I was no longer cold.

I looked back at him lying there. He slept with his arms stretched right out, like a starfish – the most vulnerable position there is; afraid of nothing. I had always slept with my arms hugged into my chest, covers pulled up past my ears, needing to feel cosy and secure. That was probably why I couldn't swim – and why he swam like a fish, a starfish; free-floating.

As silently as I could, I took my notebook out of my bag. It may have been Eric, it may have been the ancestral healing; but, whatever it was, I started to write. And write. I didn't stop until the next morning, when Maura knocked on the door to warn us that breakfast was imminent.

234

32

Eric pulled me back into his warmth. I couldn't have been happier if someone had offered me a six-figure book deal and a Mercedes Benz. I had my man – and I had the first three chapters of my next novel. Was it the sex or the ancestral healing? Whatever it was, the curse of the writer's block had been lifted from my head.

Eric was kissing the dip between my shoulder and neck, the soft bit just above the clavicle. He mumbled something into my flesh.

'What was that?' I said.

'I knew you'd taste like this.'

'Like what?'

'All spicy. Like oranges and cinnamon.'

I smiled and hugged myself inwardly, while Eric hugged me outwardly. And I wasn't even wearing any perfume; the Opium would have been washed away hours ago.

'We'd better get up,' I said. 'It's nearly time for breakfast.'

'So?' His voice was muffled in my neck again.

'So Maura will be annoyed.'

'Who's Maura?'

'The B&B lady.'

'Oh, her.'

'Come on. You must be starved after last night. What do you feel like eating?'

'Cinnamon and oranges.'

I'll admit it was a leading question.

One melty, chocolaty orgasm later, neither of us gave a toss about Maura's feelings – nor, indeed, about rashers and sausages. But when she rapped on the door for the third time, harder than before, we got up. Unshowered – I was reluctant to wash away Eric and the beach – we made our way into the breakfast room, which was the inevitable conservatory with indoor fountain and artificial flowers. We sat across the table from each other and grinned. Eric's hair was all mussed up and he had his T-shirt on inside out. I was in a similar state of disarray.

'Did you have a good sleep?' Maura asked pointedly, whacking the plates down on the table in front of us, just like my mother did when she was pissed off with me. We were the only people in the breakfast room; no doubt all the other lodgers had risen and eaten their breakfasts at the allotted time. My sausages were a little burnt, but there was no way I was sending them back. What cared I for food, anyway? Who needed it at a time like this?

Eric did, clearly. He was milling into his food as if it were his last supper. 'Are you going to eat those sausages?' he asked me.

'No. Work away.'

He speared them up with his fork and began munching them with great gusto.

Maura reappeared. 'More toast?'

'No, thanks,' I said.

'Yes, please,' said Eric.

Maura smiled as if to say, *I like to see a man with a healthy appetite.* 'I have a son just like you,' she said. 'He's a bottomless pit – I could never fill him – and there's not a pick on him, either. You must put it all in those great big long legs of yours. I remember now, you were like this the last time too. Tell you what: I've a few rashers left over. Would you like them?'

'That'd be great, thanks.'

Maura went off, all delighted with herself. *Oh, yes,* I thought. *The last time he was here.*

'So,' I said, 'when did you say you stayed here before?'

'About a year and a half ago.'

'With whom?'

'The woman I was seeing at the time.'

Now we were getting somewhere.

'Your girlfriend?'

'It was a bit more complicated. She was one of the college lecturers.'

I waited for him to continue, but he didn't.

'Very Mrs Robinson,' I said – urged.

Eric shrugged. 'She was separated at the time, but she ended up getting back with her husband.'

'That must have been hard on you.'

'It was. Very hard.' He was looking down at his plate, so I couldn't see his expression.

'Was she much – older than you?'

'Not really. She was only in her thirties.'

Yes. That was really very young indeed. 'So you like older women, then.'

This time Eric looked up. He smiled and waggled his eyebrows up and down. 'Depends on the older woman.'

He caught my knees between his, under the table, and gave them a squeeze. This small gesture alone made me feel so happy that I was fit to burst. Never mind the college lecturer; he was with me now. (I could get the skinny on her at a later date.)

'So,' I said, 'we don't have to head back to Dublin right away – do we?'

'Well, I kind of have to.'

'Why?'

'I'm going to Hamburg tomorrow.'

Hamburg? *Tomorrow?*

'Our manager has arranged some gigs for us over there.'

'Like the Beatles.'

He smiled. 'Just like the Beatles.'

Well, they had an equally stupid name, anyhow. 'How long will you be away?' I chased several cold mushrooms around the plate with my fork, in an effort to appear casual.

'Six weeks.'

'Six weeks!' I couldn't stop myself.

'It's not that long.'

Not that long? Anything could happen in six weeks. Goodness knows how many buxom, blonde Vikingettes (or was it Vikingesses?) he could meet in that time. And he looked so good on stage... They'd be flinging themselves and their bras at him. I knew all about what these rock bands got up to on tour. I was no fool. I'd seen *Almost Famous*. I was now well and truly down off my high.

Within an hour, we were showered and packed and ready to go. Eric carried the bags out to the car and I followed him, my feet dragging on the tarmac. At least we'd have the journey home together – another four hours or so of intimacy; and maybe we could stop off somewhere nice for lunch...

Eric turned the key in the ignition, and the car made a sound like a nasty cough. He turned the key again: the same sound. I looked at him, but he was concentrating hard. After several more failed attempts at lift-off, he popped the bonnet and hopped out of the car.

I got out as well, and began walking around the top of Maura's garden. I took in as much as I could of my last view of Streedagh strand.

After a few minutes, Eric came and stood beside me.

'What's the prognosis?' I asked.

'I'm afraid it's not looking good.'

'Major surgery required?'

'I don't think so. But it could take a while to get her up and running again. I'd better call a taxi to take you to the station, and you can get the train home.'

'What? Why? I don't mind waiting here with you.'

'It could take hours, Liz. You'd be bored out of your tree. And we're miles from anywhere; it's not as if you could walk into town. No, I'll get you a cab. Maura!' he shouted, heading back towards the house. *Shit*. This was not good, whatever way you looked at it.

When the cab arrived we stood awkwardly beside the open door, looking at each other. Eric took my face in his hands and gave me a kiss that made me feel a little bit better. I got into the back seat, slammed the door and wound down the window. Eric ducked his head down.

'I'll call you,' he said.

Famous last words.

I berated myself all the way from Sligo to Dublin. How could I have been so stupid? How? Surely I was old enough and ugly enough to know that, given the opportunity, most men would have sex with anything that moved. I couldn't believe I'd fallen for it again. After George, I'd sworn that I'd be smarter the next time around, but I never knew how to play these situations right, impeded as I was by excessive emotion. I'd been so sure Eric liked me, last night *and* this morning, but clearly he couldn't wait to get rid of me. It made no difference now, anyway: he was off to Germany, where he would be plied ceaselessly with cheap blond beer and cheap blonde groupies – and cheap blonde prostitutes. Oh, yes, I'd seen all the documentaries.

God, what an idiot I was. I should have suggested going over there for a weekend. In fact, *he* should have suggested it. The fact that he hadn't was further proof of his intention to be unfaithful – but unfaithful to what? I wasn't his girlfriend; I was just some woman with whom he'd had sex on a beach in Sligo – and on two single beds pushed together in a tawdry B&B. The journey home in the car would have been the proper time to sort all that stuff out. But here I was on a train, and Eric was miles away, trying to get that banger to work. And tomorrow – and for the next six weeks – he'd be even more miles away. Anything, absolutely anything, could happen in six weeks.

There was no doubt about it: a fool and her knickers are soon parted.

By the time I got home, I was tired and cranky. I sat down heavily on the front doorstep and searched my handbag for my keys. In a fit of temper, I emptied the contents of the bag out onto the ground. It was as if all the debris from every handbag I'd ever owned had gathered together into one gigantic mound. I began to sift through. An earring I'd been looking for, a hair-slide, enough loose change to open my own bank. A book token. Where had that come from? It wasn't even in euro; it was for thirty pounds, which made it years old. What a waste. I wondered if I could convert it... *Aha!* Keys.

My bunch of keys had grown quite voluminous over the years. I still had the keys from the bookshop, and the key to my locker in college – the college from which I'd graduated a decade earlier. There were several mystery keys in the mix, too; I was afraid to throw them out, in case they matched the lock to something really important (a secret garden, perhaps).

As I shovelled everything back into my handbag, the front door opened.

'Hello.' My mother stood there, smiling at me. 'You must be exhausted. Let me help you with your bag.'

I followed her into the kitchen, pleasantly bemused. Jim was already in there, milling into what looked like a quadruple-decker sandwich.

'You're not back, are you?' he said, his mouth full, starting to leave.

For some reason – maybe I was overtired and overwrought – this really got to me. The rage spurted up inside me and out of my mouth.

'You know what?' I yelled. 'I'm part of this family too! I have just as much right to be here as you do.'

Jim turned on his way out the door and stared at me; his mouth opened in surprise, revealing half-masticated morsels of ham, crisp and ketchup. Then, wisely, he retreated upstairs.

I expected my mother to give out to me for speaking to my little brother that way, but instead she said, 'Sit yourself down there and I'll heat up a bit of dinner for you. You must be hungry after your journey.'

'Yes, I am. That'd be great. Thanks. Just let me ring Auntie Kit first and find out how Granny is.'

'I'm only after ringing.'

'Are you?' I said, startled. 'How is she?'

'No change. If you like, I'll drive you over there tonight.'

'That'd be brilliant. Thanks a lot.'

'No problem.'

Mam placed the food before me, and I started to eat. This was nice – very nice. And the food wasn't bad, either.

'Oh, I almost forgot,' Mam said. 'This came for you yesterday.'

She handed me a package. It was a small, brown jiffy bag with a Dublin postal code. What could it be? I wasn't expecting anything.

I tore it open. There was nothing inside except something very small wrapped up in a piece of white tissue paper – and a compliments slip from the hotel in which I'd had my dalliance with Carlos and his band. All it said was, 'Found behind the bed in room 301.' The signature was illegible.

My mother read the note over my shoulder. 'When did you ever stay there?' she asked.

'Oh, it was ages ago.'

I brushed her question away and excitedly tore open the tissue paper. The locket fell onto the table with a clank. I picked it up and examined it. It seemed OK on the outside. I opened it up: everything perfect on the inside, too.

'What's that?' said my mother, peering down. 'I never saw that before.'

I had always been careful to keep it hidden. I handed it to her. She looked at it for some time, stroking both sides of the broken love-heart with her thumb, before handing it back to me.

'It's lovely,' she said. 'And very nice of the hotel to send it back to you.'

Yes, it was. But, personally, I felt that Mary McClancy should get the credit.

33

One small box of toilet rolls had made its way back into Kit and Granny's hallway. I interpreted this as a good sign, an indication that things were returning to normal. An alien car was parked outside. At first I assumed that it belonged to a friend or well-wisher, but no: my two aunties had arrived from Australia. This I interpreted as a bad sign.

Kit looked relieved to see us. 'Reenie's here,' she whispered, as she all but pulled us in. I witnessed my mother draw to a halt for a second or two and take a deep breath, as if rallying her resources.

Two middle-aged women who had to be relatives were sitting in the good room. One of them had hair identical to Kit's – improbably black and drawn back into a severe bun. The other had short hair, which had been allowed to grey naturally.

Black Bun was the first to speak. 'Well, Róisín Madigan, as I live and breathe.' Madigan was my mother's maiden name. 'And this must be Elizabeth. By God, she's the spit of Auntie Aggie, all right. God bless us and save us, it's uncanny – isn't it, Stacia?'

Stacia merely nodded and smiled at me.

Reenie had this in common with her brother: the thirty-odd years that she had spent in Melbourne hadn't taken so much as the edge off her Dublin accent. It was almost as if she'd been secretly hiding out on Clanbrassil Street all this time. 'Well, Róisín,' she continued, 'I'd know you anywhere. The years have been kind to you.'

'And to you, Reenie.'

This was a big, fat lie – unless Reenie had resembled a shrivelled-up old prune in her twenties. She had the worst case of Australian woman's skin I'd ever seen; she looked as if she sunbathed daily directly under the hole in the ozone layer. Aunt Stacia was distinctly less wrinkly and more natural-looking.

'So, Róisín,' Reenie asked, 'how's life been with you since you killed my brother?'

And there you had it. Right for the jugular.

'Now, Reenie,' Stacia jumped in, 'we all know that Robert died in a tragic accident—'

'How dare you, you – dried-up old crone?' My mother was instantly on her feet. 'My Robert went to London in spite of me. Not because of me.'

Did she just say 'my Robert'?

'Codswallop,' said Reenie. 'We all know he would never have gone off like that if it wasn't for that row you had.'

'Robert was his own man, and nobody could stop him once he got an idea into his head – not even me. That was one of the things I loved most about him.'

I was speechless with amazement. In my living memory, she had never before used my father's name and the word 'love' in the same breath.

'You never loved my brother!' Reenie was shouting now. 'You just used him and discarded him, because that's the type of woman you are. You couldn't even be bothered coming to his funeral. And the way you cut my mother out of your life and wouldn't even let her see Elizabeth, her own granddaughter – nothing short of shameful, it was. Absolutely shameful.'

'I didn't go to his funeral because I couldn't stand the pain!' Mam's voice cracked. 'And I couldn't stand having his family around, reminding me... I had to move on, for my own sake and

244

for Elizabeth's.' Her voice dissolved into sobs. 'Libby,' she said, 'I'll wait for you out in the car.'

We all stared at the vacant space my mother left behind. Then we looked at one another. Reenie's face was the colour of port wine and her breath came hard.

'I'm sorry, Elizabeth,' she said, 'but some things just have to be said.'

I glared at her and got up. 'Maybe I should go out to her.'

'No – don't do that.' Stacia had risen to her feet too. 'Leave her be for a while. Come on up with me and we'll see if your granny is awake – although, if she wasn't, she certainly is now.' She gave Reenie a pointed look, and the other woman looked away.

I followed Stacia up the stairs. Halfway up, she stopped and looked back at me. 'You all right, love?'

'Fine, thanks.'

'Don't mind that one. She doesn't know what she's saying half the time. She's probably drunk.'

I giggled. This didn't seem likely.

'You know,' she said, as we reached the landing, 'it's a real pleasure to meet you after all these years. I remember you when you were a tiny baby. Gorgeous, you were – like a little doll. I'm looking forward to getting to know you properly.'

'You too, Stacia.'

'You're very welcome to this family. I hope you know that.' Her accent had a distinct Aussie twang.

'I do.'

'Good. Now, I'll see if she's awake.' Stacia tapped lightly on the door and stuck her head into Granny's room. I heard Granny's muffled voice coming from inside.

'Go right in,' said Stacia. 'I'll see you downstairs.'

Granny's room resembled a small florist's shop. You could barely turn without knocking over a rose, gypsophila or gladiolus.

'Ah, Elizabeth, love,' she said. 'You're back. Would you ever do me a favour and get rid of some of these bloody flowers? I'm not dead yet.'

'Right you are, Granny.' I removed several bouquets to the hall and opened a window. Then I sat down beside her bed. I noticed that the telly had been moved up to her room. All the better to watch the wrestling.

'How was your trip?' Granny asked.

'Lovely.'

'Tell me all about it.'

So I told her all about Streedagh strand: the golden sand, the smooth grey rocks, the undulating dunes and the bladderwrack; the irises in the fields, the elderflower, buttercups and ox-eye daisies in the hedgerows; the ash and the sycamore; the bonfires. But not our bonfire.

She closed her eyes as she listened to me, as if trying to picture it all. When I had finished recounting every detail I could think of, she opened her eyes and peered across at me.

'The locket,' she said.

'What? Oh, yes.' I reached up and held it between my thumb and forefinger.

'You found it.'

'I didn't lose...' I trailed off.

'Here. Let me have a look at it.'

With a strength she definitely hadn't possessed a few days earlier, Granny hoisted herself up on her elbows and examined the locket, turning it this way and that, unclasping it to feast her eyes once

246

more on the precious contents. Eventually, she closed it and lay back down.

'Did Kit tell you about the gnome?'

'No. What about it?'

'He came back.'

'Really? That's great, isn't it?'

'It is. You could almost call it a miracle. You wouldn't happen to know anything about it, would you, Elizabeth?'

'Who, me? No.'

I hadn't even had to pay the ransom money. Those nice gentlemen in the Gnome Liberation Front had clearly elected to do the honourable thing, once they'd read my letter.

'What was all that commotion about earlier on?' Granny asked.

'Oh, nothing. Just Reenie and my mother having a difference of opinion.'

'They used to have a lot of those while your mammy and daddy were courting. They always clashed, that pair. Two women with such strong opinions can never get on, if you ask me; it's like having two red-headed women in the one kitchen. What's she doing here, anyway, that Reenie? Sitting around like a vulture, waiting for me to die. She's always had her eye on my good china, that one.'

'Now, I'm sure that's not true, Granny. She could have bought herself some very nice china with the money it took to buy a plane ticket from Australia.'

'Ah, but mine is antique. You couldn't buy it in any old shop.'

Fair enough.

Granny sank further back into her pillow and sighed a weary sigh. 'It won't be long now,' she said.

'I wish you'd stop talking like that.'

'Sorry, love.'

I hoped she was wrong. If Granny died, a piece of old Dublin would be dying with her, never to be recovered. And, apart from that, I'd miss her too much.

Graham was still up when we got home. Since it was past his bedtime, I could only assume that he'd been waiting up for us. Mam, who had sniffled silently all the way home in the car, went straight up the stairs to bed, avoiding all conversation.

'Cup of tea?' I said to Graham, switching on the kettle.

'You're all right. I was just going up. There was a call for you while you were out; some lad by the name of Eric.'

I nearly dropped the kettle.

This wasn't wasted on Graham, who was watching me carefully. 'Nice lad, is he, this Eric?'

'Nice enough.'

'What does he do?'

'He's a part-time student, part-time musician.'

'Like your father.'

I turned and looked at Graham, who was staring at me fixedly. 'I suppose.'

I sat down beside him with my mug of tea. I'd never really considered Graham's position in all this. 'It must be quite hard for you,' I said.

'What?'

'All of this – stuff from the past being dragged up after all this time, stuff about Mam's former husband… I'm sorry.'

'Now what are you sorry for?'

'It's all because of me.'

'It's not all about you, Libby. It's your mother's past too.'

'If she hadn't got pregnant with me, he might have been just another long-forgotten ex-boyfriend.'

'No,' Graham said quietly. 'Your father was the love of her life. I've always known that.'

I didn't know what to say. I ached to reassure him and tell him that it wasn't true; yet he seemed so sure. And I wanted it to be true myself. I wanted my father to have been the love of my mother's life; I wanted the union from which I'd sprung to have been something good and special, after all, not something unfortunate and accidental, as I'd always believed.

Graham smiled at me, but the smile failed to reach his eyes. He scraped back his chair and stood up. 'I'm going up. Don't forget to pull out all the plugs.'

Halfway out the door, he turned. 'Eric said he'd ring again. Be careful this time, Libby. I don't want to see you hurt again.'

'I will. Good night, Graham.'

'Night.'

Right on cue, the phone rang. I practically jumped out of my skin, as if it were an air-raid siren.

'Hello,' I said.

'Hello. Can I speak to Tallulah, please?'

I smiled and relaxed a little. 'Hi, Eric.'

'How are you doing?'

'Good. You?'

'Good. I made it back to Dublin.'

'You did? How long did it take you?'

'Three hours fixing, eight hours driving.'

'Jesus. You must be wrecked.'

'I am a bit. I'm only back an hour.'

'And how's the car?'

'Let's just say I'll be getting a taxi to the airport in the morning.'

Ah, yes: the airport. My heart sank. 'What time is your flight?'

'Eight.'

'You should be getting your beauty sleep,' I said, trying to keep my voice light.

'I'm in bed already. I just had to ring you before I left.'

'You did?'

'Of course.'

There was a brief silence, during which I imagined Eric in bed. *No, Liz, you can't ask him what he's wearing.*

'I'm sorry I have to go off like this,' he said at last. 'Just as...'

'Just as what?'

'Just as we were getting to know each other better.'

So that was what we'd been doing. 'Well, I'm sure they have phones in Germany.' Eric was one of the few people – perhaps the only person – I knew who didn't have a mobile phone.

'Yes. I think they call it *"Das Phone"*.'

'Do you speak any German?' I asked.

'Not a word. But music is the international language, so I'm not too worried.'

'I thought it was the language of love.'

'That too.'

I was dying to say that we could meet up when he got back; but, somehow, I couldn't summon up the courage.

'Well,' said Eric, once it became clear that I wasn't going to say anything else, 'guess I'd better go and get a few hours' kip while I still can.'

Yes, I thought. *Because once you get to Hamburg, you'll be down the red-light district every night.* 'Yes,' I said. 'Very wise.'

'We could always...' His voice was unusually hesitant. 'We could always meet up when I get back.'

'I'd like that,' I said, trying not to sound quite as overjoyed as I felt.

'Great.' He sounded genuinely delighted. 'Well, I'll give you a call when I'm settled in – and I'll see you when I get back.'

'OK. Bye, Eric. Safe journey.'

'Bye, Liz.'

I put down the phone.

Glee – that's what I was filled with: pure glee. I downed the rest of my tea in one go, put the mug in the dishwasher, pulled out all the plugs and turned off all the lights. Then I got ready for bed, humming 'Wuthering Heights' to myself as I went – although it was difficult not to sing it at the top of my lungs.

In bed, I turned on my laptop. By three-thirty that morning, I had written another two chapters. Then I decided it was high time I caught up on some beauty sleep of my own.

34

The phone rang again the next morning. After my late-night writing session, I didn't know where the hell I was. At first, I thought it was part of my dream: I was on the beach with Eric, and a siren was going off to warn us that a ship had been wrecked. I jumped out of the sofa-bed, bashed my knee against the coffee table and cursed angrily to myself as I limped towards the phone – only to have it stop ringing a split second before I could pick it up. Cursing yet more angrily, I went back to bed. I had just lain down when it started to ring again. This time, I was on it by the third ring.

'Hello,' I said.

'You're back.'

'Who is this?'

'What do you mean, who is this? It's your good friend Tom.'

'If you were such a good friend, you wouldn't be ringing me first thing in the morning.'

'It's almost midday,' Tom informed me.

I glanced at the clock. 'Oh. So it is. Sorry about that.'

'You weren't out gallivanting, were you?'

'Nothing like that. Actually, I was up late writing.' My mouth curved upwards into a smile. It was the first time in yonks I'd been able to say this truthfully.

'Ah…the famous novel. It must be nearly finished by now, is it?'

'Not quite. But you'll be the first to know when it is.'

'Will you let me edit it for you?'

'Of course. You know there's no one's opinion I value more highly than yours.' This was the truth.

'Thank you, sweetie. But enough of that. I digress. What I really want to know is, how did you get on with the Viking in Sligo? Did he impale you with his manly staff?'

'Did he what me with his manly what? These Viking metaphors are going to have to go, Tom.'

'OK. But did he?'

'I'm not telling you.'

'Come on,' Tom coaxed. 'Who else are you going to tell?'

Good question. Once upon a time it would have been Helen, but not any more. 'I won't be telling anyone. It's nobody's business.'

'That means he did.'

'It means no such thing,' I said with dignity. 'Besides, he's gone to Germany for six weeks. So he's bound to hook up with some fräulein over there and forget about me.'

'Germany! How inconsiderate of him.' Tom sounded disappointed. This made me even more convinced that the chances of my 'relationship' with Eric surviving the Hamburg trip were slim.

'Yes, isn't it just?'

'Pity,' said Tom. 'Because I was planning to invite the two of you around for dinner tonight.'

'I am capable of eating without him, you know.'

'Quite right. Come around on your own.'

'I'd love to, Tom, thanks. But only if you promise not to pester me about Eric all night.'

'I promise.'

'And only if you promise not to invite Helen and try and instigate a reunion.'

'As if,' said Tom. 'Everything's not always about you, you know.

253

Mindy and I happen to have some news of our own that we'd like to share.'

'Really?' I was intrigued. 'How exciting. Any chance of a sneak preview?'

'None whatsoever. You'll have to keep your powder dry until tonight.'

'Would you like me to bring anything with me? Dessert?'

'You can bring anything at all, as long as you don't attempt to make it yourself.'

'Bitch. See you later.'

'Half seven for eight,' Tom said. 'Dress is smart casual.'

'I'll wear my best jeans,' I promised.

'And a tie.'

I replaced the receiver. A bottle of wine would do. I'd wear the new second-hand skirt I'd got in the Cerebral Palsy shop the other day, and the earring I'd found in the bottom of my bag last night. I wondered what news Tom and Mindy could have. A new little brother or sister for Clarissa?

I arrived at Chez Tom and Mindy at eight-fourteen precisely.

'You're late,' said Tom, opening the door for me. He was wearing an ensemble that most people would deem too fancy for a fancy restaurant.

'But fashionably so,' I said, sweeping majestically into the hall in my own striking vintage ensemble. 'Where's the lady of the house?'

'The big one or the little one?'

'Little one first.'

'TV room, of course.'

Clarissa was dug into the latest Barney video – for only the third

254

time that evening, apparently. Her eyes lit up when she saw me, and she ran over to greet me on her tiny little legs. I was incredibly flattered. I bent down and prepared to scoop her up in my arms; but she stopped, about a foot short of me, and held out her right palm.

'Sweeties,' she said.

Oh, well. I handed her a pack of M&Ms and two tubes of Smarties. Clarissa snatched them from my grasp, an expression of wicked delight on her face, and ran back to where she'd been sitting – about two inches away from the TV screen.

'Thanks,' said Tom. 'Packed full of all her favourite E-numbers. You'd easily know you don't have any kids of your own.'

'Well, the time I brought her fruit she had a tantrum.'

'She's always having those. She takes after her mother.'

Speaking of whom, Mindy came into the TV room, carrying a dripping wooden spoon and wearing an apron that depicted Michelangelo's David. His family jewels hung at the join between her legs.

'Liz,' she said, smiling broadly. 'Good to see you. It's been ages.' She embraced me. It was like hugging a centre forward, or a tank. 'Did Tom tell you our news yet?'

'No, he didn't.' I looked more closely at her. Was she 'blooming'? I could never tell.

'Will we tell her?' Mindy asked Tom.

'Well, tell her your part of the news, then.'

'I've got a new job,' Mindy said happily.

'Really? Congratulations.'

'As a prison officer.'

'Really? A prison officer? Well…that's great! Well done, Mindy.'

Mindy had been a secretary – and a miserable one – ever since I'd known her. Being a prison officer was quite a change, and it had to be a tough job – but then again, it was perfect for her, really. She already had the haircut; and she'd scare the shit out of the most ferocious criminal.

For a prison-officer-to-be, Mindy was a stupendous cook. We started with a weird and wonderful concoction of black pudding and apple, followed by beef Stroganoff for the main course and baked Alaska – a cherished memory from childhood – for dessert.

Belts had been loosened, buttons opened and chairs moved back. Tom was letting the third bottle of wine breathe. It was to live a short life.

'You still haven't told me your part of the news,' I said to Tom.

'Ah, yes. My news.'

There was a pause. It was Tom's version of a drum roll.

'Well, go on, then.'

'A woman has to retain an air of mystery, you know.'

'Spit it out.'

'Today...' Another pause for dramatic effect. 'I handed in my notice.'

'You did not!'

'I did so.'

'Have you got a new job?'

'Indeed I have. Assistant editor at Dingbats Publishing House.'

'Tom! That's fantastic.'

'I know.'

I got up and flung my arms around his neck. He was beaming; he was clearly thrilled with himself. 'I'm so pleased for you,' I told him. I was. This was what he'd wanted for as long as I'd known him.

'Who knows?' he said. 'Maybe one day I can edit one of your books and actually get paid for it.'

'How did George take it?' I asked.

'He was none too pleased.'

I grinned. 'I'm fucking delighted.'

'I thought you would be.'

'Cheers,' I said, raising my glass. 'A toast. Wishing you both every success in your new careers.' We all clinked glasses. Everybody seemed to be moving on. It was just a pity that some were moving thousands of miles on, to Hamburg. 'So what exactly did George say when you told him?'

'Never mind what *he* said. Wait until you hear what *I* said.'

'What did you say?'

'I told him I wasn't prepared to work another moment for a man – if he could call himself that – who treated his employees, and people in general, like dirt.'

'You didn't!'

'I did. And, furthermore, I told him I'd had enough of working for a cretin who wore a goatee beard that was way too young for him and too much ill-advised gold jewellery.'

I clapped my hands together in delight. 'I'm proud of you, Tom.'

'I'm proud of me, too.'

'And so am I, dear,' added Mindy.

'Of course,' Tom continued, 'I made sure I took some headed notepaper from the office before I left, so I could write my own reference.'

'Good idea. So what did George say?' I would have given just about anything to see George's face when Tom criticised his goatee.

'What do you care?' Tom said. 'Haven't you got a fabulous new man in your life?'

'Oh, yes,' said Mindy. 'Tom told me you went away with Eric. Did anything happen?'

Usually you could rely on Mindy to be reasonably non-invasive, but that had all been swept aside on a crimson tide of wine.

'It doesn't matter now,' I said. 'He's gone to Germany.'

'So something did happen?'

'Might have done.'

'I knew it!' said Tom. 'Any good?'

'Very good.'

'A rating, please. How many stars?'

'If he were a hotel, he'd be that seven-star one in Dubai.'

'Excellent recommendation. It's about time you two kids got it together.'

'Yes,' agreed Mindy. 'I knew he liked you after that night in Whelan's. He kept watching you from the stage.' Had he? I hadn't noticed. I'd been too busy trying to avoid a broken bottle in the face. 'Do you like him?' she asked.

'What does it matter? He's gone away now.'

'Only for six weeks. It's hardly a lifetime,' said Tom.

'Might as well be,' I said gloomily.

'Oh, don't be so negative. He'll be back before you know it.'

'Yes. Together with a variety of sexually transmitted diseases he'll have managed to pick up in the red-light district.'

'What part of Germany, again?'

'Hamburg.'

'Oh, yes,' Tom said reminiscently. 'Hamburg does have a very impressive red-light district, now that you come to mention it. I went there on a stag weekend once.'

'Tom!' said Mindy.

'Sorry.'

'Don't mind him, Liz. I'm sure Eric isn't the type to go to brothels.'

'What about the groupies?' I said.

'Sure, how could they have any groupies? They're unknown over there.'

I took a deep draught of wine. I wasn't convinced that the blond, six-foot-something lead singer of a rock band would be spending all of his free time in libraries and museums. Still, it was nice of Mindy to try and comfort me. In fact, I think it qualified as our first girly chat – if you deleted Tom's interruptions.

Later on, we were half passed out on the settee in the sitting room – in fact, I think Mindy *had* passed out. Tom was giving me a foot massage while I dribbled red wine onto his cushions. Nina Simone was warbling in the background, and I was thinking about Tom leaving the shop. At this rate, George would have no one left working for him. He was lucky Helen was going back.

'When is Helen back off her maternity leave?' I said.

It was the first time her name had been mentioned all night. Tom and Mindy hadn't brought her up out of deference to me, although I knew they still saw her.

'That's actually another bit of news,' said Tom. 'I've been waiting for the right time to tell you, and I think it might be now.'

I sat up as upright as the massive, squishy cushions would allow. 'I'm all ears.'

'George has gone back to his wife.'

George has gone back to his wife. The words were nothing more than meaningless sounds.

'Did you just say George has gone back to his wife?'

'That's what I said.'

'So…he's left Helen?' I said, trying to absorb this astounding new piece of information.

'Apparently.'

'And gone back to his wife.'

'That's what the man said.'

Well, holy cow. 'What about the baby?' I asked.

'He's with Helen, of course,' Tom said. 'The last I heard, Grainger was applying for access.'

'When did this all happen?'

259

'While you were away.'

'You should have told me straight away.'

'Give me a break. You're only back a day.'

I didn't respond. I got up and started pacing unsteadily about the room.

'How is she?' I asked, finally.

'Helen?'

I nodded.

'Why don't you give her a call and find out?'

'Oh, I couldn't do that.'

'Why not?'

Why not? 'Because she'll think I'm gloating.'

'Would you be?'

Would I be? 'No.' Was I sure? 'No. Definitely. I definitely wouldn't gloat.'

'Well, then. Give her a call.'

I did better than that. The very next day, I called around to her flat.

35

Helen lived in a ground-floor flat on one of those roads in Ranelagh I'd always dreamt about. These were the leafy suburbs at their best. The lawns were manicured, and so were the fingernails. How idyllic it all looked from the outside. I rang the bell and admired the stained glass in the front door.

Even though I heard her coming, I still jumped when she appeared. She was holding the child under her oxter, head first, like a battering ram. We stared at each other for a few seconds – well, really, she glared at me. 'Come to gloat, have you?' she said, before turning her back on me and going back inside, Royston's padded blue bottom bobbing along behind her.

What to do? She hadn't invited me in; then again, she hadn't slammed the door in my face, either. I stepped hesitantly into the hall and gently shut the front door. It was easy to work out where they'd gone. I just followed the wails.

The living room had probably once been very elegant, but today it was strewn with nappies – not all clean – and brightly coloured plastic objects. A peculiar stench – rusk, piss and Sudocrem – hit me in the nose, forming a kind of sensory force field that I was just about able to penetrate.

Helen was sitting in an armchair with the wailing Royston draped across her shoulder. She was rubbing his back and rocking him back and forth.

'What's wrong with him? Is he sick?' I said, bringing all my vast knowledge of babies to bear on the situation.

'He's teething,' said Helen. She looked as if she might be teething herself. Her cheeks were very red, and she looked as if she could start drooling at any second.

'Are you having a bad day?' I said.

'Is there any other kind? Look, Liz, what are you doing here? If you've come looking for all the gory details, I'm afraid I really don't have the time.'

'Actually, I just came to see how you were,' I said quietly.

I could see Helen trying to work out if I was for real. It turned out I was. I'd found out, to my surprise, that – now that I didn't want George any more – Helen was amazingly easy to forgive. And, now that she'd been left in the lurch in the cruellest of ways, I found that the only emotion I felt towards her was sympathy.

'Do you want a cup of tea?' she finally said.

'I'll make it,' I said.

I found the kitchen easily enough. Nice units; they were the same ones I'd picked out of the B&Q catalogue myself. All in all, this was my dream apartment. I carried back in two mugs of tea and an open packet of ginger nuts I'd found in the back of a press.

Royston had given up wailing and taken up whimpering. Helen, it seemed, had given up the ghost. Even in the midst of labour, she had never looked so wretched. She'd lost any baby weight she had gained and was now way too thin; her skin seemed to hang in folds from her gaunt face. It was as if she'd aged five years in the same number of months. The clothes she was wearing were baggy, but her form underneath seemed skeletal.

'Are you sick, Helen?'

'No.'

'You look sick.'

'So would you if you hadn't slept in six months,' she snapped.

'OK, OK. I'm sorry.'

262

She looked away and began stroking Royston's head.

'I know you won't believe me,' I said, choosing my words carefully, 'but I'm very sorry about the way this has worked out for you.'

'Yeah, right. I'm sure you're fucking thrilled.'

'Now, Helen. You know me better than that.'

She glared at me, then looked away again. Royston resumed his caterwauling, and I saw her eyes fill up with tears.

'Why don't you go and lie down for an hour?' I said. 'I'll mind Royston.'

'I can't leave him with anybody. He's making strange.'

'You wouldn't be leaving him with *anybody*. You'd be leaving him with me. What's the worst he can do? Cry? Stick him in his buggy and I'll take him out for a walk. With a bit of luck, he'll fall asleep too.'

I could see her weighing up her options: going without sleep versus entrusting her precious son to a woman of dubious moral character, not to mention breathtaking incompetence, whose knowledge of babies could fit inside a matchbox – one of those tiny ones that they give you for free in some hotel bars. She must have been really desperate, because she agreed.

I watched her prepare Royston for his outing like a seasoned pro, manipulating his tiny, flailing arms into the sleeves of his jacket and securing the convoluted plethora of straps on his buggy over his wriggling little form. When she was finished, he looked like a midget fighter pilot ready for take-off. Royston regarded me fiercely, an expression of pure belligerence on his countenance. His hands were balled into fists, and he looked as if he was about to have either a shit or a fit. Fit it was.

'Maybe this isn't such a good idea,' said Helen, her brow a mass of wriggly lines.

'Nonsense. We'll be fine. He'll calm down after a while. You go up and have a sleep, and we'll talk properly when I get back.'

She nodded and plodded up the stairs. I turned my attention back to her son. How bad could this be?

Pretty bad, as it turned out. Royston screamed the whole way to the Swan Centre in Rathmines. He refused his dummy, his juice, his bottle and his rusk – in that order – and as for his rattle, forget it. That offending item was swiped away in no uncertain terms. By God, he had his father's temper. I was just about to tip him into the canal, buggy and all, when all of a sudden he fell silent. I looked down at his nut-brown head. He was fast asleep. Hallelujah, praise the Lord. He'd live to scream another day.

I sat down on a bench and looked at his dreaming little face. How angelic could one child look? Like a miniature Jekyll and Hyde, so he was. Fearful of waking him, but unable to resist, I reached out and touched his cheek. It was unimaginably soft. It reminded me of that time in Sligo when I'd taken the petal of a wild rose between my thumb and forefinger.

In spite of Royston's previous appalling behaviour, I was almost toppled off the bench by an overwhelming surge of broodiness. I longed for my own baby. (Did I really?) My own little blond, blue-eyed boy, who never cried, to dandle on my knee and sing lullabies to. *Forget it,* I told myself. *It'll never happen. If you had to look after a baby, you'd only wind up leaving it on the bus or something.* But, then again, I wasn't doing too badly with Royston, and the circumstances were hardly ideal – him being a little bugger and all. It wasn't his fault that he had half of George's genes.

I stayed out for as long as I could. Poor Helen needed her rest. But, instead of returning to a quietly sleeping house as expected, I found Helen waiting at the front door, hopping from one foot to the other, like when you're standing on hot sand on your holidays.

'Where have you been?' she said, her voice high-pitched and frantic.

'Rathmines.'

'You've been gone ages!'

'I wanted to let you sleep.'

'I thought something had happened.'

'Did you get any sleep at all?'

'A little. About half an hour. Then I woke up and started to worry. I thought the two of you were in the canal or something.'

'Now, how would we have ended up in the canal?'

'I don't know.' Her voice shrank as she crouched in front of Royston's buggy and started unbuckling him. Royston continued sucking his dummy and eyed her expectantly. She took him out and hugged him fiercely into her chest. Then she stood up, turned her back to me and disappeared into the house. I presumed I was meant to follow her in again.

Back in the living room, Helen had plugged up Royston's mouth with a bottle, and he guzzled noisily.

'Have you finished breast-feeding?' I asked.

'I had to. I got mastitis.'

Wasn't that a disease for cows? I sat on the edge of the settee and looked at Helen. She looked back at me. Her eyes were less suspicious now, less wary; the trust was seeping back in.

'Helen,' I began, 'why don't you move back home?'

'I've thought about it. But it would feel like taking a step backwards.'

I considered this. 'Would you kill me if I said that sometimes you have to take one step backwards to take two steps forward?'

'I think I'd probably have to, yes.'

I could see her trying to hide a kind of half-smile. She hadn't decided I was worthy of a full one yet.

I felt the question building up inside of me, but it took several attempts to get it out. *OK. This time. Say it… No. Now.*

'So what happened with George?'

Helen's expression hardened again. 'I'm afraid the harsh realities of family life proved too much for him.'

'But he has another small baby at home – I mean, at his other home.'

'No, it's his home,' she said sadly. 'True. But they have a nanny and a housekeeper. I'm afraid even George couldn't afford two sets of domestic staff – not that I'd want anyone else looking after my baby.'

'But he has other kids. He must have known what he was letting himself in for.'

She shrugged. 'It wasn't just that. His wife served divorce papers on him, and she was threatening to take him to the cleaners. It was right about that time that he decided they should try "making a go of it".'

I nodded. That sounded about right. 'So where does that leave you?'

'Up shit creek without a paddle, that's where.'

'But he is paying you maintenance?'

'Sort of. He pays the rent on this place.'

'Ah, Helen. You don't want to stay living here like some sort of kept woman. He'll think he has the right to come and go whenever he feels like it.'

'Why should you care?'

'I care because I'm your friend.'

'Really? You certainly haven't been acting like it lately.'

'Oh, come on, Helen! What did you expect? You went behind my back and stole my boyfriend.'

'Ex-boyfriend. I didn't start seeing him till April. You broke up with him in March.'

'I was still seeing him.'

'What?' Her voice was tiny, as if it had retreated halfway down her throat.

'I started seeing George again. I didn't tell anyone about it because I was too ashamed. You would have been three or four months gone at the time. So you see, he was doing us both at the same time – and probably his wife, too.'

Helen's mouth gaped open and her eyes were huge. 'I don't believe you,' she said.

'Why would I make it up now?'

Helen was patting Royston's back so hard that he was starting to protest. She laid him down on his baby gym, whereupon he began beating the living daylights out of a little purple elephant that had probably never done any harm to anybody in its life.

'You swear it's the truth?' she said eventually.

'I swear to you. I wish it wasn't.'

'The bastard,' she said.

'I know.'

'The low-down, stinking, lying, rotten bastard.'

'I know.'

'I can't believe it. Why didn't you tell me this before?'

'Because of the baby. I knew you wanted to make a go of it as a family.'

'But – I don't know – didn't you think it was your duty to warn me, or something?'

'I thought about it – agonised over it, really. But in the end I decided to say nothing. I'm sorry it was the wrong decision.'

'No,' said Helen, '*I'm* sorry. I should never have done what I did. I knew you were still in love with him when I started the affair.'

'Affair,' I said, half smiling. 'It sounds very grown up, doesn't it?'

'But it's not, is it?'

'No.'

'Can we be friends again?'

'Yes, please.'

Helen moved over to my side of the settee and hugged me, as fiercely as she had hugged Royston minutes previously. It made me feel precious. I hugged her back, just as hard.

'Let's never do anything like this again,' she said.

'Agreed.'

'You know,' she said, 'I have a confession to make.'

'What?'

She looked at me hard. Then: 'No. I can't. I'll put the kettle on.'

I pulled her back down. 'I don't want tea. Tell me.'

'OK, then.' She shuffled about on the couch, trying to compose herself. 'Right,' she said. 'Here we go...'

I waited.

'Right...'

'Oh, come on, Helen.'

'All right! I only went after George because I wanted to be more like you.'

I stared at her. 'What? Are you mad? Why on earth would *you* want to be more like *me*?'

'Because you're different. You've got this bohemian thing going on. You're a published writer, for pity's sake. And here I am – boring, staid old Helen... I got sick of being me.'

'But, Helen, you're so—'

She held out her hand as if to push my words away. 'Don't say it,' she said. 'Whatever you do, don't say that word.'

'What – perfect?'

'I told you not to say it.'

'What's wrong with it?'

'Look at my life. Look around this room, for God's sake. Does this look like perfection to you? And look at my tits.' Here, she grabbed each of her breasts and shook them hard. 'They've gone all loose and droopy, and my stomach feels like a bowl of jelly. And look at my hair – it's falling out in chunks.' She demonstrated by tugging out an alarming number of strands.

'Jesus. That is terrible,' I said.

'And I don't have a job. There's no way I'm going back to work for that fucker. So I'm an unemployed, unmarried mother.'

'You're not an unmarried mother. You're a lone parent. Remember?'

'Whatever. Either way, I'm fucked.'

'You know what else has deteriorated?' I said.

'What?'

'Your language.'

We both started to laugh.

'Stop,' Helen said. 'It's not funny.'

'I know,' I said, making a real effort to stop. 'It's not a bit funny.' This made us both laugh even harder.

Royston stared at us both. Then he flipped himself over onto his belly and tried to wriggle frantically towards us, as if swimming without any water. Helen bent over and gathered him up in her arms.

'Come on, you,' she said to him. 'Let's go and put the kettle on and make your Auntie Liz a nice cup of tea.'

Auntie Liz. I liked the sound of that.

I listened to the two of them clattering around in the kitchen. Helen wanting to be more like me...imagine that. And there was I, thinking it was the other way around. Maybe I wasn't such a lost cause after all.

The doorbell rang. 'Do you want me to get that?' I called, heading out to the hallway.

'No, it's all right.' Helen brushed past me, the baby in her arms.

I watched as she opened the door. Then I watched as she stood aside to let him in. She took a couple of steps backwards, until we were level with each other. I wished I had a camera, to record that beautiful moment when George first saw us both, standing there together, side by side – one tall, honey-blonde and magnificent; one small, dark and straggly.

'Well,' said Helen. 'What have *you* got to say for yourself?'

George wore a peculiar, stunned expression. 'What are you doing here?' he said to me.

'Visiting a friend,' I said.

'Helen...' He turned to her. 'I need to discuss some things with you.'

'You can discuss them with my solicitor. Tyrone Power is his name. Now...' Her voice rose to a shout. 'Get the fuck out of here, and don't come back!'

Helen slammed the door and turned to face me.

'Jesus,' she said. 'How could we have been so stupid?'

36

As happy as I was to have Helen back in my life, my happiness was nothing compared to that of my mother. For the previous six months, she'd had me pestered to death. 'Where's Helen these days? Why doesn't she ever call around any more? Have you two had a falling-out? What about? Whatever it is, it's not worth it. You two have been friends for years…' She'd guessed that it had something to do with the fact that George, rather than Phil Gallagher, had fathered Helen's child; but the details had stayed tantalisingly out of her reach.

I'd invited Helen around to ours for breakfast, a couple of Saturdays later. I was woken by the intoxicating scent of bacon frying. I followed my nose down to the kitchen like a snake being charmed.

'Morning.' My mother was all smiles, spatula in hand, flipping the rashers in the pan; the sausages were browning away under the grill, each one split down the middle in order to make them cook faster. 'Be a love and cut a few slices of soda bread for me, Libby.'

I did as instructed, hoping she might stretch to a few potato cakes. The woman made a mean potato cake.

The doorbell rang. 'I'll get it,' Mam said, running out to the hall. 'Watch they don't burn.' I could hear her greeting Helen effusively at the front door, and then the squeals as she clapped her eyes on Royston for the first time. Funnily enough, I didn't feel the slightest bit jealous.

They came into the kitchen en masse – two mammies, one baby

and a veritable shitload of miscellaneous equipment. Royston didn't believe in travelling light.

'Hi!' We embraced. Helen still felt like a bag of bones, but she did look a bit better.

'Look at you. You're as skinny,' said Mam, echoing my sentiments. 'Sit yourself down there and eat. You look as if you could do with a good, hearty breakfast.'

Helen did as instructed, Royston perched beside her in his portable high chair, and for the next half-hour or so, the kitchen was filled with sunlight and laughter. It was like all my sunny Saturday mornings rolled into one.

Helen told us all about her plans to open her own bookshop-*cum*-coffee-shop. 'Maybe you'll come and do a few shifts for me?' she said to me.

'In the bookshop or the coffee shop?'

'Either – both.'

'Maybe I could make some cakes for you to sell in the coffee shop.'

Helen and my mother looked at each other and then fell around the place laughing.

'What?' I said.

'When was the last time you baked, Libby?' said Mam.

'I don't know. I used to bake all the time when I lived in the flat – didn't I, Helen?'

'Did you? Oh, yes – so you did. I remember you made fabulous chocolate Rice Krispie cakes this one time.'

'Yes, I did.' The nerve of them both, implying that I couldn't bake. And I'd even made fettuccine once, when I'd had a dinner party – although Tom had had the cheek to call it fetid-ccine.

Royston – who had been behaving impeccably up until now – was starting to get restless. He wriggled fruitlessly around in his seat and made angry little whingy noises.

'May I?' asked my mother, her eyes wide with excitement.

'Be my guest,' said Helen.

As if she did it every day of the week, Mam undid Royston's straps and eased him out of his chair. He looked back at Helen for reassurance; apparently satisfied that she wasn't going anywhere, he allowed my mother to snuggle him against her breast. She closed her eyes momentarily and breathed in his baby scent. Then she held him away from her and looked into his face.

'Hello, baba,' she said.

'Baba,' replied Royston, smiling broadly at her. I could see my mother's heart melting right through her clothes. She hugged him to her again.

'Oh, you precious, precious boy! You know...' She gave me a sidelong glance. 'I'd love a grandchild of my own.'

'Would you really?' I said.

'Oh, yes.'

'It wouldn't make you feel old and decrepit – being a grandmother?'

She laughed. 'I already know I'm past it. A grandchild wouldn't make any difference there.'

My mother, wanting to be a granny? She'd never said so before.

'There you go, Liz.' Helen smiled. 'That sounds like a challenge to me.'

'Not going to happen,' I said.

'Oh, I don't know. Eric might have something to say about that.'

I attempted to kick her ankle, but made contact with the leg of the table instead.

'Who's Eric?' said my mother.

'Oops,' Helen said. 'Have I let the cat out of the bag?'

'Yes, you have. Well done.'

'Who's Eric?' Mam demanded.

'Eric is this lovely man who used to work in the bookshop with us,' said Helen.

'The blond lad that drove you to Sligo?' The woman knew more than she let on.

'Yes, that's him. Only he's gone off to Germany now, so nothing more will be happening there,' I said.

'Don't mind her. He'll be back in a few weeks.'

'Please, Helen.' I gave her a look and she shut up.

'Oh, I almost forgot to tell you!' Mam said. 'You'll never guess what I heard down the ladies' club last Wednesday night.'

'What?' I grabbed the opportunity to change the subject.

'You know that lad, Phil Gallagher?'

Did we what? Helen kept her gaze directed steadfastly at the table.

'Well, he's only gone and got some poor young one up the pole.'

'He's what?' Helen's gaze swung upwards – then downwards again.

'Sixteen years old is all she is. He's in serious trouble now – knows it, too. He's gone on the run, apparently.'

'Did his mother tell you this?' I asked.

'You must be joking. It'll be a long while before Philomena Gallagher dares show her face down the ladies' club.'

As Tom would have said – indeed.

Then, as if to serve as a warning of what cute little Royston might grow up into, in walked Jim. Unusually, I found that his appearance in the kitchen came as a welcome distraction. As he entered the room, his face wore its habitual scowl – but, when he saw Helen, his entire expression changed.

'Oh, hi,' he said, smiling, for all the world like a pleasant human being.

274

I watched him take his usual route to the fridge, preparing to be embarrassed as he swigged from the carton of orange juice, but no: he took the carton out of the fridge, poured the juice into a *glass*, put the carton back in the fridge and sat down to eat. For the first time since he was twelve. His white T-shirt was unusually silent today.

Then he proceeded to have a mature, polite conversation with Helen, almost like an adult. I looked across at my mother, and she winked at me. Sometimes I almost hated Helen for the effect she had on men. Or was it possible that our Jim was in fact growing up – that he'd at long last realised that he was no longer a teenager, and had decided to act accordingly?

And the morning of revelations wasn't over yet. Tim was the next to arrive, the cooking smells having finally woken him from his adolescent slumber.

'That's never Tim!' said Helen. 'I can't believe it. You've got so grown-up, Tim.'

The colour of Tim's face deepened, clashing violently with his orange hair. He skulked around the kitchen, avoiding eye contact with everyone. I examined my youngest brother closely. He did seem to have got very grown-up-looking all of a sudden. These kinds of things are easy to miss when you're looking at somebody day in, day out, but he was considerably taller – although his torso hadn't quite kept up with his limbs, so he had the air of a half-grown Labrador – and he had the worst case of bum-fluff I'd ever seen in my life.

'Do you want some breakfast, love?' Mam asked.

Tim shrugged his shoulders and kept his face turned resolutely away from everyone. I guessed he was trying to hide the pimple on his right cheek. My mother, clearly adept at reading his body language, took this as a yes and cracked an egg into the pan for him.

'What have you got planned for today, Tim?' she said.

He shrugged again. 'Dunno.'

'Poor Tim,' said Mam. 'His two best friends are both on holiday with their families, and he's at a bit of a loose end.'

'Oh, really, Timmy?' I said. 'I'll play a game of *Lord of the Rings* with you later on, if you like.'

Tim turned puce. 'I don't play that any more. It's stupid.'

I stared at him in amazement. Since when?

'Tim has a girlfriend now, did you know that?' said my mother.

'Ma!' Tim said loudly, his eyes almost popping out of his head. 'I'm eating this inside.' He picked up his plate and stomped out of the room.

Lose one teenager, gain another.

When the second pot of tea had been drained and the breakfast plates had been cleared away, Helen and I took Royston for a walk. This wasn't as easy as it sounds. The presence of the afternoon sun, sitting high in the July sky, necessitated much preparation. Every inch of his new baby skin had to be smeared with special suntan lotion – factor 115, I think it was. Then he had a peaked cap, with flaps to protect both his ears and his neck from the unforgiving rays. And, finally, there was a parasol, which was designed to fit snugly onto the side of the pram but which, in actual fact, swayed precariously from side to side, striking passers-by in the ribs or groins. You'd think the little blighter would have appreciated all this effort on his behalf, but no: he grumbled for the entire time and had to have various bits of food and squeaky toys waved in front of him at regular intervals.

We did manage to talk a little. It was Helen's first real opportunity to grill me about Eric, and she had no intention of wasting it. I hadn't said anything about him to her at all. I wasn't sure why, but it felt strange – partly because we had both always regarded Eric as the odd, lanky kid who worked in the stockroom, but partly because the last man I'd spoken to her about had been George, and look how well that had worked out. So I hadn't said anything. Big-mouth Tom was the culprit, as usual. But, I reasoned, if it hadn't been for his big mouth telling me that George had returned to his wife, Helen and I wouldn't have been walking along together today. So three cheers for Tom and his big mouth.

'So. You and Eric,' she was saying. 'How did it come about?'

'Good question.' It was a good question. 'I'm not really sure. I suppose the first time I began to view him differently was that night we went to see him play in Whelan's. From that night on, I saw him with new eyes.' *Saw him with new eyes*...where had I heard that before? I had a peculiar sense of déjà vu.

'But nothing happened until Sligo, right?'

'Right. It was amazing. It happened on the beach.'

'You had sex on the beach?' Helen's eyes widened.

I grinned. 'Yes. And we're not talking cocktails here.'

'Did the sand not – you know?' She looked embarrassed.

'Did the sand not get into all of our cracks?'

'Well – yes. Trust you to put it so nicely.'

'No. We did it in the sea.'

Helen's eyes got even wider. 'In the actual water?'

'Yes. And he sang "Wuthering Heights" to me.'

'Really? One of your all-time favourites. I never heard a man singing that before.'

'Me neither. It was sublime.'

'The singing or the...'

'Everything.'

'So what happens when he gets back?'

277

'I don't know.'

'Have you heard from him yet?'

'He called the day after he got there, but he got cut off after about ten seconds. And I've got two postcards since.'

'Well, that's not bad – one postcard per week. Shows he's thinking about you.'

'But I can't help thinking of all the women he's going to meet over there. Remember all those groupies that night in Whelan's?'

'Yes, but he's not with any of them, is he? He's with you. He chose you.' That was true. But was that 'chose' in the past or in the present tense?

We wheeled the buggy in silence for a while – at least, Helen and I were silent; Royston continued his grumbling. A minute or two passed before I asked the question that had been bugging me for the last two miles and six months.

'Helen, you know when you went out with Phil Gallagher that time?'

'Yes.' Her voice tensed up, as if she knew what was coming.

'Did you only do that so I wouldn't be suspicious about George?'

'Well…kind of, yes.'

'Did you ever actually have sex with Phil?'

'No.'

Well, what did you know? Phil Gallagher's mother had been right about that one Helen Staunton all along.

It was late afternoon by the time I got back home. I headed straight for my bedroom-*cum*-sitting-room and switched on my laptop. I'd been itching to write all day – not that I hadn't enjoyed the time I'd spent with Helen (and even her noisy and demanding

278

son), but the book was flowing so well that I was loath to interrupt my roll.

There was a knock on the door. The muse would have to wait a few minutes longer. My mother came in, looking uncharacteristically apologetic.

'Sorry to disturb you, Libby. I heard you come in.'

She closed the door behind her and sat down on the sofa. She had a smallish object, wrapped in white tissue paper, in her hand. I looked at her, waiting for her to speak.

'Did you have a nice time with Helen?' she said.

'Yes, lovely. We went to that new café in the village.'

'Oh. What's it like?'

'Great,' I said. 'Beautiful carrot cake. You should try it sometime.'

'I will.'

What was this about? It wasn't like Mam to be coy.

Finally, with obvious effort, she said, 'I was sorting through my bedroom the other day, and I found something I thought you might like.'

I went over and sat down beside her. 'What is it?'

She handed it to me. I began to unwrap the tissue paper, realising that it was a lot older than I had thought: it felt brittle and thin, and it was yellowed in places. Layer after layer I unwrapped, feeling I was about to reveal a mummy, until finally a small silver picture-frame rolled out onto my lap. I picked it up and examined it closely. It was chunky, solid silver and embossed with roses, their stems and leaves forming intricate, scroll-like patterns.

'Your dad bought it for me,' she said. 'In the Dandelion Market, about a month before he went to London. It was the last thing he ever bought me.'

I ran my fingertips along the frame again. Dad had actually held this very picture-frame in his hands. Perhaps his fingerprints were still on it.

'He meant for me to put our wedding photo in it – you know, the one you found before. But I never did. I think you should have it now.'

'But, Mam, it's yours. You should keep it to remember him by.'

'I have all the memories I need, up here.' Mam tapped the side of her head. 'And I've done nothing to keep his memory alive for you over the years. And I'm...' Here she took a deep breath, in an effort to control her emotions. 'I'm very sorry about that. It was wrong of me.' Without looking at me, she reached across and squeezed my hand.

I found I couldn't say anything at first, struggling as I was with my own emotions. Then I reached over to my handbag, opened up my wallet and took out my parents' wedding photo. I began to open the back of the frame.

'You don't have to,' she said.

'I know. I want to,' I said.

I inserted the photo and wiggled it around in the frame until it was centred. Then I closed the back of the frame and held it aloft.

'There. Perfect,' I said. I looked at Mam. 'Will I put it up?'

'You can do whatever you like with it.'

So I moved the cactus in the pink pot a few inches to the right, and put the photo on top of the telly, dead centre, where everybody would see it.

37

It was about a week later, and so engrossed was I in my writing that it took me a while to figure out that the doorbell was ringing. It was like when the telephone wakes you up from a dream – those few seconds when you're not sure which is a dream and which is reality. But, when it did register, I knew I'd better answer it. The only other person home was Tim, and he'd given up answering the front door ever since he'd transmogrified into the hideous creature he had currently become. I'd miss him, and I looked forward to seeing him again sometime in his early twenties.

So, to cut a long story short, I opened the front door – and it was Eric.

My combined joy and shock at seeing him had to compete momentarily with my horror concerning my own appearance. I was wearing a pair of grey tracksuit bottoms, pulled up under the loose white T-shirt that had doubled as a nightdress the night before. My feet were bare, with chipped red nail polish on the toes, and I hadn't so much as dragged a comb across my head that morning. And I'd had such ambitious plans for how I would look at our first meeting... Eric also looked as if he'd just climbed out of bed, but in that sexy, tousled way he seemed to have completely mastered.

In spite of it all, my first instinct was to fling myself upon him and kiss him to death. Two things stopped me: the knowledge that I hadn't yet brushed my teeth, and the awareness that Tim was lurking behind me, somewhere between the kitchen and the hallway. (I couldn't see him, I couldn't hear him – but, by God, I could smell him. He had recently taken to stealing Jim's Lynx. Not only did he drench his entire body in the stuff; he also sprayed his shirt once he was dressed.) So instead I just said, 'Hello.'

'Hello,' Eric said back.

'Not that it isn't nice to see you or anything, but – what are you doing here?'

'I thought you might like to go for a walk.'

'You came all the way from Hamburg to ask me if I'd like to go for a walk?'

'Well, I do have some other business to attend to while I'm here.'

'I don't know what to say. Come in.'

I opened the door wider, and Eric walked into my house for the first time. He was wearing aftershave too, I noticed as he walked by me, but just the right amount. I showed him into the kitchen, having heard Tim scuttling up the stairs a few seconds earlier.

'I just have to get ready,' I said. 'Would you like a drink while you're waiting?'

'No, I'll just sit here. Hurry up.'

I did. I ran into my room and scuttled around in a panic. What to do, what to wear? I settled on a pair of neutral cropped trousers – although they were almost full-length on me – a hot-pink sleeveless top and matching flip-flops with a large, plastic daisy on each. Then I tried to do something with my head. I snuck into the bathroom, brushed my teeth and put on almost as much deodorant as Tim. I had to write off my hair; it looked equally tragic up or down. My face was relatively tanned, so I just put on blusher and lipstick. It was a far cry from how I'd planned to look on our first meeting, but it would have to do.

Eric was standing up, looking out the kitchen window, hands in pockets. He turned to me and smiled. 'You look nice.'

'Thanks. Not too dishevelled-looking?'

'Just dishevelled enough.'

I smiled. 'That's a relief.'

'Any nice walks around here?' Eric asked.

'The Botanic Gardens?'

'Lead the way.'

We stepped out onto the street, and I felt like skipping – the sun was shining, and Eric was back. I wasn't sure whether or not to hold his hand. Until I knew exactly where I stood, I decided to keep my hands clasped firmly behind my back, out of harm's way.

As we drew closer to the Botanic Gardens, I noticed that the gardens of the houses we passed were increasingly well kept; perhaps the owners were inspired, living as they did beside such floral magnificence. 'I haven't been here since I was a kid,' said Eric, as we walked through the wrought-iron gates. I conjured up an image of Eric as a child – a beautiful, blond, blue-eyed little boy. I'd have had no trouble holding *his* hand.

Our random strolling brought us to the entrance of one of the Victorian glasshouses. In we went. The glasshouse was dominated by what looked like a giant version of the aloe vera plant we had in the kitchen back home – except this one had a massive, pink *thing* protruding out of the top, curving towards the ceiling and ending in several rows of yellow spikes. I recalled a half-forgotten David Attenborough programme – possibly *The Life of Plants*: plants could be male or female. I'd guess that this particular one was male.

'So,' I said, 'you've only been gone three weeks. Did something go wrong over there?'

'No. This is only a flying visit. I head back tonight.'

'Tonight!' I hadn't meant to say that – at least, not with such an obvious note of dismay.

'Yes. We've still got a good few gigs lined up.'

'So it's going well, then.'

Eric smiled. 'It's going great.'

'That's terrific, Eric. And the Germans themselves – did you find them...friendly?'

'I suppose so, yes.'

'And what do you do when you're not working?'

'There's a lot of hanging about. Sometimes we try and sight-see, or travel around a bit if we have two days off in a row.'

That sounded harmless enough. 'And at nighttime?'

'We're mostly working.'

And so did that. Still, he was hardly going to tell me about all the fräuleins.

Our meandering had brought us to the door of the next glasshouse. This one seemed to be housing conifers and ferns, with water features interspersed throughout. The passageways between the plants were narrower here, as the greenery tumbled down in lush fronds; we had to walk close together. Of course, looking back, we could have walked in single file, but this didn't seem to occur to either of us at the time. *Is it hot in here or is it just me?*

Our next stop was the orchid house, crammed with impossibly exotic-looking blooms in hot pinks, yellows and whites. I was beginning to feel like a tropical flower myself; my top blended right in. Every so often, it seemed as if one of the flowers was moving, but on closer inspection it would turn out to be a gardener, going about his business as unobtrusively as possible – as if they liked to give the impression that no effort was involved, that all these plants were occurring naturally. They reminded me of Oompa-Loompas.

'Hey, would you look at that,' said Eric.

I tore my eyes away from a speckled orchid that was doing its best to imitate an insect. He was pointing at the herbaceous border outside, in all its blazing July glory.

'Shall we?' said Eric, holding the back door of the glasshouse open for me.

'We shall,' I replied, stepping through.

Side by side we walked. My hands were still behind my back, and so were his – behind *his* back, that is. It was like walking through a tunnel of colour; like when Dorothy woke up in the Land of Oz, on the other side of the rainbow. I wasn't wearing ruby slippers, but my flip-flops were close enough. Instead of Toto, a resident black cat padded nonchalantly across our path. If somebody had told me at that moment that this was what heaven looked like – and felt like – I would have been very happy.

I *was* very happy. I looked up at Eric and beamed.

'Let's sit down,' he said, as we reached the end of the border.

We sat down on the nearest bench and looked out over the gardens spread before us. It occurred to me that this would be the ideal place for a romantic hero in a Jane Austen novel to propose.

'Here – I got you this,' said Eric, handing me a pear.

'Another pear?' I said. 'I'm not sick, you know.'

'Well, I'm sorry, but I don't know what kind of flowers you like. I only know you like pears.'

'I do like pears. Thank you very much. And, for future reference, I generally prefer to see flowers growing, rather than in a vase – but the odd bunch of freesias wouldn't go amiss.'

'Noted.'

I, for my part, noted that Eric had his arm draped across the back of the bench, behind me, in the manner of a teenage boy at the cinema. Was it hot in here, or was it just me? For the first time that day, the pause in the conversation felt awkward – to me, at least. I wasn't sure why, but it was as if something was hanging in the air between us.

'Will you marry me?' asked Eric.

I turned my head and stared at him. 'What did you say?'

He repeated the words. I could see his lips moving, but no sound appeared to be coming out – although this could have been because of the gushing sensation going on behind my ears. I needed further confirmation.

'Did you just ask me to marry you?'

'Yes.'

Blimey. If I'd thought the pause was awkward before…

Eric glanced at his watch. 'Do you think you might have an answer for me sometime soon, or would you like to go to lunch first? It's almost one, and I'm pretty hungry.'

'Eric,' I spluttered, 'you can't ask me such a – a profound question and expect me to answer right away, and then ask me if I want to go to lunch.'

'Well, I thought you might be more comfortable with a smaller question for the time being. Take it in bite-sized chunks, as it were.'

I just stared at him. Was he taking the piss or what? He was hardly acting like a romantic hero in an Austen novel – but, then again, I was hardly romantic-heroine material. If I were, I would have been either accepting with tears of joy, perhaps even swooning, or – if he was a cad, or somebody unworthy of my intellect – rejecting him fairly yet firmly, and possibly giving him a sound telling-off. Still, where was the bended knee? The diamond ring?

'What about my ring?'

'You'd want one of those, would you?'

'Of course I'd want one of those. Why wouldn't I?'

Eric shrugged. 'I just didn't have you down as the traditional type.'

'I'm not. But that doesn't mean I like jewellery any less than the next girl, or deserve it any less. Apparently all I'm worthy of is a pear. Is it an engagement pear?'

'A Conference pear, I think.'

'Stop smirking. It's not funny. Some women get twenty-four carats; I get one pear. And what about getting down on one knee?'

'These are new trousers.' He was laughing openly at me now. I punched him in the arm and tried to keep a straight face.

'You're very relaxed,' I said. 'For a man who's just proposed to a woman who hasn't even said yes.'

'Well, what do you think? Is it a good idea?'

'I don't know. I don't know what to say. I really like you...'

'I like you too.'

'Thanks.'

'You're welcome.'

'...But we haven't known each other for very long.'

'We've known each other for about three years.'

'You know what I mean. We've only just got to know each other properly. We've only spent one night together, for God's sake.' Again, not very Austen.

'That can be easily remedied,' he said. And, all of a sudden, there was the thrilling feel of his hands on my waist, then his hot breath, then his lips hard on mine. We exchanged a kiss that bordered on pornographic. I eventually pulled away, not wishing to frighten the group of American tourists who were about to pass our way.

Eric kept his eyes closed. 'You still taste the same,' he said.

'So do you.'

'So, if we have sex again, that'll help you make your mind up?'

'Maybe. The thing is, Eric, I don't feel ready for marriage.'

'That's OK. Neither do I.'

'What? Why are you asking me, then?'

He opened his eyes and took my hands in his. 'Because I know that you're the woman for me, and that's not going to change – whether we get married or not.'

I looked into his eyes, which were serious now. I could be Eric's woman, if I wanted to be. I didn't think I'd been anyone's woman before – not properly, anyhow. I'd never been George's woman, just his bit on the side.

'Maybe I should amend my offer,' Eric said.

'To what?'

'Will you marry me someday? It's a genuine offer.'

'I know it is.'

'Well, then?'

I started to smile. 'OK, then.'

'OK?'

'I mean, yes. I will marry you – someday. But not for ages, probably.'

'Thank God for that. I thought we were going to be here all day.' Eric stood up. 'Let's go and get some lunch.'

'You romantic devil, you.'

He pulled me to my feet and we walked back down the herbaceous border – the tunnel of flowers – the tunnel of love. This time, my arm was around Eric's waist and his was around my shoulders. The black cat crossed our path again.

'Eric,' I said suddenly, 'you know you said you had some business to attend to?'

'Yes.'

'Was that it?'

'Yes.'

So I guess this meant that he liked me.

38

Tom took the drinks orders – vodkas and tonic for me and Helen, Scrumpy Jack for Mindy, Guinness for Deji and Smithwicks for Eric – and headed up to the bar. We were spending the night in Killarney, having just attended the first Gypsy Kings concert in Ireland in ten years, and spirits were high. Spirits were about to be sunk, too – the liquid kind, and lots of them.

Eric went up to the bar to give Tom a hand, which gave Helen and Mindy the opportunity to pounce on me that they'd been waiting for all evening. 'So,' Helen said excitedly, 'how's it going, then?'

'How's what going?'

'Don't play the innocent. You know what I mean – you and Eric.'

'Oh,' I said, pretending to consider the question. 'Not bad, I suppose.'

'I like the ring,' said Mindy. 'Is it meant to signify something?'

'No. It's just a ring.'

Since we were only sort of engaged, Eric had bought me a sort-of-engagement ring – silver, with semi-precious stones. He'd bought it in Germany, and I wore it on the third finger of my right hand – or the wrong hand, depending on your perspective.

I wasn't concerned about what verbal arrows Mindy might sling in my direction tonight. You see, I had plenty of ammunition of my own – because tonight, Mindy was wearing a dress. Yes, you heard right, a dress – and a flowery one, at that. And she was clearly self-conscious about it. When Helen had mentioned it earlier, Mindy had got quite defensive, and she kept crossing and uncrossing her legs as if she didn't know what to do with them. The rest of us hadn't even known she had legs. My first guess had been that Tom had put her up to it, but no: it seemed that Clarissa had got into a fight with one of the other little girls in her crèche, who had accused her of having two daddies, so Mindy was trying to change her image.

But Helen had no such weakness, and she was not to be deterred. 'Are you engaged?' she demanded.

'No, Helen. Don't be silly. What gave you that idea?'

I hadn't told her about my sort-of proposal. It felt private. Besides, I knew she'd never approve of such an anti-Austen scenario. In her book it was roses, diamond ring and bended knee all the way – preferably on top of the Eiffel Tower, or on a gondola in Venice. And as for my response…I'd never hear the end of it.

To my tremendous relief, Tom and Eric returned from the bar, bearing much-needed refreshments. Tom doled out the drinks, then reached deep into the pocket of his waistcoat.

'I almost forgot,' he said. 'I have new business cards.' He handed out cards to all and sundry – including Mindy, who told him in no uncertain terms where to go.

'Thomas T. Burke?' said Helen. 'Who's that?'

'What does the T stand for?' I said.

'Nothing. I don't have a middle name. I just thought the extra initial added a touch of class.'

'Like Captain James T. Kirk,' said Eric.

'Now you have it,' said Tom. 'At least someone understands me, even if my own wife doesn't.'

'Good Jaysus, I'm married to one pretentious prick,' said Mindy, downing at least half the bottle of Scrumpy.

'Assistant editor,' Helen read. 'Well done, you.' She leant over and gave Tom a kiss.

'A toast,' I said. 'To Tom and his fabulous new career in publishing.'

'To Tom!' We all raised our glasses and knocked back our respective drinks with such enthusiasm that it was almost time for another round.

'I have a few toasts of my own to make,' said Tom, rising to his feet. He cleared his throat loudly, causing the people at the nearby tables in the small, packed Killarney pub to stop what they were doing and look at him. This was intentional on Tom's part; he loved nothing more than a captive audience. I must suggest that he give a talk to Mindy's charges in Mountjoy Women's Prison.

'We have multiple causes for celebration this evening,' Tom began, his chest puffed up with importance, his face aglow. 'First of all, I shall turn my attention to the very beautiful and fragrant Ms Helen Staunton.'

'Oh, God,' said Helen, shrinking into her seat.

'Helen has – this very week – signed the lease on her brand-new bookshop-*cum*-coffee-shop, Tomes and Scones. We all hope you'll pay it a visit next time you're in Dublin,' he added, to his ever-increasing audience. 'It's just a stone's throw away from Grafton Street. We know that she'll make a fantastic success of it – just as she makes a fantastic success of everything.'

'Apart from my love life,' mumbled Helen.

'Well, indeed,' said Tom. 'I didn't like to mention it, but now that you bring it up…you have made a bit of a pig's ear of that, haven't you, my dear?'

'Tom!' said Helen and Mindy and I.

'But don't worry,' Tom continued. 'Look at Liz here. She was the biggest disaster of them all, and even she's got her act together now.'

'Cheers, Tom,' I said.

'Any time, Liz. But back to Helen.'

'Thank God,' I said.

'As I was saying. I know her shop's going to be a great success, and I know that she's going to stock all the books I publish and that she's going to give all her friends free scones whenever they happen to drop by.' Small localised cheer. 'And I would like to reassure everybody that Liz Clancy will not – I repeat, will not – be making the scones.'

Big localised cheer. Who needed enemies? Even Eric cheered. I punched him in the arm – the same arm that had encircled my waist for the entire concert. (I'd felt sorry for the person who'd had to sit behind his big, blond head – not that there had been much sitting; everyone had been on their feet, dancing.)

'So, ladies and gentlemen – and those of you who aren't quite sure what you are – please raise a glass to the lovely, the delectable, the delightful Ms Helen Staunton!'

We all clinked glasses and drank some more. This time, another round was definitely in order.

'Barman,' boomed Tom, without leaving the table, 'another round, please.' I'd never have had the nerve to do something like that. But, sure enough, two minutes later another round of drinks materialised.

'Good man, good man,' said Tom, distributing the drinks and tipping the lounge boy generously. 'You can put that on my tab.'

The boy gave Tom a doubtful look and retreated hastily. Tom took a deep sup, removed the thin line of Guinness foam from his moustache with his bottom lip and rose to his feet again.

'Next, I would like to propose a toast to my good friend Deji – the only one of us here tonight who still works in Grainger's Bookshop.'

I looked around the table. I'd never given it much thought before, but it was absolutely true.

'I had the privilege of working with Deji, albeit for a very short time, and I must say that he filled the enormous shoes left by the inimitable Eric with wonderful aplomb. And may I also say that he makes the most charming drinking companion? And, furthermore, I hear that he's become the star player of Clontarf rugby team and reversed their failing fortunes absolutely. So raise your glasses, please, to Deji.'

'To Deji.'

More standing, more drinking. Deji clinked each of our glasses and smiled serenely. 'Thank you, my friends.'

'Now for Eric.' Tom didn't even sit down this time. He was in full flight.

I leaned across to Mindy. 'How many times has he been best man?'

'Six times.'

'And what's the record for his longest speech?'

'An hour and a quarter.'

'Maybe we should get another round in.'

'Good idea.'

'Eric,' Tom went on, 'I admit that it's only in recent times that I've begun to get to know you properly. I must apologise for all those years of calling you "the Viking" behind your back.'

'That's all right, Tom. I got a band name out of it, didn't I?'

'Indeed. You should be thanking me, really. But seriously – hearty congratulations to you, Eric, on your new record deal. May you go on to make many hits and even more spondulicks. And the heartiest congratulations of all on your new girlfriend. OK, she's kind of scruffy, and she can't cook; but she's fun to have around, and you certainly could have done a lot worse.'

'Thanks a lot, Tom,' I said.

Eric laughed and gave me a squeeze as they all raised their

glasses to him. 'I couldn't have done any better,' he whispered into my ear.

'Which brings me nicely on to my next toastee – if that's a word: my good friend Liz. You'd think she'd be too busy seducing young Eric here to have any time for writing, but no: she's only gone and finished her third novel. And maybe she'll actually tell us what it's about, at long last.'

They were all looking at me expectantly. I couldn't disappoint them.

'It's about a woman who uncovers the secrets of her past.' To my tremendous relief, Marian had loved the new manuscript and had agreed to publish it instead of the memoir, which I'd gratefully put back in my drawer. Maybe in a few years' time, I'd be ready to let it see the light of day.

'So tell us,' said Tom. 'We're dying to know: does she find true love and live happily ever after?'

'But of course.'

'Excellent. A toast to Liz, and to finding true love and living happily ever after.'

I was duly toasted – just true love and me.

'What about me?' said Mindy.

'Oh, yes. Last but not least, to my marvellous missus Mindy – mostly for having the balls to wear that appalling dress this evening.'

'To Mindy!' At this stage, most of the neighbouring drinkers were joining in on the toasts – much to the delight of the publican, who was having his most profitable night in weeks.

Tom's ample arse was about to hit his seat at last, but it didn't quite make it. 'I almost forgot,' he said. 'Two very important people.'

'Get on with it!' shouted Helen.

'No heckling, please, Ms Staunton. This concerns you too. I'd like to propose a toast to Mr George Grainger.'

A silent pall fell over the table, and we all looked at one another. Why did Tom have to bring *him* up? We'd been having such a nice time.

'Because if it hadn't been for good old Georgie boy, I wouldn't have met any of you people here tonight – with the exception of Mindy – and I, for one, think that would have been a terrible tragedy. So, ladies and gentlemen, please raise your glasses with me and drink a toast to the abominable, the unfaithful, the diabolical – Mr George Grainger!'

'George Grainger,' we all chorused.

'And let's not forget his wife Judith.'

Helen and I shared an uncomfortable look. That was one name I'd have preferred to forget – and so, no doubt, would Helen.

'My sources inform me,' continued Tom, 'that, as of earlier this week, Mrs Grainger has left her erstwhile husband for a younger man.'

'How do you know that?' I asked, thrilled and scandalised.

'I bumped into Rachel from the shop.'

'How does she know?'

'Her best friend's mother's bridge partner is the Graingers' cleaning lady.'

'Must be true, so,' said Helen.

'And not only that,' said Tom. 'I'm also reliably informed that she's served divorce papers on hubby, and that she's intending to fleece him for everything he's got. So good for her.'

'Amen,' I said.

'By the way, Helen,' Tom added, 'I believe you're named in her divorce papers as an adulteress.'

'What?' said Helen.

295

'Only kidding. So, for one last time – please raise your glasses to Mrs Judith Grainger!'

'Judith Grainger,' we all agreed.

'Right,' said Tom, sitting down at last. 'Now for some serious drinking.'

I could tell Granny was getting better because she had a pair of tights on her head. (For the uninitiated: in certain parts of Dublin, it is customary to wear a pair of tights on one's head in order to preserve one's set and blow-dry.) We were sitting in her back garden, enjoying the late-summer sunshine and two glasses of warm, fizzy 7-Up – gentle on the stomach, don't you know. Granny had offered to 'do my cards', and I'd accepted, once she explained that she needed to keep her hand in.

She laid down the first card. 'Oh, that's a good one,' she said. 'It means your book is going to be a huge success.'

'Really, Granny?' I was sure that card had meant something completely different the last time.

'Oh, yes. It'll wing its way all around the world.' International publishing deals – I liked the sound of that. 'This book…am I in it, by any chance?'

'There might be a character quite like you.'

'God bless us and save us.' She clapped her hands together. 'I've always wanted to be in a book.'

'Now, I didn't exactly say—'

'God bless you, child.' She ignored my protestations and laid down another card. 'Oh, you're getting a great reading today. This card symbolises fertility. I see many children in your future – little blondies.'

My head whipped up and I stared at her. She'd never met Eric, and, as far as I knew, nobody had ever provided her with a description. Many children...I wasn't sure what I thought of that. I only wanted two, max.

'Next card,' I said.

Granny placed a third card alongside the previous two. 'Harmony,' she said, definitively. 'The end of conflict in your life.' I liked that.

I was allowed to pick one more card from the shuffled pack. Granny placed it on the tray that was sitting across her lap, and looked up at me.

'You've found him, then?'

I nodded briefly and looked away. She took up the cards slowly, with her arthritic hands, and put them back in their shabby box. We both resumed sipping our 7-Up.

After a while, Granny said, 'Make sure you bring him to see me soon. Because it won't be...'

'I know, Granny. It won't be long now.'

Epilogue

My life has changed unimaginably since the success of my third book – and the birth of my first child. David is one today. Just this morning, we brought him to visit his great-grandmother and his great-auntie Kit, both of whom are besotted with him, of course. That's 'we', my mother and I, rather than Eric and I. He's touring England right now. We'll be joining him next week.

So I didn't get my father figure in the end; it turned out I didn't need one. And I didn't get my dashing Spaniard, either. I got something better. (Although he does allow me to call him Julio on my birthday and on those other special nights.)

As for Mam and me, we're getting along OK these days. She's visibly proud of my success. We haven't quite booked the private jet to the Oscars yet, but we're getting there. I'm not only writing women's fiction these days. There are also the children's books I've written under the pen name 'Tallulah Jones'. My friends still call me Liz, however, and my family still calls me Libby.

My mother dotes on David. It's as if she's lavishing upon my child all the love she should have lavished on me – the love that skipped a generation, like a talent for music. This is fine by me. I want him to have it.

He's not as I imagined him, my little boy. He's not blond. That renegade gene that keeps resurfacing has blackened his hair and eyes and turned his skin dusky.

We're in the city-centre apartment I share with Eric and David. We've finished lunch, and we're looking out onto the roofs of

Dublin – some old, some new. My mother swings David up into the air above our heads, and his peals of laughter fill the apartment with joy and spiral down onto the rooftops. She looks up into his face, his joy mirrored on her own.

'He's just like your father,' she says.

Also by Tara Heavey

If you're looking for a fresh and funny read,
this is the book for you.

Legal secretary Fern can't quite believe her luck when posh barrister
James Carver takes a shine to her. With her mahogany brown hair –
'I blend in with the office furniture' – and green eyes, she doesn't feel
in any way special. After all, a typing speed of 60 wpm and a failed
artistic career hardly make her a catch.

Flattered and thrilled at the attention, Fern is smitten, even when
James turns out to have some very strange habits.
When will Fern see that he is a total rat? When she gets the sack –
for slapping a judge – or when she realises he's already got a girlfriend?
With her family breaking apart and her love life in disarray, Fern refuses
to see the truth about James – or about herself, and why she's running
away from a man who really loves her.

'*A Brush with Love*... is a fantastic first novel. The main
character, Fern, is a delight, and her madcap romantic
adventures are compulsive reading.'
Sarah Webb

Available wherever books are sold
or order online at **www.gillmacmillan.ie** to save **20%**

Also by Tara Heavey

The countryside has never looked so exciting!

Elena is a solicitor of the regular kind, the only unusual thing about her is her name (her mother had a passion for Russian ice dancing). She shares a flat with two friends and, occasionally, her uptight accountant boyfriend, Paul. Elena's future seems to be mapped out in its own unexciting way.

That is, until her boss calls her into his office, and promises her a partnership if she sets up a new office for him in his hometown of Ballyknock. Elena is horrified; after all, the country is full of wildlife and strange noises!

But the promise of a partnership prevails and she takes off for nine months' purgatory in the back of beyond. However, as Elena gets to grips with the wildlife of this picturesque little town - both animal and human - she discovers quite a lot: that she actually likes the countryside, that her former life was stressful and boring, and that the local publican has not one but seven, handsome sons.

'A real page-turner'
The Independent

Available wherever books are sold
or order online at **www.gillmacmillan.ie** to save **20%**